BLACK OPS FAE

A SPY AMONG THE FALLEN

C.N. CRAWFORD

Copyright © 2018 by C.N. Crawford

All rights reserved.

No part of this book may be reproduced in any form or by any electronic or mechanical means, including information storage and retrieval systems, without written permission from the author, except for the use of brief quotations in a book review.

CHAPTER 1

*I*n the forest outside Hotemet Castle, I nursed a small, silver flask. In the amber morning light, Hazel and Elan walked by my side.

Just three fae out for a walk among the oaks. Two of us pretending to be demons.

I scanned the forest, my chest tightening as I thought of Johnny. I'd buried his scrawny angel ass in a shallow grave out here, but angels were immortal. I had no idea how long it would take him to recover. At any minute, he could come bounding out of the soil, hunting for me with murder on his mind.

I'd just be keeping that particular image to myself for now. No reason to spoil our evening stroll.

"I like it here." Hazel chomped into the cheese and onion pasty she'd snagged from the kitchen, the crumbs flaking over her black clothes. "We get to go outside and talk to each other and stuff."

Elan frowned. "And you couldn't in the dragon lair?"

"Nope." Hazel's mop of black curls tumbled over her shoulders. Like me, she was glamoured as a succubus, which meant that wisps of shimmering magic lifted from her body in steamy tendrils.

Warm light washed over Elan's pale skin and gaunt features. He grabbed the flask, taking a sip of Irish coffee—spiked with just the right amount of scotch.

Don't judge. Things had been stressful lately.

Another spray of crumbs over Hazel's clothes. "And the dragon food wasn't this good," she said through a mouthful of pie. "They ate a lot of sheep. Not flavored or anything. Just sheep they caught and then roasted in their fire-breath."

I finished the last bite of my own pie. "I guess that would make sense." I *really* didn't want to talk about dragon shifters, or think about them, or know what I might find on their menu. "Since they're giant, disgusting lizard people."

In her leather outfit, Hazel looked so much older than the last time I'd seen her—older than a sixteen-year-old should look, and I was pretty sure she'd spiked her own flask of coffee with the scotch.

But considering she'd spent a year among the dragons, I supposed a few changes were to be expected.

Our feet crunched over leaves and twigs as we walked.

Smiling, Hazel nudged Elan with her elbow. "You know what you remind me of? A starving egret."

"Hazel!" I snapped. The dragons certainly hadn't taught her any manners.

Hazel widened her dark eyes. "What? It's not an insult. It's just because of the paleness, and the thinness, and the haunted look in his eyes. As if he'd spent years in captivity eating frogs."

"A hundred forty-seven years," he confirmed. "Working in troll mines. Frogs were an infrequent delicacy." He scratched his cheek. "From what I understand, some people like the haunted bird look."

"There are all kinds of people," Hazel agreed and sipped her coffee.

Elan took another swig from the flask, then wiped the back of his sleeve across his mouth. "I should probably get back to my cooking duties before one of the angels vaporizes me. I've been asked to roast a pig for lunch. Kratos's favorite." He turned, stalking off through the forest without another word.

And at last, I was alone with my sister. Considering we'd only reunited yesterday, we still had a lot to talk about.

As soon as Elan was completely out of earshot, I grabbed my sister's arm. "Hazel. I need to fill you in on a few things."

"Let me guess," she whispered. "You're pretending to be a succubus so the angels will let you stay in the nice castle with the nice food."

Honestly. How shallow did she think I was? "Not exactly. I mean, I'm not complaining about the food, but I'm here as a spy. I'm working with the Institute to stop them from wrecking the earth any more than they already have."

"Why the hell would you do that?"

My jaw dropped open. "Because they kill people, Hazel, in case that's escaped your notice. Please don't tell me that you're fine with that."

She pursed her lips, shrugging. "It doesn't matter if I'm fine with it. It's happening, and we can either adapt to the new world, or starve like peasants in the dirt. Those are our options."

Anger flared. She'd become a bit jaded in the past two years, but maybe living among fire-breathing reptiles did that to a girl.

"I'm not adapting," I whispered. "I'm fighting them. You should be, too." I scanned the forest again, my heart thudding at the idea that Johnny could be lurking out here somewhere.

Hazel arched an eyebrow, whispering back, "And how do you plan to fight them?"

I took a sip of my coffee. "With information. And a little faith."

After everything that had happened recently, I'd become a believer in the Old Gods. The angels were powerful and terrifying—yes—but there were older beings, ones who'd been born native to the earth itself. And in the past couple of weeks, I'd started to believe they were providing us with everything we needed to combat the angels.

Hazel sneered. "Faith. Right."

"Yasmin was right to believe in them."

"Who?"

"My handler from the Institute. I'll arrange for us to meet soon. Anyway, she told me when we needed something, the Old Gods provided. And watch this." I scanned the skies for sentinels, making sure none were in view. Then, I stood still, lifting my hand in front of my face. Since I'd jammed a knife into the silver tree branch yesterday—mainlining the power of the Old Gods—some of their magic continued to live inside me. I'd stayed up late last night, summoning a faint glow around my fingertips.

I concentrated, trying to bring up that beautiful light.

Hazel loosed a sigh. "Am I supposed to keep watching you stare at your fingers?"

"Hang on." After a few moments, the tips of my fingers started to gleam with incandescent light.

"Hmmm..." said Hazel. "What does it do?"

"I'm not sure yet. This is just the beginning. But it's something, right?" I let the glow die out on my fingertips.

Hazel looked unimpressed. "Or—instead of fighting the heavenly horde with your glowing hands—we could just stay in the luxurious castle. A servant brought me breakfast this morning, and then I had a hot bath. I have a brilliant idea.

How about we don't mess it up? Do you know that every time you try to change something, you have the distinct possibility of making it worse?"

I shook my head. "It can't get any worse. And anyway, I don't have a lot of choice at this point. Apart from the fact that the angels are psychopaths, Johnny is lying out here in the dirt somewhere. Still alive. He knows I'm a fae, that I've been lying the whole time. I shot him with a poison-tipped arrow. When he wakes up, he's going to remember that I was the one who put him in the ground. If I don't find a way to end his life for good, I won't be drinking any wine or having any baths, because I'll be dead, or possibly locked in a torture room for eternity. And you will be too. Understand?"

For the first time, she looked rattled. "Maybe he won't wake up for years. Maybe he won't remember."

"That's a risky dream to pin your hopes on."

She sipped her coffee, her gaze never leaving mine. "Between now and then, we have time to charm the other angels. We'll take care of this whole...shooting and burying situation you created."

"Don't take this the wrong way, but I'm not sure charming people is in your skill set."

She glowered at me. "What makes you say that?"

"You just met Elan a day ago and you already called him a starving, haunted egret."

"He didn't seem to mind. Anyway, the dragons liked being mildly insulted. I was their favorite."

I *definitely* needed more whiskey in this coffee. "You're telling me you *charmed* the dragons. After what they did..." I let the sentence trail off, didn't want to give life to that particular horror with words.

Her jaw tightened. "Yeah, I got on their good side. How do you think I survived? How do you think I was able to control them? It doesn't matter if I *liked* them, Ruby. What mattered was that they liked me. That meant they protected me, gave me food and a place to sleep. All I had to do was entertain them and keep them happy."

I gritted my teeth. "Did they know you were fifteen?"

She glared at me. "Yes, and I didn't entertain them like that. I told them jokes, told them stories, filled their drinks. I flirted." She scowled. "Oh, don't look so shocked. You and I are the same. I lived among the dragons, pretending to be someone else. You lived in a castle, pretending to be someone else. And it doesn't matter if we liked it, or if other people would approve. Dragons and angels will do what they want. Our job was to survive."

"We can do more than just survive. We can fight them."

"We can't. I remember, Ruby. I remember when dragons killed our parents. I remember when they ripped Marcus apart. He was trying to save us, and—"

I held up a hand, cutting her off. "Let's not think about that, Hazel. You're right that we need to survive, but it's not going to happen by dwelling on all the terrible things that ever happened to us."

Something dangerous sparked in her eyes. "And ignoring all the terrible things will get you killed. Don't underestimate the forces working against you if you try to cross the angels. No one is looking after us, Ruby. We need to look after ourselves, and we can do that by pleasing the people in power."

"I will look after you. We just need to return to our roots. If we can end the Great Nightmare, we'll have a normal life. A cottage in the woods, with a fireplace, venison that I hunt, and…I don't know… root vegetables. Just like our ancestors. We can even bring along the haunted egret if you like. In any case, we don't belong among the angels *or* the dragons. We belong among our kind, and I'm going to do whatever I can to protect the only family I have left."

Her jaw dropped. "Are you out of your mind? Root vegetables and fireplaces? How do you expect to achieve this domestic dream?"

I loosed a long breath. The answer sounded ridiculous, even to me. And yet, I was starting to have faith in something older than the angels themselves. "The Old Gods are helping us. They've always been here—we just never knew about them. They're the reason why I was able to put Johnny in the ground in the first place."

She arched an eyebrow. "Sounds like bullshit. And even if the Old Gods are real, everything has a price. You realize that, don't you? *Everyone* has a price."

"So cynical for sixteen." As we walked, I fixed my gaze on hers intently. "Hazel. What I'm about to tell you is important, and you *have* to keep this to yourself, do you understand?"

She nodded. "I can keep a secret."

"Not all the angels are on the same side," I whispered. "Adonis says he's working against the others. I don't really understand why, and I don't trust him, either, but there are fractures in their alliance. He is the only one here who knows what I really am. I don't know what his motives are, but he let me live."

Hazel ran her fingertips along the leaves of a nearby shrub. "Now that is interesting."

My jaw tightened. I wasn't sure she was getting the severity of the situation. "Hazel. If Johnny wakes up—*when* Johnny wakes up, I'm going to need to leave here, fast. In fact, a smart person would probably leave *before* he wakes up. And you'll need to come with me, because he'll blow your cover, too."

She shot me a sharp look. "Maybe. Or maybe I stay here and use my own skills to keep Johnny and Kratos from coming after you. Then I can continue to eat Elan's food, because let's not overlook the fact that I just ate a pie for the first time in two years."

"That's wonderful. And your plan is to charm Johnny enough so that he won't care that I'm a lying fae spy who wants to kill him."

"Maybe charm isn't the right word. I'm good at confusing people."

"You don't say."

She grabbed my arm. "I'm not joking. I'm can *persuade* people, just by talking. Like, I confuse them, and then they forget what they were angry about, or they forget what they want me to do. How do you think I explained to the dragons why I was suddenly a succubus?"

"You confused them." I narrowed my eyes, an idea sparking in my mind. "Little sister, you just might have inherited the ancient fae skill of befuddlement."

Hazel smiled. "See? Our problem is solved. We can stay here with the pies and the fireplaces, and we won't end up out on our asses trying to hunt rabbits in the woods. I'll just befuddle them."

I shook my head. "No, Hazel. This isn't just about us. Look, we're going to dinner tonight with the remaining angels. If you really do have these powers of befuddlement, I could use your help. Kratos has asked both of us to dinner tonight, but he wants to keep me as far as possible from Adonis. I'm not supposed to go into Adonis's corridor, or leave my tower, or walk anywhere near the Dark Lord."

"A gilded cage."

"Pretty much. But we can see Kratos. Any chance you can persuade Kratos to invite Adonis to this dinner? And then find a way to get us alone?"

"Easy." She studied me closely. "And of course you'd like to get him alone. I caught a glimpse of him in the courtyard. Looks like a god."

"It's not like that. I need him for information, but I don't trust him as far as I can throw him. He hates the fae as much as he loves himself. Whatever his motives are, they're not altruistic. If I had to guess, he's angling for even more power than he already has."

"So stick with him, then. In this world, when power dynamics shift, you'd better make sure you're on the winning side." She snatched my spiked coffee and took a sip.

I didn't even try to stop her. Right now, I was pretty sure "little Hazel"—the one who'd once crawled into my bed to stave off nightmares about closet monsters—was well and truly gone.

In this world, maybe a loss of innocence wasn't the worst thing.

CHAPTER 2

I spun across the dance floor, my body thrilling at its own movements. Kratos had installed this studio for me, with a wooden floor and everything. I was only now getting to use it for the first time. Truthfully, a fae preferred to dance outside, but since he didn't know my true nature, the wooden floors would have to do.

That morning, I'd taken a quick mirror call from Yasmin—just a few flashes of the candle to signal to my handler from the Institute that I was in no immediate danger. Then, I'd quickly found my way to the dance studio.

As I moved, arching my back in an arabesque, a thin sheen of sweat spread over my body. *Gods* it felt good to dance again, and now that Hazel had returned to me, I could finally truly enjoy myself for once. I glimpsed myself in the mirror as I danced.

Twirling, a familiar ecstasy rippled through my ribs. This was what I was born to do. And ever since I'd connected to the Old Gods in the forest outside—since I'd harnessed their light—I felt connected to the earth, to my body, more than ever.

Closing my eyes, I twirled, a smile lighting up my face—until I spun right into a powerful chest that felt a lot like a wall of steel.

I opened my eyes, finding myself face-to-face with a muscled chest dressed in a finely cut crimson shirt, and the sweep of coppery wings. Then, I looked up into the chiseled face of Kratos, his eyes blazing like sunlight as he stared down at me. A vein throbbed in his neck.

From somewhere behind him, one of his ivory hounds growled, as if sensing the tension in the room. As if *I* were a threat to *him*. The creature padded over, his claws clicking against the hardwood floor, and stood next to his master. Kratos reached down, giving the hound an affectionate pat.

"Culloch, I'm fine. You can go away."

With a low whine, Culloch turned and padded in the other direction.

Kratos's golden stare turned on me again, and energy crackled between us. Suddenly, I felt intensely aware of the sheer amount of skin I had pressed against him, seeing as I was only dressed in a leotard.

"Good afternoon," I said sweetly. "I was wondering how you were doing." I knew he was going out tonight to kill, to hunt humans, and I still smiled at him. Maybe Hazel and I *were* more alike than I was admitting, pretending to be people we weren't. "Thank you for bringing my sister back."

A muscle twitched in his jaw as his gaze swept over my body. "I want you to be happy."

"I am. This dance studio is everything I want. Dancing and Hazel, who you found for me." A sharp pang of guilt coiled through me. He was standing here telling me that he wanted me to be happy, while I'd come here to find a way to destroy him. I'd already taken down one angel—at least temporarily—and maybe Kratos would be next.

Of course I needed to stop them. What the hell was I

feeling guilty for? They'd destroyed New York, London, one city after another. They hunted people and sowed death and destruction across the world. I had no loyalty to his kind, and I could never forget that.

"You belong here." His voice was a low murmur that warmed my skin.

Every word of his seemed like a command, so powerful that I wanted to obey. And sometimes, when he looked down at me with his golden eyes, like he was doing right now, I had to fight the urge to fall to my knees before him. Something about his raw magic compelled me to bend to his will, to worship him. The wooden floor called to me, urging me downward to kneel in supplication. My legs practically shook as I resisted him.

Kratos's gaze swept lower over my body, and his muscles visibly tensed. He wasn't allowed to touch me—not *really* touch me. He'd been cursed for his whole life, and that meant that if he gave into earthly temptations, he'd fall. He'd turn into a demon, all leathery wings and horns.

And yet, he seemed entranced by my throat right now. Without entirely realizing what I was doing, I tilted my head back.

"Must you dance in something so revealing?" Tension laced his voice.

I swallowed hard. If I tempted Kratos to fall, the consequences would be terrible for everyone, but I wouldn't let it go that far.

I just needed to distract him enough that he kept his mind off slaughtering everyone, but not so tempted that he'd actually fall. If he did, the terrifying archangels known as the Heavenly Host would fly to earth to finish off the last of the living.

"Maybe you could take the night off hunting," I suggested. "Stay here to watch me dance."

His golden eyes darkened to a deep umber. "I can't skip the hunt. The curse compels me to do it." He ran his fingertips over his chest. "When I don't act as the curse commands me to, I burn from the inside out." He closed his eyes, breathing in deeply as if some strange sort of ecstasy were overtaking his body. "But sometimes I wonder if it would be worth it to burn." He opened his eyes again, trailing his gaze over my body, and I had the disconcerting feeling that he could see right through my leotard to the bare skin beneath, to the freckle just below my left breast.

Maybe I shouldn't get too close to Kratos—maybe an angel tempted to fall was too much of a dangerous thing.

Now seemed as good a time as any to dig for information, now that Kratos seemed completely entranced by my body. "And Adonis is the only one of you who isn't cursed?" I still didn't understand these angels.

For just a moment, a cold fire flashed in Kratos's eyes, and his coppery wings spread out behind him. "You need to stay away from Adonis." His voice was almost a growl. From his back, his hound snarled in warning.

I reached up to touch Kratos's cheek as if soothing him. "What do you think will happen if I don't?" I asked, widening my eyes innocently.

He was looking at me the way a predator sizes up his prey. Instinctively, I took a step away from him, backing up into the wall.

But Kratos moved with me. In the next instant, his hands were around my waist, then lower, sliding down over my hips. I gasped as his fingers tightened possessively.

He leaned in, his breath warming the shell of my ear. "If I weren't cursed, I'd be pulling that scrap of clothing off you right now and..." He stopped himself, fighting with his impulses.

I was certainly doing my job of distracting him. His

fingers moved up my body, until his powerful hands curled around my biceps, pinning me to the wall. Something wild and untamed blazed in his eyes.

"Are you trying to tempt me to fall?" he asked, his voice a growl.

No, that would be bad. I shook my head. "I don't know what you're talking about."

He was breathing deeply, his golden magic burning from his body like sunlight. "I see you walking around the castle, the way you sway your hips, the way your clothing hugs your body. You want to turn me into a demon, like you. Maybe I want to know what that feels like. I want to know what *you* feel like."

I clenched my jaw, suddenly realizing what a dangerous game I'd been playing. "I think you should let me go now. Get a cold shower in."

"You're making me insane, Ruby." His voice was a snarl, and it rumbled over my skin.

Despite myself, my back was arching into him.

"Ruby." My name sounded like a command on his tongue, and once again I had to fight that overpowering urge to drop to my knees, to pull off my clothes like I knew he wanted me to.

My body was trembling now, and sweat dampened my skin again, this time for another reason. I raised my hands to push on his powerful chest, but it was like trying to shove an oak tree. "This is a bad idea."

He tightened his grip on my arms, and in the next moment, his mouth was on my neck, teeth grazing my skin. He growled as his tongue replaced his teeth. He was kissing me—*hard* and possessively, as though he were claiming his territory—and he really shouldn't have been. I tried pushing against him, my hips bucking, but he had me pinned.

One of his hands slid up my back, and I heard the tear of

fabric as he ripped my leotard. Cold air whispered over my skin, peaking my breasts as he tugged it down.

"Stop." I slammed my fists against his chest. "Stop!"

The words seemed to hit him like a slap to his face, and he stared at me, stunned. I gripped the top of my leotard, holding it up to cover myself. From behind him, Culloch was snarling.

My breath was coming rapidly, my cheeks flushed. *I can't stay here.*

At the sound of footsteps, I realized another presence had entered the room—this one draped in shadowy magic.

Adonis crossed the wooden floor smoothly, as though moving through water. His dark magic trembled up my spine. "Get away from her, Kratos. Now." An unmistakable threat of violence laced his tone, a ruthlessness under his perfect exterior.

Kratos growled, almost inaudibly, but took a step away from me.

As he did, Adonis's cold rage seemed to disappear like smoke on the wind.

Adonis shoved his hands into his pockets, completely at ease now, a wicked smile on his lips. "Has it occurred to you that maybe having a succubus in your home is a bad idea?"

Kratos clenched his fists, his eyes still locked on me. "I'm fine. I just need to hunt soon. That's all."

"Let's go, then." Adonis's tone brooked no argument.

Gripping my leotard, I stared after the two angels as they left the room, and dread began to bloom in my chest. I *definitely* needed to end this as soon as I could.

CHAPTER 3

Until tonight, I'd never been in the Celestial Room—the crowning jewel on top of the Tower of Silence. Nor had I ever sat below an enormous glass dome, with a canopy of stars twinkling above me.

It might have even been relaxing, if it weren't for the sentinels drifting above us, their dark eyes glinting with suspicion.

Below the dome, I sat at a round table with Kratos and Hazel. Red candles burned in iron candelabras, casting a wavering light over the flagstone floor. It wasn't the coziest place I'd ever been, but it had a certain stark elegance. Perfect for an angel, I guess.

I took a sip of my Bordeaux, trying to ignore their ever watchful eyes. If it hadn't been for the whole apocalypse issue, maybe Hazel would have a point about how we should just stay here enjoying the food, luxuriating in our silk dresses.

Kratos leaned over the table, refilling Hazel's wineglass. Considering we were supposed to be thousand-year-old succubi, I couldn't exactly point out that she was only sixteen. And Hazel certainly wasn't turning it down.

"Cheers!" Hazel beamed, lifting her glass. "To the angels and their amazing castle!"

Kratos lifted his glass, his rings glinting in the candlelight. "I never imagined I'd be dining with *two* ancient succubi."

Well, that's because you aren't.

His golden eyes slid to me. I still hadn't quite gotten used to the look of them—the eerie gold that faded to a burnt umber around the edges. Everything about him blazed with an inner golden light—and yet, according to Adonis, *I* was supposed to be the Bringer of Light. Whatever that was.

I'd already eaten at least half a roast quail, plus a good amount of potatoes, and Adonis still hadn't made an appearance. Had Hazel been able to persuade him to join us, or had she overestimated her befuddlement powers?

Kratos's gaze was slowly lingering over my sheer, pewter-gray dress. I watched his body tense, glowing brighter with that honeyed light. "I must get you some more concealing clothing."

He sounded almost angry this time. Clearly, my wardrobe was straining his ability to keep a leash on himself.

"You don't like my dress?" I asked.

His gaze was locked completely on me, as if Hazel weren't in the room at all. "I'm starting to wonder if it might be worth it to wear the wings of a demon."

I bit my lip. "I can almost picture you as a demon. Maybe some horns."

Hazel cleared her throat. "You guys remember that I'm here, right?"

When Kratos glanced at her, he looked almost surprised to find that she was still there. Then, his brow furrowed. "Did you ask me to invite Adonis to dinner earlier?"

Hazel widened her eyes and blinked. "When I spoke to

you in the forest's edge? No, we talked about the sparrows and the rowan trees, and I wondered about poisonous plants and you said there were many in the woods, and then you thought of Adonis and inviting him to dinner. That was, of course, before your thoughts turned to my sister's body and how she would look completely naked in a rainstorm. But the point is, you wanted to invite Adonis because you're the same, really, and your fates are the same, like a pair of oaks grown intertwined. Can I have more wine?"

Now *that* was befuddlement.

Kratos simply nodded at her, a faint line between his brows. Before Kratos could answer, the sound of footfalls echoed off the stone floor outside the room.

Adonis pushed through the oak door, a sly smile curling his sensual lips. As usual, he wore finely cut, dark clothes, and shadows seemed to cloak his body. Dark tendrils of midnight magic swept into the room, rushing over my skin like a night breeze. "Sorry that I'm late."

"You really didn't need to come at all," said Kratos sharply.

Adonis arched an eyebrow as he pulled out his chair. "You did invite me."

Kratos leaned back in his chair, sipping his wine. "For the life of me, I can't remember why."

"For my scintillating company." A smile ghosted over his sensuous lips. "Obviously."

Kratos winced, nearly dropping his wineglass, and clutched his chest.

"Okay there?" I asked.

"I must go hunting soon." Kratos's eyes burned deep gold. "You should return to your tower."

Kratos really didn't want me anywhere near Adonis, did he?

"Kratos," Hazel chirped. "Golden one. Can I walk you

outside? I just want to see where you keep the hounds, and I was saying earlier that I had a burning desire to see the hounds, and I thought you might want to take me to them now, and to fulfill your heart's desire by going to the hounds *now*, and you really just wanted to hunt and feel that sweet release in your chest like a great explosion of joy." She rose, her chair scraping over the floor, and beamed a smile at Kratos. "Shall we go?"

Brilliant. My sister was a brilliant manipulator.

Kratos frowned, confusion clouding his features. "Right. Hunting." He rubbed his chest, wincing for a moment. "I need to go."

"Of course you do," said Hazel. She strode out of the room, and Kratos trailed after her.

At the threshold, he turned back to me, his body flashing amber. A corona of light beamed around his head, and his copper wings appeared behind him, cascading down his back. "You'll want to get back to your room, Ruby."

As he turned and left, my stomach dropped. That was right. I couldn't forget that I was a prisoner here.

When I glanced at Adonis, amusement was dancing in his pale eyes.

"He seems awfully eager to keep us apart," I said.

Adonis picked up his wineglass. "Of course he is. I'm a monster."

A shiver danced up my neck. Sometimes, his beauty had a cruelly mocking edge to it.

I took a long sip of my wine and glanced around the room, taking care that no servants lurked in the shadows. "If you're a monster, why are you working against the other death angels?"

"Their vision is limited. They're slaves to the commands of the Heavenly Host. They don't want what I want."

"And what do you want?"

His masculine scent wrapped itself around me, bringing with it promises of dangerous pleasure. "To rebel against those who seek to control us. To maintain my free will, to drag the gods from the heavens, and make them suffer, just a little." The ice in his eyes hardened. "To put them in their place."

"And you need a Bringer of Light to achieve…your rebellion?"

"Precisely. Powerful as I am, I can't kill the other angels. Funny, isn't it? You're a fae from nowhere, but only the Bringer of Light can stop them."

"What exactly is a Bringer of Light?"

He leaned closer, his dark magic curling around his powerful body. "Someone who can control the magic of the Old Gods. A power grew in the rowan branch. I couldn't see it like you could, but I could feel it. When you fought Johnny, I watched you harness that power. You're a vessel, Ruby."

"I see. And you want to use me, but you haven't explained what I need to do."

In his eyes, I saw nothing but the cold, staggering arrogance of an ancient god. "It's quite simple, Ruby." The candlelight flickered over the chiseled planes of his face. "As the Bringer of Light, I want you to serve me. I don't want to rule on earth. Worship from humans is hardly an achievement. I want to rule the celestial realm. You can help me achieve that."

"How? And what's in it for me?"

A wicked smile. "What's in it for you, my little feral fae? You get to live."

CHAPTER 4

My chest tightened. Of course, he'd keep his cards close to his chest. Bringer of Light —whatever that was—obviously came with some serious power, and he wasn't going to give me access to it without keeping complete control.

"You want me to *help* you gain even more power than you already have?"

Adonis's magic moved in menacing whorls around him. "Yes."

"Call me crazy, but I'm not sure I'm keen to give more power to a monster."

The air thinned around me. "You're surrounded by monsters. You just have to decide which ones are your allies." An easy smile, a predator toying with his prey. "I must say I find it interesting that you were perfectly happy to kiss a monster on Eimmal. I heard your heart speeding up, felt your blood racing. I saw the look in your eyes, how much you wanted me. Tell me, Ruby. Does death lure you in?"

I tightened my grip on my wineglass. "No. The spring fever affects me that way because I'm fae. I kissed you because you were there. That's it. I would have preferred Kratos." I wasn't sure why I added that, except I thought it would help to keep Adonis at a distance.

Adonis's eyes hardened like chunks of ice, and a cold draft whispered over my skin. "Is that right?" His powerful, shadowy magic slid through to my bones, making my body shiver. "Then you're a wise one, Ruby. And you're right to think me a monster. I've killed scores of humans. I've spread plagues over continents. When I lived among the fae, I helped them kill for fun." His eyes gleamed with a terrifying intensity, and his magic coiled around my ribs. "I killed my own parents, Ruby. That is what I am."

The hair on the back of my neck stood on end, and I swallowed hard. "Wonderful. Sounds like a promising partnership. Why the hell should I choose you as an ally?"

"Because I'm the only one here who knows the truth about you. Kratos's reaction to your deception is an unknown. And what's more, if I rule the celestial realm, I won't be here. We both have the same goal, don't we? Get me away from this world."

"You make fair points."

"You don't have the first clue how to fight the Heavenly Host, or even what you're looking for. I suppose I could fill you in on a few details, except that I don't trust you at all."

The wheels began to turn in my mind. He had a book in his room—*Bringer of Light*. If I could steal that from him, maybe I could learn this information on my own. Then I wouldn't have to rely on a death angel.

"So in this partnership of ours, you're not going to tell me what we're looking for, or where we're going, or anything remotely useful."

He traced his fingertips over his wineglass. "What would be the fun in that? Besides, I don't need you running off to the Institute with every little morsel of information I give you. And I don't need you turning your powers on me."

Bastard was holding all the damn cards. "Hazel will never come with us if we can't tell her where we're going."

A cruel smile. "And what makes you think I have a use for your sister?"

My fingers tightened into fists. "I'm not leaving without her. You need me, and I'm not going without her."

"You do realize I can compel you to act. The fun I could have with a beauty like you." His sensual voice promised excruciating temptation.

I sucked in a sharp breath. "But you never have compelled me. How do I know you're not bluffing?"

Adonis's eyes flashed with a pale light, and I felt his magic ripple over my skin in a dangerous caress. The hair rose on the back of my neck, and an invasive power crawled through my blood, wrapping itself around my bones like a vine. Against my will, I felt my arm rise, my fingers reaching out for Adonis's face.

I couldn't control my voice anymore, but if I could, I'd be screaming at him. His intoxicating magic gripped me against my will. He had complete control over my body. I stared, entranced, as my fingertips stroked down his smooth cheek. He closed his eyes, breathing in deeply.

As soon as the magic loosened its grip on my body, I yanked my hand from his cheek. Snatching my wineglass from the table, I flung the contents in his face.

"Don't ever do that again," I snarled.

He leaned back in his chair, wine dripping from his skin in red rivulets. That infuriating, amused smile curled his lips as he dabbed the wine from his cheeks. "You did ask for a demonstration."

Once again, he had a point, but that didn't negate the primal outrage I felt at being controlled by an outside force. I tried to still the shaking in my body. I had nothing to threaten him with, no power of my own to stop him. Just my own impotent fury. "Promise me one thing. If you rule the celestial realm, will you be able to stay the fuck away from our world? Because angels like you don't belong here. This is our world. The demons, the fae, the humans. And we want it back."

Adonis seemed completely unperturbed. Bored, even. He held my gaze for a long moment, shadows pooling in the air around him. "Johnny could wake at any moment, and when he does, you'll be faced with not one, but two angels you've betrayed. I'm your only way out of here."

True. I refilled my glass, not answering him.

"Here's what you need to know for now," he continued. "We're going to my castle first. I have some informants there who can tell us about our next move. But if you think I'm going to tell you where to find *that*, you may as well dig yourself a shallow grave next to Johnny's."

I raised my eyebrows. "You have your own castle?"

"Where do you think I've been living all these years?" He rose from his chair, his pale gaze sweeping over me. "Get your things ready to leave quickly. Whether you like it or not, it's me and you against the world."

I shuddered, and his footsteps echoed off the high ceiling as he stalked out of the room.

Screwed. Adonis had all the power here, and I was truly and completely screwed.

Unless, of course, I could steal that book from his room and learn a few things of my own.

I LURKED outside Adonis's door, my ear pressed to the wood. I heard nothing inside his room. I sniffed the air—I couldn't smell his exotic scent, either.

Darkness had fallen outside, and only a few guttering candles lit the hallway. My pulse raced as I thought of sneaking around inside his room without his permission. What would he do to me if he found me?

I grabbed one of the candles from the sconces. Best if I got in and out of there fast, before I had the chance to find out.

Slowly, I turned the doorknob, opening the door into darkness.

I loosed a sigh of relief when I found the room empty. With a slow, careful movement, I shut the door behind me. Adonis had closed his curtains, and shadows seemed to climb the walls. I glanced at Adonis's bed, wondering for just a moment if he ever entertained women there, what it would be like to give in to his seductive power.

None of my business.

I crossed to the bookshelf, and a spark of hope lit in my chest when I spied the thin, black volume, *Bringer of Light* etched on the spine.

I pulled it from the shelf, holding the candle above it. I opened it with one hand, turning to the first page—a hand-drawn picture of light beaming from a tree branch.

That was when I felt something else in the room—a seductive, exotic presence that whispered over my skin. I froze at the sensation of breath warming the back of my neck, fingertips skimming my hips.

"Ruby, my darling," Adonis purred in my ear. "Did you think you could steal from the Dark Lord?" His voice was a dangerous caress.

Goose bumps rose on my skin. Of *course* he caught me. But how did he sneak up on me so quietly? My pulse raced, breath speeding up at the feel of his body's warmth behind mine.

I snapped the book shut, speaking to him over my shoulder, my heart pattering like a frightened animal. "I just wanted a little more information. Since you won't just tell me things."

"No one steals from me. But I suppose I have to let you live." His fingertips skimmed my hips again, a subtle promise of tormenting pleasure. "I can think of one way you can make it up to me."

Heat swooped through my belly. I pivoted, shoving the book at him. "You can keep your book. I'll find out the truth, one way or another."

Adonis plucked the book from my fingertips. "Honestly, this one doesn't contain anything useful anyway. You need to know Phoenician and cuneiform for that."

"Whatever." I stalked out of the room.

A part of me wanted to give in to the torturous pleasure he promised, but I'd never submit to the seductive allure of a monstrous angel of death.

CHAPTER 5

A howling noise woke me from my sleep—something inhuman that chilled me to my marrow.

I glanced quickly at Hazel, who snored gently by my side.

But that ragged keening kept winding through the air, piercing ice in my blood. I pushed off my blankets and crossed to the window. I pressed my hands against the cold panes, jumping as a sentinel drifted past, dark eyes wide, soaking in everything.

Even as a creature rent the night air with its cries, the sentinels were watching me. The only creatures the sentinels didn't watch were the angels.

I swallowed hard. Johnny couldn't have risen already, could he? It had only been a few days. Granted, I had no idea how long poisoned angels stayed unconscious. It wasn't like there were reference books for this kind of thing, and if there were, Adonis would probably just yank them from my hands.

I focused my vision, summoning my keen fae senses to search through the dark for signs of movement in the trees, but I could see nothing outside.

As I pressed my hands against the glass, a flock of ravens burst from the trees, squawking as they swooped away from the forest. They soared over the castle walls. More birds followed—crows, swallows—desperate and writhing murmurations that fled the dark forest in a chaotic panic.

Johnny. He was waking. I could feel it like a deep, gnawing hunger between my ribs, an emptiness I could never fill. I'd had the same feeling before, when I'd gotten too close to him on the castle parapet.

Adonis was right. These angels never belonged on earth.

A chill rippled over my skin at the sight of gray mist curling from the trees.

"Hazel," I said quietly.

"Mmmm." She rolled over, pulling the sheets tighter around her shoulders.

"Hazel," I said a little louder.

This time, she sat bolt upright.

My mouth had gone dry. "I think Johnny is waking already. We have to get out of here."

She rubbed her eyes, yawning. "Why?"

"Because he's going to tell everyone what I did." I spoke in a harsh whisper. "He's going to tell Kratos that I'm a fake, that I'm trying to kill them all."

Hazel blinked, suddenly becoming more alert. "Oh, right. I thought we had more time."

"So did I."

Her dark eyes were wide, skin pale, and her forehead furrowed. "Is that him? That terrible howling sound?"

"I think so. Doesn't sound happy, does he?"

In an instant, Hazel was by my side, hands pressed against the glass. Our breaths fogged the window as we stared outside. When a sentinel swooped past, my heart leapt. Would they report us—the two succubi with their faces

BLACK OPS FAE

pressed up against the window—as we waited for the angel to crawl from his shallow grave in the woods?

That hunger in my gut intensified, and I clutched my stomach. I'd never be full, never satisfied. My soul itself was starving, desperate for life. It was Johnny's strange magic—ripping through the air like a tornado.

Kratos made me want to fall to my knees and submit to his power, while Adonis lured me toward either death or seduction—I wasn't sure which. Johnny, on the other hand, filled me with an agonizing hunger.

Hazel pressed her palms to the window, and I could have sworn her cheeks looked thinner. "I'm starving," she said listlessly. "Do you know what it feels like to starve?"

Dear sister. I've fought men over scraps of rat meat.

"Not really," I lied. Through the confusion of hunger, I tried to scramble up a plan. Maybe we could pack what clothing we had, grab a few things from the kitchen—some bread, cheese, butter, a bit of meat...

Hazel's eyes had taken on a haunted look. "I want to stay where the food is." She shook her head. "We can't leave. We'll starve out there."

"Hazel. Our minds are being clouded by Johnny's magic. We'll bring food with us."

Bread, cheese, the pastries, lamb, venison, fruit... My mouth watered, and a wild hunger tore through me. How could we leave all this behind?

As we gaped out the window, dusty gray magic swirled from the trees, a sickly light tingeing the fog. And from the mist, a figure emerged—punctuated like a black hole against it. An angel stalked from the forest, his wings ragged, body gaunt and hunched.

My stomach dropped.

Definitely Johnny.

Frantically, I pushed all thoughts of starvation out of my mind, trying to focus. I ran for the wardrobe and yanked open the wooden doors. Unfortunately, these clothes weren't made for survival—they were made only for strutting around a castle, looking pretty. I had two sets of leather leggings, a sweater, and one jacket, plus a pair of boots. The rest was a useless collection of flimsy dresses.

Fast as I could, I dressed in the warm clothes. As I scrambled to put them on, I tossed a pair of leggings at Hazel.

With my sweater and my jacket on, I snatched my poison-tipped knife sheathed in its holster from the wardrobe and tied it around my waist.

Hazel still stared at the window, her body shaking. Didn't she realize what was going to happen here? I didn't even want to think about how they'd execute us. Kratos had tolerated me because he thought I was a succubus. I didn't think he'd tolerate betrayal. He demanded loyalty—worship, even.

My mind whirled in a fog of hunger, and I was dimly aware of Hazel babbling on about food—

Another sharp pang of famine ripped through my stomach, and I doubled over. In the hollows of my mind, images flashed of a woman starving, her ribs protruding through her back. A vulture circled overhead.

My fingernails were digging into my flesh, and I glanced at Hazel. *We have to get out of here.* I was ready to wrestle those leggings onto her slender body.

"Hazel," I said through gritted teeth. "Get dressed, or I'm going to have to kill you and eat your corpse."

"I'm going to the kitchen," Hazel declared.

In the next moment, she was rushing for the door.

I took off after her, our footsteps echoing down the corridor. She slammed through the door to the stairwell.

We didn't get very far when Hazel doubled over,

clutching her stomach. She leaned against the stairwell wall for support. "It's killing me."

Only one thought could drown out the oppressive hunger, and only one thing terrified me more right now. It was the sound of the heavy footfalls coming up the stairwell.

"He's coming," I whispered. He'd chosen this tower—the Tower of Wrath—the one where I slept. He was coming to kill me.

I pulled the knife from its sheath and stepped back up the stairwell. "Hazel," I whispered, grabbing her by the arm. "He's coming for us." She only seemed to care about one thing right now, so I'd have to focus on that. "That feeling of hunger that's ripping you apart—it's coming from Johnny. We have to get away from him."

We'd have to find another way out—another stairwell.

She nodded listlessly, seeming to listen to me for once.

Quietly, I pulled her back up the stairwell, backing away from Johnny. Gray magic, tinged with that pale green light, climbed toward us.

Shaking with hunger and exertion, I backed through the stairwell door—and into a powerful body. Slowly, I turned, looking up into Adonis's pale eyes. His midnight wings cascaded behind him.

Bizarrely—I actually felt relieved to see him.

"Johnny's coming," I whispered. My whole body was trembling. Pretty sure I was just a few minutes from passing out.

Adonis grabbed me by the biceps to steady me. "Johnny's magic is affecting you. He's not able to control it right now."

He touched my shoulder, and a soothing sensation rippled through my core, assuaging some of the hunger.

"Can you get us out of here?" I asked.

Adonis nodded, but the starvation kept intensifying. A tortured scream from Hazel ripped through the quiet castle. I knew what she was feeling—that death hovered over her like a bird of prey.

Adonis let go of me, then swooped down to scoop up Hazel. She wrapped her arms around his neck. Just as we began to move, the stairwell door slammed open, and Johnny's giant figure loomed in the doorway.

CHAPTER 6

*D*irt covered his face, and streaks of green smudged the side of his mouth, as if he'd been eating moss and grass. His shirt hung ragged and torn over his bony frame, and his blue Mohawk hung limp and dirty over his skull.

There, in his chest, an open wound gaped through his clothing. Where his heart should've been was instead a ravaged, corrupted hole. Right where I'd stabbed him.

The three of us—Adonis, Hazel, and I—stared at him, waiting to see what he would do.

Johnny reached for the wound, tracing his fingertips over it. Then, he smeared the blood down the front of his torso. His eyes were locked on me as he moved, wide and staring.

I clutched my stomach, leaning on Adonis for support. The closer I stayed to Adonis, the more his magic seemed to protect me from Johnny's, soothing that crippling hunger.

Johnny pointed a bony, blood-covered finger at me, and his jaw dropped.

Adonis cleared his throat. "Johnny. Wonderful to see you again. You look well."

As if this situation weren't terrible enough, I felt the presence of a third angel moving closer—this one beaming with gold.

Kratos strode toward us, his coppery wings radiating light. "Johnny," he boomed. "I thought I felt your presence. What the hell is going on here?"

Johnny just kept staring at me, pointing with his bloodied finger.

Adonis broke the silence. "It seems our favorite drunken angel has returned to us after one of his benders. No idea what happened to him, except that he seems to have had a brush with Devil's Bane. I'd hazard a guess that he doesn't remember the full story either. A tankard of vodka or two will do that to you."

Kratos narrowed his eyes. "Why are the succubi clinging to you like that?"

Adonis shrugged. "Johnny's famine magic is ripping their minds apart right now. Mine helps to soothe their pain."

"Johnny," Kratos said evenly. "Control yourself."

Johnny continued to glare at me, hatred burning in his eyes. Yet he wasn't saying anything, and his silence unnerved me.

He grunted, rubbing the wound on his chest again. His pale lips opened and closed. Maybe that Devil's Bane had gone straight to his mind, because he didn't seem to be firing on all cylinders anymore.

Without another word, he lunged for me, his eyes shot through with incendiary red. The next thing I knew, his hands were around my throat. I reached for the knife at my thigh—poison-tipped. If I poisoned him in front of Kratos, the jig would be up. Wouldn't take a genius to figure out who'd been messing around with Devil's Bane.

Through the blood roaring in my ears, I could hear my sister screaming my name.

My heart slammed against my ribs, my lungs burning as Johnny squeezed. Frantic, I lifted the knife—

Fortunately for me, I didn't have to make the call about whether or not to stab him, because Adonis was ripping Johnny away from me by his withered, blue mohawk.

"Subdue yourself," snarled Adonis, still gripping Johnny by the hair.

For a moment, Johnny seemed to grow calmer, some of the fire in his eyes dulling, even if his gaze was still locked on me. He took deep, ragged breaths, and a thin stream of drool slid from his lips.

Slowly, Adonis let go of Johnny's hair.

Then, like a wild beast, Johnny howled and whirled on Adonis.

Midnight feathers scattered into the air, and I watched with horror as Johnny tore a brutal rip in the top of Adonis's wing. The sound of a wing tearing is something I don't think I'll ever forget—the shredding of tendon and bones.

Adonis roared, and the temperature around us plunged, shadows swallowing up the light. With a feral snarl, Adonis rushed at Johnny. It took only a few moments for Adonis to snap the punk angel's neck, and the crack of bone echoed off the stone walls.

Kratos looked down at Johnny's crumpled, filthy body on the flagstones, his expression betraying nothing. "I've come to expect dramatic entrances from Johnny, but this one has surpassed my wildest dreams."

Adonis grimaced with pain. His hand hovered protectively near his wounded wing, but he didn't seem to want to touch it. A bit of bone jutted from the top of it, and streams of crimson blood trailed down his dark feathers.

I swallowed hard. "That looks like it hurts."

"I'll live."

Kratos's gaze slid from me to Adonis and back again. "Anyone care to tell me what the fuck is going on here?"

Hazel stepped closer to him, blinking her dark eyes innocently. "Johnny was drinking again. He reeks of vodka. Must have been quite a bender, and he found himself—yourself—tangled in the forest's brambles, unable to remember what got him there. When he tried to think back, it's all a foggy mist of vodka, moss, and the elder roots that pulled you deep into the earth, deep until the secrets are forgotten and questions plague you no more."

Kratos cocked his head, mesmerized by Hazel's rambling, as though she'd just uttered the wisest jumble of sentences in the history of the world. Fortunately for me, I seemed immune to her skills. And given the way Adonis was frowning at her, I had a feeling he was too.

Another set of footsteps echoed down the hall as Elan approached, his arms full of pastries and an entire baked ham. Some sort of custard coated his cat sweater and was smeared over his cheeks.

His eyes were on Johnny. "He returned! Is he all right?" Crumbs rained from his mouth as he spoke.

Hazel rushed over to the lanky fae. She grasped for the baked ham, while Elan clung to it, dropping all of the other food in his arms.

"Adonis," Kratos said sharply. "Can you stifle Johnny's magic? It's still creating chaos in here."

Still shielding his wing protectively, Adonis whispered something under his breath. His dark magic swooped around Hazel and me, soothing some of our gnawing hunger.

Kratos stared after him. "I'm going to find some stronger servants to drag Johnny back into his room until he recovers." He glared at Elan. "Share your food with the succubi, and see that they get back to their room." He stalked away, a golden glow in the gloom.

With Adonis's magic whispering over my body, some of the raw pain of famine began to bleed out of me, even if my stomach still rumbled.

While Elan and Hazel scooped food from the floor, I raised my eyebrows at Adonis. "How long will that take to heal?"

He looked positively murderous. "I won't be flying anytime soon."

"Thanks for pulling Johnny off me. I thought of stabbing him, but..." I glanced at Elan, unwilling to continue the conversation about poison-tipped weapons in front of him.

"Come." Adonis nodded at my bedroom, then quietly slipped into the fire-lit room.

While Elan and Hazel continued to gnaw on food in the hallway, I followed Adonis. He stood on the flagstones, and warm firelight wavered over his perfect features. The door closed softly behind me.

"How long until Johnny blows my cover?" I asked quietly.

"When Johnny wakes, his mind will be addled. He was already confused from being underground for days, and the poisons are probably still working their way through his brain. When I snapped his neck, I bought you more time. But he's immortal, and he'll recover eventually. You can't stay here any longer."

I swallowed hard. How could I trust Adonis? Everything he did was self-serving. Not to mention that I'd seen him vaporize people.

Kratos—for all his faults—had reunited me with my sister. He'd done it because he actually seemed to care for me on some level.

But what would Kratos do once he learned that I'd been lying to him this whole time?

I heaved a deep sigh, stuck in an impossible situation. "I'll go with you. But I want to take my sister."

The door creaked as Hazel opened it, and she crossed to my side. She'd chomped halfway through the ham already. "I heard that. And I'm staying here," she declared.

Irritation sparked. "Don't be ridiculous. I'm not leaving you here."

Adonis folded his arms, wincing just a bit at the movement. "She should stay here until Johnny shows the first signs of recovery."

"What are you talking about?" My voice came out a little too harshly.

Adonis stared at me. "If Johnny recovers within days, your sister can keep him confused for as long as possible. She has a remarkable skill."

Grease smeared Hazel's lips, and she wiped it off with the back of her hand. "Yeah. See? I have a purpose here."

I cocked my hip. "I really don't see how that's safe."

Hazel fixed her dark eyes on me. "I'm staying, Ruby. You go do what you can, and I have my own part to play here. You have to trust me. I survived the dragons, and I can survive the angels."

Adonis smirked. "See? She'll be fine here. Useful, in fact."

I clenched my jaw, pointing at my sister. "At the first sign of danger, you need to flee, okay? I don't care how hungry you are."

She nodded. "I'm going to keep a bag packed with food and clothing at all times, ready to go. Don't forget that I can summon dragons if I need to, so like, it's really not a big deal."

I frowned. "You can?"

"I told you. I charmed them." She pulled a gold dragon's tooth pendant from her shirt. "Right before I left, Uthyr the Harvester of Souls gave me this. Says he'll come for me when I need him. He's actually quite nice once you get to know him."

BLACK OPS FAE

Well. I didn't see that coming.

I turned to Adonis. "What are you going to tell Kratos? He doesn't want me anywhere near you."

Adonis was already heading for the door. "You pack your things for tomorrow morning, and you leave the rest to me. Meet me outside the Tower of Wrath after the sun rises tomorrow morning."

The door closed with a final click, and his footsteps echoed off the hallway outside.

The farther he moved from me, the more that gnawing hunger began to return, and I pulled the ham from my sister's reluctant hands. "Tomorrow morning, I need you to make contact with Yasmin, from the Institute of the Watchers. I told you the signal, right? She'll let you know where to meet her. Tell her everything. Johnny came back, he could recover his memory, and Adonis is taking me somewhere. Tell her that he plans to rule the celestial realm, I'm the Bringer of Light, and that's all I know."

"And how will you and I communicate when you're away?"

"We won't. That's why I didn't want to separate from you in the first place."

She crawled into the bed, pulling up the covers around her. "Such a worrier. What's the worst that could happen?"

My mouth dropped open. "The world could literally end and all living things could die?"

She blinked. "I have faith in you, Ruby. You'll figure something out."

A memory clawed at the recesses of my mind—a dark pool of glistening blood and gore on the pavement. *If I couldn't save Marcus...* I slammed an iron door over the memory. No point dwelling on the past.

A fae believed in beauty, in pleasure—dark thoughts were wasted moments.

After a final bite of ham, I crawled into bed next to my sister, listening to her breaths as they grew heavier.

CHAPTER 7

With the morning rays streaming into our room, I shoved my meager, useless clothing into a backpack. My chest ached at the thought of leaving Hazel again—but maybe she was right. I had to trust that she was smart enough to survive. And considering she could apparently summon a dragon at will—as well as befuddle anyone around her—I had to admit she had her own set of protections in place.

Dressed in my warmest clothes—my berry-blue wool coat from the night before, my leather leggings—I crossed to the bed. Rolling over, Hazel blinked sleep away. For just a moment, I caught a glimpse of my sister as she had been—the little twelve-year-old who'd cried when a boy at school dumped milk onto her backpack.

She smiled sleepily. "Ruby. You're dressed already."

"I have to go. I can't tell you where I'm going, because I don't know. Only that I'm going to Adonis's castle, and that we're looking for...something."

Hazel rubbed her eyes. "I'll keep Johnny and Kratos off your case."

"Just keep yourself safe. And check in with Yasmin to tell her what we know. Remember—use the candle to summon her. She'll want to meet you by the cave at the northern edge of the forest, near the mulberry grove. Find it as soon as you can."

She nodded. "Got it."

It was no wonder Adonis was keeping me in the dark. I took all the information I had straight to the Institute.

I pushed through the door into the frigid hallway. Every step away from my sister felt like a growling hollow in my chest, and I blinked away my tears.

Still, I had to do this. We couldn't stay here. There was only one way out of this situation alive, and that involved stopping the apocalypse itself. Unfortunately for me, I had to rely on one of the angels of death himself to get what I wanted.

I traced my fingertips down the cold stones as I descended the stairs. What made me a Bringer of Light? Yasmin had said something like "you can be our beacon, but first you must descend into the shadows." Maybe she meant it literally.

At the bottom of the stairs, I used my gloved hands to pull the iron bar from the door. I pushed outside into the frigid February air, and the sunlight dazzled my eyes for a moment. When they adjusted, I gaped at the slightly terrifying sight of two angels on horseback, their wings on full display.

Kratos sat on top of his powerful white horse. Sunlight streamed over his copper wings, blazing off his head like a crown of light. He wore his battle gear, and given the rigid set of his shoulders, he looked as if he were about to rip Adonis's heart out.

Adonis didn't look any more approachable. His midnight wings swooped out from a dark cloak, and he and his pale eyes blazed from within a dark cowl. His left wing hung at an awkward angle. I winced at the sight. I guess now I knew where to attack an angel. An angel could rise from the dead in just a few days, but a wing injury seemed like it could lay them out for weeks.

A sheathed sword glinted on his back, the hilt studded with red gems. His horse was a color I'd never seen before—a sort of purple-gray, like a fading bruise, with eyes of pure white and a silver mane. A large, black satchel hung off his saddle.

Another saddled stallion stood to Adonis's side, his fur a murky blue-green, like seawater. A gleaming, silver star shone from his forehead, and his mane flowed over his shoulders, the creamy color of seafoam. Clearly, these were not ordinary horses. In fact, they were creepy as hell.

As I drank in the scene, it took me a moment to realize both angels were glaring down at me.

"What?" I asked.

Kratos's hands gripped his horse's reins rigidly, looking like he was about to snap the leather through sheer force of will. "Adonis tells me that you're not safe here. He tells me that Johnny is coming for you. Something about his drunken escapades, a fixation on you."

"Is it any wonder?" A half smile curled Adonis's lips. "Succubi were created to tempt. Johnny is fighting his urge to fall, and Ruby is making it hard for him."

Kratos's golden eyes studied me. "Is this true, Ruby? Has Johnny been coming after you?"

I shot him my most innocent, baleful expression. "Yes. You saw him last night, pointing at me. He seems to blame me for something. Whatever got him into that state he was in. But I think Adonis is right. He's scared that I'll tempt him to fall, and he hates me for it."

Kratos's jaw tensed. "I should be the one to take her from here. You can't even fly."

I wished that Kratos had been the one to discover my secret, and that he and I were the ones going off together. He might be a monster, but he was a monster who'd returned my sister to me. That was worth *something*.

"I don't need to fly." Adonis's voice was pure ice.

Kratos grimaced, stroking his chest. He clearly hadn't been hunting enough to keep the pain away. "With that crippled wing of yours, you won't be able to disguise yourself. An angel traveling through the countryside will attract every vengeful demon in the country."

"Since when have I let a hostile demon get anywhere near me?" asked Adonis. "In any case, you won't be able to take her anywhere, Kratos. You're as tempted as Johnny is. I *saw* you with her, ripping her clothes off. If I leave the two of you alone for ten minutes, the Heavenly Host will tear the rest of the world to shreds. And besides. You need to hunt."

Kratos's wings spread out behind him, and for just a moment, hot fury glinted in his eyes. After a heavy silence, he asked, "Where are you taking her?"

"I have to return to my castle. A shadow demon rebellion has been brewing nearby. It will give you and Johnny enough time to get control of yourselves, and if you still want her, I'll return her."

Kratos glared down at me. "Fine. Go with him. You'll be back here as soon as I get control of Johnny."

He didn't give me any choice in the matter. I was his to command, apparently. I no longer felt quite as guilty about plotting against him.

Adonis nodded at the seafoam horse. "I hope you can ride."

I nodded. One of the many fae gifts my parents had given to me—not that I was particularly practiced at it. "Kind of."

BLACK OPS FAE

Kratos met my gaze evenly. "If you need me, write my name on a piece of paper and burn it. I will hear the summons and come for you."

Like a magical text message. "Thanks, Kratos."

Without another word, Kratos reared his horse and galloped off into the forest. I had a disturbing feeling he'd be exceptionally savage on his hunt tonight.

Adonis peered down at me. "Do you need any help mounting Nuckelavee?"

I frowned. That name seemed somehow familiar. "Nuckelavee? Isn't that...a demonic horse monster?"

Adonis shrugged. "He's not as bad as people make him out to be."

Wonderful. "No, I can mount him fine." *I think.*

I crossed to the horse. I knew this was insane, but I could have sworn the thing narrowed his dark eyes at me as I approached. I stroked his mane, and the creature snorted, steam rising from his nostrils. He jerked his head away, not wanting anything to do with me.

Shit. Well, charming a horse couldn't be any harder than charming humans, could it?

I stroked his mane again, trying to conjure my inner horse-whisperer. "We're going to be friends," I whispered.

He snorted again, then reared on his hind legs.

"Nuckelavee!" Adonis barked. "Stop it."

I grabbed the stallion's reins, trying to gain control of the situation. Clearly I wasn't getting anywhere with charm. I scrambled to slide my left foot into the stirrup, clutching the saddle as if my life depended on it. With a loud, ungraceful grunt, I swung my right leg over the saddle.

Nuckelavee took off in a gallop.

As the stallion carried me away from Hotemet Castle—away from my sister—I felt more alone than ever before. I'd only just reunited with Hazel, and maybe she wasn't even quite the sister I remembered.

Still, she was all I had left at this point. Since the Great Nightmare had begun, every separation had the overwhelming potential to be permanent.

CHAPTER 8

Three hours into our journey, I wanted to die. The word *uncle* rang in my head like a curse. My thighs were not coping so well with the situation. In fact, they'd been trembling and screaming for the past hour, and I'd started to look forward to Nuckelavee's little grass-eating detours.

Still, my pride stopped me from calling out to Adonis. When I used to play Mercy as a kid, grappling with older boys who twisted my arms behind my back, I was never the first to cry *uncle*. I wasn't about to start giving in now.

Leaning into the wind as he rode, Adonis seemed completely impervious to exertion, silver-flecked wings sparking with sunlight. He was supposed to be the one who was injured. Why did this seem so easy for him?

He hadn't been one for conversation so far, which gave me nothing to think about but my shrieking thighs. I clenched tighter onto the reins, willing myself not to fall off.

"What's your horse's name?" I called up to him as we rode through yet another windswept, grassy field.

Adonis slowed his pace, turning back to look at me. "Thanatos."

I frowned, pulling on Nuckelavee's reins until he slowed to a trot. Good. I'd stalled our pace. "Thanatos. Doesn't that mean *death?* Like, a Greek god of death?"

"Yes." He slowed his horse to a trot by my side.

Circling above us, Adonis's pet, Drakon, screeched, piercing the quiet countryside. The black-scaled dragonile's cries slid through my bones, and I shuddered. Given that Drakon's larger, dragon-shifter counterparts had killed my parents *and* my boyfriend, I didn't have particularly warm feelings about demonic, reptilian creatures.

I blocked out the dragonile's cries and heaved a sigh of relief at our slowed pace. Maybe I could keep Adonis talking about his favorite topic, which I imagined to be himself.

I nudged Nuckelavee onto a patch of clover, and he wandered to the right. "Can't control this thing," I said. "I think he needs a snack, and we can just have a little chitchat for a minute."

"A chitchat," Adonis repeated with no inflection.

I needed a snack. Didn't Adonis know that the fae needed to eat?

He reared his horse to a halt by my side. "I can help you control Nuckelavee if—"

Distract him. "So you named your horse after a Greek god of death?"

"Not exactly." The wind toyed with his cloak.

"Care to elaborate? How did Thanatos get his name, then?"

"Thanatos is my true name, and my horse and I are inextricably linked. He appeared when I was born."

My mouth went dry, and I swallowed hard. "So…you're a literal god of death."

"Archangels. Gods. Humans use these words interchangeably." A nearly imperceptible shrug. "I suppose 'god' suits me, but I don't like to brag."

I snorted. "What do you mean your horse—"

A squirrel scampered across the field nearby, and Nuckelavee jerked me toward it in a chase. Pain screamed in my thighs. I grimaced, struggling to rear my horse to a halt again, when Nuckelavee stopped and began munching on a dandelion.

"We should go," said Adonis.

"Hang on." I caught my breath. "The horse needs to rest. You can't run these beasts into the ground. Anyway, I don't think you've explained your death-god thing to me well enough. What does it mean?"

"It means that I'm incredibly powerful and destined to kill. You already know this."

Lovely. At least I'd found a way to stall him. "Can you escape your destiny? Who makes the rules, anyway?"

"It's a very interesting question, Ruby. One probably best left to philosophers and people who like to hear themselves speak."

"I took a psychology class in high school. Have you ever heard of the Thanatos drive?"

"What *are* you talking about?"

"Humans aren't just driven to live, or to procreate, apparently. That's Eros." I chewed my lip. "Wait, is Eros a real god, too?"

"He's a demon." Adonis arched an eyebrow. "He's awful. Thousands of years old and he acts like an eighteen-year-old. What was your point exactly?"

"Humans have a Thanatos drive. They're attracted to death. It's why they smoke, start wars, drive fast cars... Why they drink themselves into comas."

He nodded slowly. "Humans crave oblivion as much as they fear it. They crave release."

"Why?"

His eyes pierced me, his dark magic curling around him in sharp whorls. "So they can have some peace and quiet, I should imagine. It's an idea I empathize with at the moment."

I blinked, watching as Adonis took off at a gallop. Of course, he just expected me to follow. I gritted my teeth, spurring Nuckelavee on. Pain shot through my thighs, and I groaned.

After another five minutes of cantering, I glimpsed an iron-gray river cutting through the field. Willow trees lined its banks, and an old stone bridge spanned the rushing water.

How *good* it would feel to rest against the trunks of one of those glorious trees, or the stone bridge. How much I wanted to drink some water and lie down in the grass…

Desperation screamed in my mind.

"Adonis!" I bellowed, blood roaring in my ears. "Uncle! Uncle! Uncle!"

He halted Thanatos, his eyes wide as he turned around to look at me. "Why on earth are you shouting the word *uncle*?"

"I'm done!" I shouted. "I don't care anymore. I'm tired. This is ridiculous. You win!"

He cocked his head, his dark magic swirling around his horns, his leathery wings. "What do I win?"

I swallowed hard. I wasn't sure exactly why I was so angry, except that I hadn't wanted to admit defeat, and now I'd done it. Humiliatingly, I felt tears sting my eyes, and I blinked them away.

A shadow swooped over my head, and I glanced up to catch sight of Drakon soaring in lazy arcs above us. He opened his throat, breathing a hot burst of fire into the air.

I cleared my throat, taking care to speak with a steady voice, the voice of reason. "We need to rest. I can't keep riding."

"You should have just said so."

I lifted my chin. "I'm saying it now."

A small smile curled the corner of his lips. "What does *uncle* mean?"

I swallowed hard. "It's an American game. It's not important."

He nodded at one of the trees. "Let's rest under there."

I nodded, so grateful the tears nearly started again, but I clenched my jaw until I had control of myself again.

Under the naked boughs of a willow tree, I dismounted from Nuckelavee, slowly sliding down his enormous side. I walked hunched over, my legs trembling.

Adonis frowned at me with concern. "You look as if you can hardly walk," he said quietly. His pale eyes stood out sharply below the straight, black lines of his eyebrows.

"Not all creatures are made to gallop on horses for hours at a time. I'm stronger than a human. Not as strong as a death god. Plus, you're part horse or something, as we established."

"I didn't say that."

I pointed to his twisted wing. "How does that feel?"

"I can hardly feel it now." He nodded at a large rock on the river's edge. "Sit down. I'll help you."

Pain ripped through my legs as I lowered myself to the rock. "Help me how?"

Without a word, he sat next to me on the rock. "I can take your pain away if you let me."

I blinked at him. "And are you concerned about my comfort? I thought we established that you're a monster."

"I can't have you slowing me down with a broken body." A slight edge tinged his voice.

Bone-deep pain screamed up my legs, my hips. "Fine. Whatever you need to do."

With a smooth movement, he brushed his fingertips over my knees. Shadows seemed to thicken around him, and his magic wrapped around me, both soothing and electrifying at the same time. Warmth streamed from his fingertips, swirling into places I had no business thinking about right now. As he touched my legs, he pulled the pain from me.

But at the same time, his agonizingly light touch filled me with a hot ache. I wanted more of him.

"That's helping," I whispered, disturbed by my own body's reaction to him.

Slowly, he traced his fingertips farther up my thighs, his warm, silky magic penetrating my body. I stared at the dark swoop of his eyelashes, such a stark contrast to his pale eyes. I fought the impulse to kiss his skin, to press my breasts against him. *Sweet release.* I hoped he didn't notice the subtle arch of my back, or my pulse racing. I hoped he didn't hear my heart slamming against my ribs. Molten heat pooled in my belly, and my mouth opened, ready to be kissed.

As he soothed my pain, his face moved closer to mine, his breath warming my cheek. Up close, I had the chance to study the perfect, golden smoothness of his skin, the perfect, straight eyebrows. I remembered the thrilling rush of heat when my tongue had brushed against his…

Then, he pulled away, and the loss of his touch felt like a cold, sharp shock to my system. I almost grabbed his hand and put it on my thigh again, before I regained some composure.

Get a grip, Ruby. He has this effect on every woman he meets. The thought annoyed me. How easy it was for him to seduce, and how little it probably meant to him.

"Better?" he asked, completely unruffled by what might have been one of the most erotic encounters of my life. If he could do that to me by just touching my thighs, what would it feel like—

"Ruby?"

I blinked at him, trying to remember how to form a sentence. "What?"

"Does your leg feel better?"

I sucked in a deep, steadying breath. "Oh, that. Yes. It's better."

I narrowed my eyes at his wing. The wound had opened again, and a bright stream of blood spilled down the front.

"Isn't there something we can do for your wing?" I asked quietly.

"Not unless you have healing powers like I do."

"If you're a god of death," I asked, "why do you have the power to heal?"

"Because death is an analgesic."

I frowned. "This doesn't have any side effects, does it? Like necrosis?"

He smiled slowly, pulling his hands away. "No. You'll be fine."

The pain had completely left my body, replaced instead with a warm, tingling excitement. I could get addicted to his touch, like a drug fiend craving opiates.

Pretty sure the last thing I needed was to let Adonis's seductive beauty lure me in. I'd be keeping my Thanatos drive well and truly suppressed.

CHAPTER 9

I stared out over the wildflower-dappled field. "I might not have healing powers, but I'm supposed to be the Bringer of Light, right? And the Old Gods will provide. All we need to do is tune in to their beauty."

"Is that right?" I heard a faintly mocking tone in his voice.

"They've given me what I needed so far: poison, sap from the trees to light my arrows, the power of light." I sat up straight. "Let me try it."

I closed my eyes, focusing on the sounds around me—the rustling of the wind through the grasses, the gentle lapping and splashing of the river. A faint whispering floated on the breeze, the words unintelligible. A vibrating power seemed to move up my feet, up my limbs, lighting my body from the inside out. Something faintly floral wafted through the air—an unusual scent for February.

I opened my eyes, scanning the tall grasses around me, until I spotted a faint smudge of yellow in the distance. "There," I said.

"What?"

"They're giving us a remedy." I rose on my newly healed

legs. I bit my lip. "I don't suppose you have any bandages though?"

He nodded at Thanatos. "You can find a blanket in the satchel. Tear a strip off it."

I crossed to his enormous, bruise-colored horse, who reared back his head, snorting as I approached. Gingerly, I stroked his silver mane until he quieted. Then, I reached into the leather satchel, pulling out a thick woolen blanket. I slid my knife from its holster, then sliced a long, thin strip from the wool. I stuffed the rest of the blanket back into the satchel.

With the bandage ready, I hurried over to a patch of white and yellow wildflowers blooming among the grasses.

When I was a kid, my mom took me out on long treks into the New England forests. We'd walk through the forests, her pale hair gleaming in chinks of streaming sunlight, her hiking boots and jeans muddied. She always wore long sleeves, even in summer. She had some kind of brutal scar she didn't want anyone to see. An attack from a wild beast that had disfigured her—a reptile, probably. She'd never tell me the whole story.

In any case, those long nature walks were my salvation.

I smiled, then plucked a handful of the weeds and stroked my fingertips over the delicate, fern-like leaves. I remembered Mom's voice as she told me yarrow was a styptic—a substance that can staunch bleeding.

I stripped the leaves from the stem, piling them into one of my palms. Then, I closed my eyes and held my palm up to the sunlight. Warmth blazed from my palm, the sun's rays using my hand as a brazier, and an herbal smell filled the air. When I opened my eyes again, the leaves had been heated, dried to a crisp.

I grinned. Maybe I didn't know what the hell it meant, but I felt blessed by the Old Gods. This was the way of the ancient fae—live in the moment; merge with the beauty around you.

I scanned the earth for moss until my gaze landed on a bright green patch among the rocks and grasses nearby. I knelt down next to it and pried off a cool, damp chunk.

Clutching my handfuls of moss and dried yarrow, I crossed back to Adonis. When I reached him, I plopped down next to him on the rock.

He was studying me with an intense curiosity. "Communing with the Old Gods, I suppose?"

I opened my palm. "I have my own healing treatment for that shattered wing of yours."

"Is this really necessary?"

"It will heal a lot faster than if you just rely on your own magic. And what if it heals all crooked?"

"I must admit. I want to know what your hands would feel like on my wings."

My cheeks flushed. "What, is that some kind of sex thing for angels?"

A slow shrug.

"I'll try to forget I just learned that." I examined his midnight blue wings, cascading gracefully over the back of the rock. Streaks of blood pooled from the jagged break at the top.

"So I'm supposed to trust the healing skills of a deceitful, feral fae?" A seductive purr softened the harshness of his words.

"Yes. I know you hate the fae, but we have our own set of skills." Carefully, I laid out the moss and crushed herbs on my makeshift bandage. "I spent my formative years with my mom, learning about the trees, the plants, the herbs. We found a broken sparrow once, and she taught me to treat and set his wing."

A wicked smile. "And you think I'm like a broken sparrow."

"Same idea. You're just bigger." Gently, I ran my fingertips over the top of his wing.

Adonis inhaled sharply, his wing twitching, pupils dilating.

"Did that hurt already?"

"No. But wings are a sensitive area. I don't normally let anyone touch them."

"It's a closed fracture," I said. "I think the open break has begun to set itself already. This will help with the tears in your skin and muscle."

"How ever did I survive four thousand years without you?"

I leaned in closer to him and began pressing the dried yarrow against his wing, his feathers soft and silky against my fingertips. As I pressed the herbs against him, he gasped faintly, and his lids lowered. I couldn't quite tell if he was enjoying this or hating it, but I tried not to think about it either way.

"Yarrow will staunch the bleeding and clean the wound," I said quietly. I picked up the moss from the rock and gently held it over the broken wing's surface. "And this will help pack the wound." Holding the moss in place, I reached for the bandage.

Carefully, I tied it over the top of his wing, pressing the moss and yarrow to his feathers. He winced slightly, but as I threaded it gently around his muscle and bone, through the curtain of midnight feathers, his stormy eyes were locked intently on my face. I was pressing in close to him to reach his back, and his body radiated warmth.

I sat back on the rock, admiring my work. He drank me in with his gaze.

"There. Good as new." I took a deep breath. "See? Fae skills can be useful. We're not *just* beasts."

A twitch of his lip. "You didn't grow up around them, did you?"

I shook my head. "My parents left the fae realm long before I was born." I swallowed hard. "What did you mean when you said you lived among the fae, helping them kill for fun?"

Any trace of a smile disappeared from his face. "They're savage and driven to dominate."

My wild antics obviously didn't do much to dispel that notion—not that he'd seemed to mind at the time.

"If they were so savage, why did you help them kill?"

"I told you. I was born to kill." He definitely wasn't smiling now. In fact, his voice had a despairing edge.

"But why the fae in particular—if you hate us so much?"

Sharp tendrils of his magic cut at the air, and he pulled his gaze away from me.

I heaved a sigh. "Fine. Don't elaborate. I wouldn't expect you to. We can get on with the journey now that you've healed my legs." My stomach grumbled loudly.

Adonis scowled. "You should have told me you were hungry."

I rubbed my belly. "I didn't feel the hunger until now. Now that my legs are no longer screaming at me."

He cocked his head, studying me like a curious child would a dying insect. "And why didn't you tell me you were tired?"

My jaw tightened. "Because I didn't want you to know. You don't tell me things, and I don't tell you things. That's our relationship."

He quirked an eyebrow. "I see. I thought you were big on chatter." He stood and crossed to his horse. He rummaged in his leather pack for a moment, then pulled out some packages wrapped in brown paper. He pulled out a flask too.

The rock felt frozen beneath my bum, and I pulled my coat a little tighter around me. "Do you feel hunger?"

"No. But sometimes, I eat for pleasure. I understand your kind need sustenance."

I began unwrapping the food he'd brought: a package of bread, one of chorizo, and one of cheese. My mouth watered, and I had to restrain myself from throwing my arms around Adonis's neck to thank him for understanding the concept of "needing sustenance."

I drew my Nyxobian blade to slice the chorizo, before I gave up on manners and just started gnawing on it like a wild animal. When I took a break from the chorizo to build myself a hasty cheese sandwich, Drakon ambled over and snatched the sausage from the ground.

I grumbled through my mouthful of sandwich. "That was mine."

When I finished eating, crumbs littered my blue coat. "Sorry. Did you want any?"

Adonis's eyes were wide. "I honestly didn't know the fae got *quite* that hungry."

"Older fae can control it better."

"And how old are you?"

I cleared my throat. "Not as old as I'd pretended to be."

"*How old?*"

"Twenty-five."

His eyes snapped open. "Sweet heavenly gods. You were just born."

I folded my arms. "Johnny isn't that much older than me. Born in the seventies." I squinted in the sunlight. "How does it work, exactly? Why are you all such different ages?"

He sipped from his flask. "Johnny, Kratos, and I—we're different than other archangels."

"Different how?"

"The Heavenly Host is made up of ten archangels. Like us, they're nearly impossible to kill. But they're heavenly beings. Johnny, Kratos, and I—we're archangels who were born on earth."

I frowned. "And your parents were...what exactly?"

"My father was an archangel. My mother was a human."

Surprise flickered through me. "So you're...half human."

"There's nothing human about me. An archangel is defined by his soul."

"Right." His mother would have died thousands of years ago, but his father? I couldn't quite believe he was telling me all this, and I had a burning desire to know more about him. About all of this.

"Did your father return to the heavens?" I asked.

His gaze shuttered, and something about the raw look in his eyes told me not to push anymore on this question. I'd touched a nerve somehow. Still, I *needed* to know more. Needed to know how and why all this had happened.

"Why did it start?" I asked. "The Great Nightmare?"

"Once the wars started between humans, demons, the fae —the Heavenly Host decided it was time for a purification. Since the fall, they've just been waiting for the right moment to unleash us. And you all gave it to them with your infighting."

"I see." I swallowed hard. "Why does Johnny make me feel so...*hungry* when he stands near me?"

Adonis's keen eyes searched me. "He's an angel of famine."

"Famine," I repeated. "And you're...death."

"Is that what you feel when I stand near you?"

Not exactly. But I wasn't going to tell him that standing near him made me yearn for the excruciating pleasure I knew he could give me. That he made my blood heat, my breasts strain against my clothes until I wanted to pull them off.

Nope, no way I was saying that. The archangel's ego was oppressive enough as it was. Instead, I said, "Something like that. Shadows seem to cling to you. You give off a bit of a death vibe."

I almost thought I saw a flicker of disappointment in his pale eyes. He sipped his flask before handing it to me. "And what do you feel when you're near Kratos?"

My throat tightened. *Like I want to fall to my knees.* "He exudes dominance. Like he was born to conquer."

"And there you have it."

My pulse raced as a glimmer of understanding began to spark in my mind. "Death, Famine, Conquest…" My stomach clenched as I pieced it all together. "Your horse."

Adonis's pale, gray eyes pierced me. I shivered, and he widened his wings, shielding me from the wintry winds that whipped at my hair and skin. The feathered tip of one wing brushed against my skin, and I shivered.

"I thought it was a human myth," I said hollowly.

"You thought what was a human myth?"

"The four horsemen of the apocalypse."

CHAPTER 10

"I prefer angel to horseman," he said, "but either is fine."

My throat had gone dry. "So that means there's one more. War, right?"

A hint of mockery in his smile. "I think your young mind has learned all it can handle at this point."

The wind rushed over the river, carrying with it the scent of early wisteria shoots.

I didn't understand him, or the archangels, or the horsemen. Adonis was a dark and foreign power. I only knew that in the sound of the wind rustling the leaves, I felt the Old Gods calling me.

"And your purpose on earth is to kill in massive numbers." I hugged my knees to my chest. "I don't know what you have planned for me, Adonis, but I happen to believe that the good guys always win in the end. Even if you have to go through several years of hell and death to get there."

Shadows slid through his eyes. "And you're sure you know who the good guys are?"

BLACK OPS FAE

A shiver danced up my neck. "Not exactly. But I think the Old Gods are the good guys. I felt them in the forest outside Hotemet Castle. I feel them out here, even, whispering on the February wind, mingling with the early scents of spring. And I felt them on Eimmal, when their power flowed through my body like an ancient river. They're looking after the fae, the humans."

"Don't mistake them for benevolent gods. Nature gives as much as it takes. Death is as much a part of nature as life. Have you ever seen a starving grizzly take down a deer? Or watched smallpox spread through a village? That is nature as much as the pretty flowers you enjoy sniffing."

I bit my lip. "Fine. Nature is full of terrible things, but we don't need to focus on it, do we? Is the world a terrible place or a beautiful place? The answer to that is a choice. Our lives and our souls are our stories. That's where truth lies. And I want to tell the stories of love and happiness, not chaos and death."

Adonis was studying me closely. "And what are your personal stories of love, Ruby?"

The word *love* on his tongue was a sensual caress that licked up my spine, but I pushed the temptation out of my mind. "Not the kind you'd want to hear. They're not about seduction and pleasure, they're about knowing someone so well they become a part of you." A flicker in my mind, a pile of ash on the ground. I slammed my mental door down. "Before your archangel friends started destroying the world, I had that kind of love."

"What was his name?"

I didn't want to say Marcus's name in front of him. In fact, I didn't want to think about him at all, now. Because whenever I did, vicious images clawed at the back of my skull. Loss gnawed at me from the inside out. Those last, agonizing moments—

I clamped my eyes shut. "I don't want to think about this anymore. Like I said—our souls are our stories, and I want to focus on the good ones."

"But when you cut out the blood and the death and all the monstrous things that scare you, you'll start to forget the people you've lost. And you'll lose yourself, too."

My fists tightened. "Is that right?"

The breeze toyed with his dark hair, and his exotic scent wrapped around me. "There's no light without darkness, no good without evil, no meaning without death. The seeds of destruction grow in the gardens of paradise."

I scowled. "Did you just make that saying up? That is a super depressing aphorism."

"It's an old archangel saying."

"I think I preferred it when you were just making vaguely suggestive comments about touching my thighs."

His brow furrowed. "I've made no comments about touching your thighs. Would you like me to?"

He hadn't? Flustered, I rose. At that moment, I realized that my bladder was completely full. "This has been a fascinating philosophical discussion, but I'm going to the other side of the bridge. Give me a few minutes."

"Why are you going to the other side of the bridge?"

I frowned. "I need to pee, if you must know. And I'd rather not do it in front of one of the horsemen of the apocalypse. Don't come anywhere near there."

"I'll try to restrain myself."

With my arms folded, I walked briskly over the river bank, heading for the stone bridge. My mind whirled with everything I'd learned today. Strangely, instead of being overwhelmed, I felt energized. Sure, things died, nature was harsh. I'd signed up as a partner of the horseman of death. But the Old Gods thrived all around me, and I had the sense that they wanted to lure me into their realm, that they'd be on my side when I needed them.

I snuck behind the bridge, shielding myself from Adonis's view on the other side of a stony wall. After checking around me for any signs of life, I pulled down my leather leggings and underwear. I crouched on the sloping river's edge, taking care not to pee on my own shoes or pants. The wind nipped at my bare bum.

When I'd finished, I quickly pulled up my pants. In the shadows of the bridge, I took a moment to readjust the holster on my thigh. As I did, a splashing sound in the water behind me turned my head.

My heart stopped. There, in the steely, frigid river waters, stood a black hound, the size of our horses. Mist whirled around him, chilling me to the bone. His eyes blazed like hot, red coals, and his lips curled back from his teeth in a terrifying snarl. I reached for the knife at my thigh.

As I did, the creature began to shift, twisting silently in the ghostly mist—until he transformed into three humanoid forms. They looked massive, their hulking bodies dripping with water.

One of them sniffed the air, water streaming from his dark hair in rivulets over his pale skin. Tight, black clothing clung to his body, and claws grew from his fingertips. "You look like a succubus," he growled. "You smell even more delicious than a succubus, though. What are you?"

Since the Great Nightmare had begun, demons seemed to have free reign to terrorize smaller creatures as much as they wanted. My hand twitched at my knife. Should I simply stay and fight, or scream for Adonis at this point? I didn't suppose these were friendly demons.

"What do you want?" I asked quietly.

"Food and fucking," the three identical demons said in

unison. "You showed us your naked arse, and it looked good to us."

My stomach turned. *Oh, gross.*

"No thanks." I took a step back, pointing my knife at them. "I don't want to have to hurt—"

One of the demons silenced me with a sharp slash of his arm. I mean he *literally* silenced me, stealing my voice. I opened my mouth, trying to shout, and no sound came out. A jolt of fear gripped me.

As I readied my knife, one of the demons lunged for me. Heart pounding, I sharpened my senses and gripped the hilt. When the demon reached me, I was ready for him. I darted forward at the full speed of a fae, driving my knife between two of his ribs.

He clutched his chest, gurgling, and I let him slump to the ground. To my horror, two more enormous hounds emerged from the churning river waters, eyes blazing red.

In the mists, the black hounds transformed into more hulking, red-eyed demons.

"Bitch!" one of them hissed. "I will tear your flesh from your bones!"

I opened my mouth again to shout, but only a whisper wheezed from my throat. My legs shaking, I turned to run. I only got a few feet before rough hands were dragging me back over the rocks, into the water. I opened my mouth to scream for Adonis, and a rush of air puffed out.

I kicked one of them hard in the shins with the heel of my boot, and he loosened his grip on me just enough that I could wrench my knife arm free. With a clumsy gesture, I managed to nick his skin before more rough, powerful arms began dragging me under the water. One of them shoved my head into the icy river. Still, I clung on to that poison-tipped knife with everything in my power. I held my breath.

He released my head for just a moment, allowing me to suck in a frigid breath.

"You need to learn some manners," one of the demons barked. "Give a blessing to the river god." He rammed my head under the surface again.

I kicked and bucked fruitlessly. *Air. Sweet, heavenly gods, I need air.* After what seemed an eternity, my lungs started to burn, and panic ripped through my body.

At last, I tore my arm free and brought the knife down hard into the shin of one of the demons. I flailed, getting my head above water just long enough to draw a breath. That was when I felt the light burning dimly in my body, a warm glow of primordial power.

With a burst of wild energy, I wrenched free from the demons' grasp. I sucked in a sharp breath, desperate to sprint away from them. But I knew I needed to face them. If I turned my back to these hounds, they'd just pull me under again. I whirled, my blade ready, glowing with the light of the Old Gods.

As the first demon reached me, I slashed my blade across his throat, severing his jugular. Blood sprayed.

How many of them *were* there now? My heart hammered against my ribs, and I took another step back on the muddy shore, clutching my knife.

Five. Five enormous demons still standing, all gunning for my blood. Even with the power of the Old Gods…

Just as another one of these demons was running for me, Adonis's magic skimmed over my skin, snaking around the demons' bodies. Trembling, I stepped away from them. Tendrils of dark magic curled in a wild dance around them, freezing the demons in place.

Their jaws dropped, their expressions slackening. Abruptly, with jerking movements, they turned in the water, stumbling toward the bridge.

My entire body was shaking, blazing with light, with energy, with battle fury. But I just stood there, gaping at the Dark Lord's magic. So *this* was what Adonis's mind control powers looked like. A terrible sort of awe bloomed in my chest. This was the power of a death god.

I glanced back at him, standing just a few feet away from me. His silver-streaked, midnight wings swooped behind him, and his eyes gleamed like stars. He loomed above the riverbed, murmuring in an ancient language, shadows cloaking his powerful body. The sight of him sent an icy lick of dread racing up my spine.

Through the rushing water, the small demon horde trudged closer to the bridge, moving faster now. I cleared my throat, finding I could vocalize again.

My stomach jolted when the first red-eyed demon began bashing his head against the sleek stone of the bridge. More followed, slamming their heads against the rocks. I winced at the sound of cracking bone, the grunts and strangled cries that came from the demons, bashing their own skulls in. Blood and gore sprayed across the bridge's rocky surface.

Bile rose in my throat. He *did* tell me he was born to kill. And I'd wanted to kill the demons, too. Just maybe not with the same disturbing, bone-chilling brutality.

I stared grimly at the scene before me, cringing at the agonized snarls and shrieks, and my fingers tightened into fists.

Did I really want to give Adonis more power? What if he was lying about returning to the celestial realm, and just wanted to weaken the other archangels so he could assume complete control over the earth?

I found it hard to believe he wanted to take off into the heavens. I couldn't imagine him as an incorporeal being, just floating around. He was blood and bone, lust and violence, primal seduction—as bestial and full of cravings as I was.

I clenched my jaw. I'd go along with him for now to learn what I could from him, but I wasn't about to start trusting him.

When the last of the demons had slumped, bloodied and broken, into the churning river, I loosed a long breath.

"That was an interesting execution method," I said quietly.

Adonis's pale gray eyes had darkened to the color of iron. "Sometimes I like to get creative." He took a deep, shuddering breath, then winced, turning away from me. It almost looked like he was in pain. "Are you all right?"

"I'm fine. Just cold."

As he began walking back to the horses, I followed after him. Drakon circled slowly overhead, plumes of smoke curling from his mouth.

"Does that sort of magic drain your energy?" My teeth chattered from the freezing water.

"Yes, but sometimes it's worth it."

I hugged my coat tighter. "Why? What was it about these demons in particular that provoked your rage?"

"I sense what they wanted to do to you. I could practically hear their thoughts. It was repulsive, and they needed to answer for it."

I arched an eyebrow. Once again, I reminded myself never to get on his bad side.

CHAPTER 11

Adonis's magic had worked its way into my body, providing a sort of painkiller as we rode farther north through darkening fields. I'd changed into dry clothes, though I had to wait for my coat to dry before I'd feel warm again.

Neither Thanatos nor Nuckelavee showed any signs of tiring, and we were able to take them at a gallop for part of the way.

As the sun set, long shadows climbed over the fields. By the time darkness had fallen, we'd reached the north of England.

Darkness still terrified me. Now, we had only the thin moonlight to light our way, casting a dull glow over the rocky, undulating fields. My grip tightened on the reins. If a cloud went over the moon, I'd be at risk of a humiliating panic attack.

I strained my eyes, making out the short grasses that grew among the rocky hills. Was this what I'd heard was called the moors?

Farther ahead on the path, moonlight dimly illuminated a

grove of sycamore trees that stood out starkly against the flat landscape.

Even if my thighs had recovered somewhat, tiredness had sapped my energy, and my eyes started to drift closed. Under the cloak of darkness, an icy chill had fallen over me, and the February wind stung my skin. When, exactly, were we stopping? And where were we going to sleep?

My teeth chattered. I'd already admitted weakness once today. Might as well run with it.

"Adonis!" I called out.

He whirled, and Thanatos's eerie eyes gleamed in the darkness.

"Are you all right?" His voice carried over the moors.

"Fine. I just thought... Maybe we could sleep soon. I'm about to fall off Nuckelavee, and I think the beast is heartless enough to trample me to death. There's a grove of sycamores over there that can shield us in the wind. Maybe we can make a fire pit."

"Fine. But no fire. We don't want to attract attention."

Gods damn it.

I clenched my teeth, unwilling to admit the truth—that under the shadows of night-dark sycamores, I'd be left alone with my own fears. Not to mention the fact that I was going to freeze to death.

"It's freezing."

"I'll make sure you're warm." A taunting, dangerous invitation delivered in a sensuous timbre. "The fae live for pleasure. Isn't that right?"

"Pretty good pickup line, Adonis, but watching you force men to bash their heads into rocks didn't really get me in the mood."

Cruelty hardened his beautiful features once more, but he didn't reply.

We trotted over to the grove, and I shivered in my coat. In

a small clearing in the center of the trees, I pulled Nuckelavee to a halt beside Thanatos. I dismounted, practically falling off the stallion's side. When my feet reached the earth, I considered just throwing myself on the frozen ground to fall into a deep sleep.

Instead, I eased myself down against a sycamore trunk, watching Adonis as he pulled something out of his bag. A blanket, it looked like—thick and woolen. I rubbed my arms for warmth, my breath forming clouds around my face.

"I don't suppose you have more than one of those blankets? Since I didn't know we were traveling all the way across the country, I had no idea I needed to pack a duvet or anything."

He handed me the dark blue blanket. "I don't need it. I'm going to be keeping watch for hostile demons. Or for Johnny."

"You think he might come after us?"

"If he recovers his memory, he will definitely come for you. And that would ruin my plans, wouldn't it?"

I swallowed hard, suddenly intensely relieved that Adonis would be staying up. "You don't need sleep?"

"Sometimes." He sat, leaning against a tree trunk. "Not as much as you."

I lay on the blanket, then folded one half over myself, curling into a ball. I lay my cheek on the soft wool, hugging the blanket tightly.

In the shadows of the sycamore grove, my heart was beating hard against my ribs, and the darkness felt as if it were closing in on me. And in the shadows, those sharp, pointed memories—the dragon's teeth in Marcus's chest—

Sharp teeth piercing an arm—

I pulled the blanket tighter around my shoulders, trying to stave off the feeling that I was standing at the edge of a void. If I fell in, my soul would rip apart.

"I can hear your heart pounding."

My eyes snapped open, and I met Adonis's curious gaze.

"It's nothing." I loosed a slow breath. There was no way in hell I was telling him I was scared of the dark. "I just get a bit nervous being outside at night with demons roaming around."

"You'll be fine, Ruby," he said quietly. "I'm the most dangerous creature for thousands of miles. And I'm on your side. Just relax."

Somehow, I found that reassuring, and I tuned in to the strangely soothing feel of his magic, which kissed my cheeks like a night breeze.

Now, when I closed my eyes, a vivid memory lit up the hollows of my mind: I lay in a field, my arms spread out to the sides. White puffs of dandelions dappled the tall grasses, and from my spot on the ground, Hazel toddled over to me. She must have been two, and smears of chocolate ice cream streaked her chin and lips. She straddled my tummy, knocking the breath out of me, then reached for a white puff of dandelion by my side. She plucked it from the ground.

"Make a wish!" she commanded, holding to her mouth. Her dark curls framed her chubby cheeks.

"You're supposed to make the wish," I said quietly.

"Make a wish!" she shouted again, this time angrier, cheeks reddening.

I'd given in. I always gave in to her.

"I wish that you'd find another place to sit because you're crushing my stomach."

She touched the dandelion to her mouth, then blew. The filaments caught in the breeze, and some of the fluff stuck to her chocolate-streaked cheeks.

Slowly, sleep claimed my mind, and with it, the sun-drenched park of my memory receded, replaced by frozen, windswept fields. I dreamt of a barren landscape, and icicles gleaming from tree branches.

As I slept, I was dimly aware of the cold air piercing me to my bones, of shivering and teeth chattering. At least, until a blanket of warmth covered me, and my dreams shifted. A river rushed from a cavern, flowing over a cliff. It smelled of melted mountain water. At the base of the waterfall, banks bloomed with tall grasses and crimson flowers. The scent of myrrh trees coiled around my body.

When I woke in the dazzling, ruddy sunrise, Adonis was nowhere near me. He leaned against a sycamore trunk, watching as the sun streaked the sky with lurid shades of orange.

I rubbed the sleep from my eyes, then slowly sat up. Adonis had covered me in his black cloak during the night. Maybe it was the smell of myrrh, but I had the strangest feeling that I'd been dreaming of something from his memories.

The full power of his icy eyes fell on me. "You're awake. We have a whole day's riding ahead of us. I hope your legs hold up today."

I didn't want to take his warm cloak off my body. "How's your wing?"

"It's healing quickly. In a few more days, it will be good as new."

"Good." I rose slowly, my body groaning, and I handed Adonis his cloak. "Thanks for the extra warmth."

"The sound of your teeth chattering was driving me insane."

I scooped up the blanket from the earth, crossed to Thanatos, and tucked it into Adonis's leather satchel. The horse snorted, steam rising from his enormous nostrils. Then, he nuzzled my face. I smiled. It seemed Thanatos liked me better than Nuckelavee.

"Any chance you could tell me how much farther we have to go?" I asked.

"We'll be riding until nightfall, assuming we can keep the same pace as yesterday."

I suppressed a groan. Adonis's healing magic had been helpful, but it wasn't a panacea. I leaned over, rubbing my thighs. "Sure. All day riding again. No problem."

He wrapped his dark cloak around him, and the shadows seemed to thicken in the air surrounding him. "This time, tell me when you're falling apart instead of randomly screaming *uncle*, will you?"

CHAPTER 12

My pride took a serious hit that day. By sunset, Adonis's magical attempts to soothe my muscles were no longer working, and I'd completely given up.

A cold rain had begun hammering down on us as we traveled, completely drenching my clothes. When the cold had me shivering uncontrollably in my saddle, Adonis had reared Thanatos to a halt. In the icy downpour, he'd pulled the saddle off Thanatos, loaded his satchel onto Nuckelavee, and scooped me onto his horse with him.

Now, I rode wrapped in his powerful arms, with his soothing magic pulsing through my muscles. Drakon soared above us, occasionally igniting the dark air with sharp bursts of fire.

Nuckelavee cantered on beside us, completely compliant, with only the help of Adonis's orders.

Adonis's body kept me warm, his feathered wings shielding me from some of the wind and rain. As we rode into the night, I hated myself slightly for the disturbing thrill that surged through my body whenever his arms brushed against my sides, just skimming my breasts…

Don't fall for his charms, Ruby. He seduced every woman he met. Plus, that whole thing about him being a god of death, born to kill. It made sense that someone like him thought of nature as brutal and cruel—a paradise sown with seeds of destruction. The world around us was a mirror, reflecting our own souls back at us. And Adonis's was savage.

When we got to his castle, I'd be doing a bit of spying. Mainly, I needed to find out all the things Adonis was unwilling to tell me, starting with—what the hell was a Bringer of Light, and why did he need me?

Exhausted, I leaned back against his muscled chest, and the feel of his warm body against mine sent my pulse racing. I could have sworn I heard a low growl rise from his throat as I did.

Still, the movements of the horse began lulling me into a sense of calm, along with the slow rhythm of his pounding heart at my back. As I leaned into him, I breathed in his soothing smell. My eyes began to drift closed.

After only another minute, his deep voice pierced the silence. "We're here, Ruby."

I opened my eyes. There, in the darkness, a castle loomed above us. It towered over the edge of a cliff, its dark stone walls gleaming with rain in the faint light. Shadows claimed the space beyond the cliff, but the sound of waves crashing against rocks filled the air. I ran my tongue over my lips, tasting salt.

"When we get inside, I'll find a room for you." His voice was a soft murmur in my ear.

"Where are we, exactly? And what time is it?"

"Scotland, and late," he said quietly. "Everyone will be asleep."

"Everyone?"

"You'll meet them tomorrow."

Adonis led Thanatos over the rocky terrain toward his castle. Rain slid down my skin, between my breasts. Still, Adonis's warmth kept me from freezing.

As we moved closer to the gatehouse, I caught sight of the carvings in the walls—the skulls and gargoyles—haunted, human-like faces whose mouths and eyes gaped in horror.

Looks cozy.

My breath caught in my throat at the sight of the castle looming above us, the peaks and towers majestic against the dark night sky. At our approach, the heavy portcullis began to creak open. The gate's iron teeth speared the air, giving the entrance the appearance of a wild beast. The gatehouse's narrow windows gaped out onto the rocky landscape like empty eyes.

When the gate had groaned fully open, it revealed a towering, arched hall, lit by the dancing flames of torches. The horses' hooves echoed off a vaulted ceiling high above us. Vines climbed the walls, blooming with blood-red flowers.

The hall gave way to the open air—a wide outdoor passageway between towering gothic structures.

As I dismounted from Thanatos, a movement in the shadows caught my eyes. Cloaked in a cowl, a figure glided over the stones. I caught the faintest hint of bone-white skin under his hood. Creepy.

Adonis slid off his horse, and pulled our leather bags off. He handed over the reins, and the cloaked man led the two horses away, their hooves clopping over the stones. Adonis handed me my sodden bag, and I clung to it.

I surveyed the walls around me, each one carved with leering or agonized gargoyle faces. This place was built to intimidate, but I'd already lived through one horseman's castle. I didn't scare that easily.

Wordlessly, Adonis stalked to a second arched doorway, expecting me to follow him. We crossed a stony courtyard. Here, a statue loomed over the center of the courtyard—a beautiful man sitting on a pedestal, his wings arched and demonic. He looked down at the ground, and a stone snake coiled up his leg.

Drakon landed on the ground by the statue's feet. He hissed, and a flame shot from his mouth at the statue's base.

"Lucifer," I said quietly.

"Also known as Azazeyl."

"He's beautiful." I paused at the statue, frowning. "Who was he, exactly?"

"He introduced humans to the magical language. He was an archangel, and when he plummeted to earth, he fractured into the seven earthly gods. Then with him, a horde of angels fell, transforming into demons."

I hugged my sodden coat tighter. "Why do you have a statue of him?"

"The other horsemen think it's to remind us of our mission—to correct the great original sin. I have no interest in doing that. I admire him."

"Why?"

"Because he rebelled against those who would control us," he said with a touch of awe. "He broke the rules."

Like the snake at the statue's base, Drakon began scaling the statue, crawling up the stone in a slinking motion. He seemed quite at home there, almost as if the marble god were a long-lost lover.

Apparently done with our conversation, Adonis moved on toward one of the towers that loomed over us. As we neared it, an oak door swung open on its own.

I followed him into a hall—a vast, stony atrium. From here, a wide stairway led up to a second floor. Wordlessly, Adonis led me up the stairs.

Vaulted stone ceilings arched above us like ribs, and my footsteps echoed off a stone floor. Faintly, my fae senses tuned in to the distinct scent of old parchment and leather. *Bingo.* Somewhere around here, I'd find a library. Maybe the Dark Lord had one or two books about the Bringer of Light on his shelves.

He wasn't big on filling me in on things like what we were doing, or why we'd come here. Or what, specifically, a Light Bringer was going to do. He didn't seem to feel the need to tell me how I'd help him rule the heavens, or why he wanted to return there if he had such contempt for the celestial angels in the first place.

I was still a spy, though, wasn't I? I didn't need to wait for the information to come to me. I went out and found it.

At the top of a stairwell, Adonis led me down a long mezzanine. To my left, sculptures of twisting and thorny vines snaked over the walls. In the hallway's guttering candlelight, the sculptures looked half alive.

"Nice place you have here," I said. "Real homey."

"It suits me."

He paused at an oak door, and pushed it open to reveal a cavernous bedroom. Here, pale light shone through steeply peaked windows onto an ornate, tiled floor, inlaid with rubies. A canopied bed stood on a dais, the blankets a deep crimson. Black, thorny vines climbed the stone walls, and poison hemlock grew among them. A dark, arched doorway led to another room—the bathroom, probably. Candles hung in chandeliers high above us, but none of them were lit.

I swallowed hard. When I said before that I was no longer easily intimidated by creepy spaces, I was vastly overestimating myself.

"You'll be comfortable here," he said.

"You must be misreading my facial expression."

"What's the problem?"

I glanced at the marble fireplace, as gaping and empty as the gargoyles' eyes. "It's cold. Do you think we could get a fire going?"

He studied me, his eyes gleaming like stars in the shadowy room. "That's right," he said softly. He crossed to me, his hands in his pockets. "I'd nearly forgotten that you were scared of the dark."

I bristled. "How did you know that?"

"I can feel it." His eyes gleamed in the dim light. "You said darkness surrounds me. Do I scare you, Ruby?"

I wasn't sure what to say to him, so I thought I'd just go with the truth. "Yes. You were born to scare, weren't you?" *Born to seduce, too, but let's not get into that.* I turned, meeting his gaze head on. "But you don't scare me all the time."

Sometimes, he made me feel calm.

He snapped his fingers, and firelight burst into the empty fireplace. "That will keep you warm."

With another flick of his wrist, curtains fell over the windows. At least in Adonis's home I'd have some privacy from the ever-watchful eyes of the sentinels.

"You can hang all your wet clothes by the fire to dry. I don't have anything for you to sleep in, I'm afraid."

"I'll sleep naked."

His eyes widened, body tensing.

"As long as no one randomly barges in here, it's fine."

He paused, eyeing me for a moment before heading for the door. "Get some rest. Tomorrow, you meet my friends."

Or, I could find out more about all of you while you sleep.

CHAPTER 13

Pressing my ear against the door, I waited until I heard a nearby door open and close. To my surprise, the sound had been nearby. In this enormous castle, Adonis had put me in a bedroom right next to his.

Keeping an eye on me, I supposed. Still, unlike at Hotemet Castle, no one had explicitly told me to stay in my room, nor had I heard a lock click to trap me in here.

Before crossing into the hallway, I pulled off my boots so I could move more quietly. I slipped off my sodden jacket and laid it out by the fire. Then, I slowly opened the door.

Creeping into the hallway, I peered over the balcony's ledge to the stony floor below.

I searched for signs of movement around me, any flickers in the shadows.

A complete and eerie silence had fallen over the castle, and I could hear only my own breathing. I sharpened my fae senses, until the sights and lights dazzled me.

As I did, I homed in on a particular smell—one both deeply familiar and enticing. The smell of old books, luring me closer like a siren song. Books were my home, my refuge.

More importantly, a library might have crucial information.

I moved silently over the balcony floor, drawn in by the smell of paper and leather, until I reached an open archway. I'd found the library.

I just didn't want to walk into the darkness, exactly.

I pulled a torch from its iron bracket on the wall, and its light wavered around me as I stepped into the library.

Moonlight poured through a towering window onto vast walls of old books that reached to the ceiling. I let out a long breath. In Hotemet Castle, Kratos's book choices had given me a window into his mind. Would I learn anything about Adonis here?

I crossed to one of the walls lined with oak shelves, each one crammed with old tomes. Spindly ladders led up to the higher shelves.

I held the torch in front of a bookshelf, and some of the lettering on the spines glinted in silver and gold. I couldn't read it, unfortunately. The languages looked ancient and unfamiliar. One of them, I was pretty sure, was the angular markings of the Phoenician alphabet. What secrets were contained in these old books?

I moved on from there, eager to get to the books I could actually understand. It took me a few minutes of wandering around the bookshelves before I arrived at anything written in English. Bafflingly, they seemed to be books about gardening. Ancient catalogs of trees, herbs, some of flowers.

What did that tell me about Adonis? I could hardly see him tooling around in a garden, crouching down in a pair of rubber boots to do the weeding, but maybe he was into it.

I moved on again, this time to books of poetry—romantic poets like Coleridge and Shelley, Shakespeare, modern poets, ancient epic poems like *The Epic of Gilgamesh*...

So far, Adonis's book choices were a complete surprise. I

hadn't expected a death god to be into gardening and poetry, but I supposed I didn't know much about death gods.

In any case, I was no closer to learning about the Bringer of Light. I didn't suppose there was a *Bringer of Light for Dummies* book around here...

Still, I wasn't in a rush. In this forbidding castle, I actually felt like I belonged here. When I was a kid, I'd spent hours curled up in an alcove in my parents' old library, reading books about faraway places. I used to like the books that scared me—the ones about ghosts and haunted castles—and then I'd see monsters in the corner of my room when I tried to sleep at night. I'd call to my mom over and over again, asking for protections, for spells and charms. Over time, she started hiding the scary books, but they called to me.

I crossed to a dark corner of the library along the far wall, then slid my torch into an empty sconce. These books were in an altogether different alphabet—one with squat, sharp marks that looked millennia old. As I scanned the shelves, one book caught my eye, the lettering on the spine seeming to gleam brighter than the rest.

I pulled it from the shelf, and cracked open the spine to the faded parchment pages. Gently, I leafed through it. I scanned text, then drawings of angelic destruction—winged beings lighting fires, sending curls of dark magic streaming from their fingertips while piles of skeletons lay beneath them. Each one had his own horse. Halfway through the book, I found a picture—a simple, stylized drawing of a woman standing in a grove of trees, her hair painted the color of straw. Golden light beamed from her head.

The Bringer of Light?

A few pages more, and I found the woman again, this time accepting glittering blue jewels from vines that grew up around her.

"The Old Gods," I whispered.

I flipped another page. Now, the woman held the gems aloft, and a pale blue light radiated from them, forming a shield over her. And just above the shield, tiny winged angels flew for the heavens—

A screeching noise turned my head, and I jumped, slamming the book shut.

There, Drakon stood in the middle of the stone floor, his beady eyes on me. He hissed, and a stream of fire blazed from his mouth.

I hissed back at him, now feeling completely justified in my hatred of him.

I brought my finger to my lips. *Shhhhhh.* "I will give you…" What the hell did dragoniles eat? "I will give you rabbits if you keep quiet. Just shut the fuck up, okay?"

Drakon ignored my warning, stepping closer as he screeched again.

"Chickens," I whispered. My heart began to sink.

Let's hope Adonis and these friends of his weren't too precious about their library.

Just as I was shoving the book back onto the shelf, a figure appeared in the doorway—a rather terrifying figure, I might add.

A demon.

She must have been six feet tall—shockingly gorgeous and pale as ivory. A short, white dress hugged her curvy body, ending just below her ass, and her dark hair writhed around her head like snakes. A crescent-moon tattoo stood out on her forehead, and her red lips curled back in a vicious snarl. She lifted her clawed fingertips, and I braced myself for an attack.

I snatched my torch from the wall, holding it out as if I were about to fend off a wild beast with fire.

"Tanit." Adonis's deep voice pierced the silence. "Call off the attack. I brought her here."

Tanit hissed at me. "*This* is the Bringer of Light? She smells like the bottom of a swamp."

I glanced down at my mud-spattered, rain-soaked clothing. "We've had a very long journey, and I haven't had the benefit of a bath yet."

Tanit growled. "You're telling me we can't kill her and feed her to Drakon?"

"No."

Her nose crinkled. "Fine. Well, I'm going to insist that she leave all her filthy, rain-soaked clothes outside her door. She smells of moss and grass and dank forests, and I want the filth burned."

I frowned. "And what am I supposed to wear?"

She cocked a hip. "I'll have the servants bring her some of mine."

"I could just wash my clothes," I suggested. "Clothes are meant to be cleaned and reused indefinitely."

"They *what?*" She widened her eyes, her expression pure frustration. "We're going to burn your things. I'll give you new ones. Just be happy I'm not suggesting running *you* through the flames."

Adonis's eyes narrowed. "Simmer down, Tanit. She's on our side." He raised his eyebrows. "Ruby, Tanit doesn't often offer to give people things. This is her version of being a welcoming host." Smooth as silk, he prowled closer to me, his hands in his pockets. "And now we get to the part where you tell us what you're doing in here."

"I can't sleep without reading before bed."

"I see. And you like to read cuneiform?"

Casually, I sauntered back to the English poetry section and pulled a copy of *Don Juan* off the shelf. "I must have gotten mixed up. My mistake." I smiled at Tanit. "My name is Ruby. Pleased to meet you."

Her eyes flashed with silver. "Okay."

Through the window, the first honeyed light of morning began to warm the sky, tingeing it with pink.

Was it really that late?

"You were searching for information," said Adonis.

"That's what happens when you withhold it. People search for it on their own. So you could tell me exactly what we're hunting for, and why you've brought me here. Or I can use my own methods."

"Sophisticated methods like failing to read ancient languages."

"What are the blue gemstones?" I asked.

A sigh slid from him. "Tomorrow, when you wake, I'll explain what you need to know. Go to sleep now, and dream of all your beautiful love stories." He spoke with a soothing, lover's purr, and nothing had ever sounded more convincing than his suggestion. He was out of the room so swiftly, I hardly noticed him leave.

Morning sunlight began warming the room with coral, washing over the towering stacks of books. I'd never felt so tired in my life, and the stare Tanit was giving me urged me to move quickly.

As I crossed back to my room, I couldn't get the image of the gleaming blue stones out of my mind. Adonis said his destiny was to kill. Were the stones my destiny?

Just as I opened my door, Tanit pushed past me, glaring. She snatched my bag from the floor, yanking out my damp clothes. "This is all going in the fire."

She pulled out my sheathed knife and holster, examining it before letting it fall to the floor with a clang.

Then, she glared at me expectantly. "The rest. Take off the rest."

I was too tired to argue, and I wasn't particularly self-conscious—as long as Adonis wasn't around. I stripped off in front of her.

"All of it," she barked. "I'll leave new clothes outside your door."

"When?"

No answer.

She left with everything but my knife, leaving me damp and naked in the room. Good thing I wasn't attached to any of the clothes.

Miserable as she was, when she left my room, a deep sense of loss bloomed in my chest—complete isolation. I crawled nude under the warm covers, loneliness eating at me.

Somehow, traveling with Adonis, he'd masked my loneliness. Now, as I lay naked and alone, isolation slid through my blood like a poison.

I pulled the covers tight around me. When I closed my eyes, I dreamt of a thorny throne on a craggy cliffside, and the desolation of that image pierced me to the bone.

CHAPTER 14

*N*aked, I stumbled out of the bathroom, still completely disoriented from a heavy sleep. In fact, I'd managed to sleep through the whole day.

A fire still burned in the marble fireplace, warming the bedroom. Its orange light wavered over the walls, overgrown with flowering vines. I closed my eyes, and for just a moment, my mind wandered back to a happier time, when I'd gone with Hazel and Marcus to the Museum of Natural History in New York. Then, further back, to my mother and father curled up next to each other on a sofa, reading books. I'd always crawl in between them, splitting them up so their attention could be on me.

When I opened my eyes again, the loneliness of my current situation hit me like a fist.

Not to mention the fact that I'd ended up in a creepy death angel castle completely naked. I shuddered, rubbing my arms.

At least I'd have fresh clothes waiting for me outside the door, just as Tanit had promised.

I rose from the bed, crossing over the cold stone floor.

Goose bumps rose over my bare skin, and the chilly air peaked my breasts. Slowly, I pried the door open, looking down expectantly for a fresh stash of clothes.

A cold stone floor greeted me.

Of *course* she hadn't brought any new clothes back. Why had I trusted the crazy-eyed demoness in the first place?

I slammed the door closed again, and a draft whispered over my skin. *Should have hung on to a few items there, Ruby.*

I opened the door, then poked my head out, looking for signs of movement in the hallway. Nothing except the shadows dancing over the stone walls, the flagstone floor. I couldn't hear anything moving in the castle either.

Well, I wasn't about to just strut around the death castle bare-ass naked. I crossed back to the bed, pulled off a soft crimson blanket, and wrapped it around my naked skin.

Here, naked in the quiet castle, with only a blanket covering my body, I felt completely vulnerable. A desperation for human contact speared me, sharp as talons piercing my ribs. Inexplicably, I wanted to see Adonis. After our journey together, maybe he was the closest thing I had to a friend in this place. Or maybe he was just the most likely to find me some clothes.

I scanned both directions in the hallway. Barefoot, I crept over to the first door and pressed my ear against the wood.

As I did, the sounds coming from inside raised the hair on the back of my neck. I let my keen fae hearing sharpen, listening closely to the sound of a stifled moan. Then, a grunt.

Was Adonis torturing someone, or screwing someone? Or a little of both—a mixture of pain and pleasure? Was it *Tanit?*

Not that I cared. Whether or not he and Tanit were screwing had nothing to do with me. Clearly, I should turn around and leave this situation alone, and yet...

I needed to know. What if those weren't noises of pleasure I was hearing? What if he was peeling someone's skin off? I needed to know what kind of death god I was dealing with here.

Pulling my blanket tight around me, I knelt on the cold ground. Then, I leaned forward, peering through Adonis's keyhole. My pulse raced as I caught a glimpse of him. He stood, shirtless, his back to me. His midnight wings spread out behind him, their feathers flecked with silver. My eyes roamed over his smooth skin, his thickly corded arms.

This is intrusive, and I shouldn't be here.

And yet, I couldn't seem to tear my eyes away.

His powerful back arched, and dark shadows appeared around his neck, his wrists—like thorny manacles of magic. Something about them looked so *invasive*—a toxic magic that didn't belong here.

Still, Adonis's exotic scent seemed to lure me in. Despite the shackles around him, something about the arch of his back screamed of ecstasy. Pure, carnal pleasure.

I felt myself reaching for his door, stroking my fingertips over the wood. I hated myself a little for spying on Adonis, but—

Then I noticed the stream of blood, pooling on the floor. I gasped, and my hand flew to my mouth, knocking the doorknob just slightly.

Adonis whirled, giving me a view of the blood streaming from his chest, the shallow wound, the knife in his hand.

What the hell was he doing? *Cutting* himself?

My jaw dropped, and I stumbled to my feet, clutching tightly to my blanket as if my life depended on it.

The door swung open, and Adonis's gaze pierced me to the core, cold with fury.

"What are you doing?" he asked, venom lacing his voice. Already, his chest had begun to heal a little, though a thin stream of blood still dripped over the savage tattoos on his chest.

"What are *you* doing?" I shot back.

"Not staring through someone's keyhole, for a start." His arctic tone cooled my body. His dark hair seemed to stand out sharply against his golden complexion, his black eyelashes stark against his pale eyes.

"I didn't have anything to wear. Your friend Tanit never returned after she burned my other clothes. I thought you could help. I heard something that sounded like pain…" *Or pleasure.* "And I just wanted to look before I knocked. For all I knew, you were torturing a human or something." I could feel my cheeks reddening. "I have to know who I'm dealing with here."

For the first time, he seemed to notice the blanket wrapped around me. Then, he cut a sharp gaze over my shoulder. "Come in." He opened the door wider.

I surveyed Adonis's bedroom—a circular space adorned with faded tapestries: a night sky, a dark-winged angel. On one tapestry, red flowers blossomed by a river's edge. And on the expanses of stone wall, actual blood-red flowers bloomed on vines.

A tall window in his room cast silver light over a large bed, the blankets and sheets charcoal gray. Below his towering window, a few fernlike plants climbed the wall. On a small, oak table lay a dark cloth and a bandage. He dropped the bloodied knife on the table. A small pool of blood glistened on the floor. Did he get some kind of pleasure from self-harm?

"Look," I started. "I'm not judging. I just… Do you do that for fun?"

"Do I stab myself in the heart for fun? Are you joking?"

My jaw dropped. He'd actually *stabbed* himself in the heart?

I swallowed hard, the soft blanket skimming against my body as I walked deeper into his room. "Okay. So—why did you stab yourself in the heart?"

I'd seen his scars before—his chest, his wrists, the knotted ridges marring his perfect skin. I'd assumed they were battle scars—not self-inflicted.

He met my gaze, and a preternatural stillness came over him—a stillness more animal than angel. It unnerved me when creatures did that. The hair rose on the nape of my neck.

"No one else knows," he said, his tone edged with steel. "You can't tell anyone."

I pulled the blanket tighter around me. "I won't tell anyone."

He grabbed the dark cloth off the table, swiping some of the blood off his muscled chest. "You know that Kratos and Johnny have been cursed. It's because their apocalyptic seals have broken, and they can no longer resist their destiny. They must kill. For a horseman, the curse is applied when the apocalyptic seal is broken. The breaking of a seal feels like an ecstatic state. An overwhelming euphoria. And once you give in to euphoria, it's all over. Your fate controls you."

"And you use pain to stop the euphoria?"

"Exactly."

I shuddered. What a miserable existence. No wonder he wanted out. "I saw something around your neck and your wrists...like manacles."

He raised his eyebrows. "You can see them?"

"Was that the seal?"

He traced a fingertip over his throat, staring at me contemplatively. "I thought only angels could see it, but yes, that's the curse emerging. I guess a Light Bringer gets the privilege of witnessing that particular magic."

"How long have you been doing this for?" I asked quietly.

Only a slow, subtle shrug interrupted that animal stillness. "A few centuries."

I grimaced. "No wonder you want to rule the heavens instead of the earth. Let me treat it, at least."

"With what, exactly?"

"With the gifts from the Old Gods." I crossed to the fernlike plants that grew under his window, but something caught my eye. Adonis's sword lay against the wall, its hilt studded with red stones formed to look like flowers. I ran my fingertips over them.

"Do you like her?" asked Adonis. "Ninkasi has been with me for thousands of years."

"It's beautiful."

"*She*. She's beautiful," he corrected me. "And you plan to heal me with her?"

I frowned. "No, I told you. The Old Gods give us what we need. And right now, we need something to take care of that bleeding." I crouched down, clutching the blanket with one hand. "Even in the lair of a horseman, they give us what we need."

I snatched a handful of the yarrow that clung to the wall. As I stood, I held up the herbs to the moonlight streaming through the window. I closed my eyes, and a warm, soothing light washed over my hand. An herbal scent curled into the air.

When I opened my eyes again, a handful of dried yarrow lay crushed in my fist.

As I walked back to Adonis, my gaze flicked to Drakon by the fire, his reptilian tail flopping up and down against the stone floor.

Adonis studied me. "The magic of the Old Gods really is fascinating to watch."

"Maybe it's in my destiny to become a healer."

I surveyed the laden table, where a bandage lay. The

tricky part would be fixing him up with one hand, but I could probably manage with his help.

"Lay out the bandage flat," I commanded.

"Quite commanding for a naked fae, aren't you?" Amusement danced in his eyes. He spread it out, the ends draping off the table.

Carefully, I offloaded the dried plants into the center of the bandage. Then, I slid my fingers under the bandage, scooping up the fabric and the dried plants together with one hand.

With a swift movement, I pressed the herbs against his heart.

This close to him, the smell of myrrh wrapped around me, sweeping over my neck, my chest. I looked up into his eyes—at the gray that blended to midnight blue, at the flecks of silver. His magic whispered over my body, stroking my bare shoulders, my hips, skimming up my thighs. The look he was giving me penetrated me to my core, and sent a dark heat racing through my blood.

I couldn't think around him, could hardly remember how coherent ideas worked. It took me a moment to realize that I'd just been standing there, pressing a bandage full of dried plants against his chest, gaping at him.

"Do you need help?" he asked in a velvety voice that curled my toes.

I swallowed hard. "I just need to tie the bandage around your back."

He arched a perfect eyebrow. "Is that right?"

Already, his wound seemed to be healing—probably some of his own magic at work.

Without another word, I tightened the bandage with both hands, then reached around his back to try to tie it—only, I could hardly reach around the width of him, and—

A cold gust of air swept over my bare skin, tightening my nipples.

Oh god, the *blanket.*

It took me a long, horrified moment to realize that I'd ended up completely naked, my breasts just inches from his muscled physique.

I dropped the bandage.

Adonis's jaw had dropped, his attention completely rapt as he stared at me. His arm muscles twitched, eyes burning with pale light.

The cool of the castle's drafty air raised goose bumps on my arms. A low growl escaped his throat. His expression shifted—no longer remote, angelic serenity, it was now pure carnal lust. He looked like he was about to throw me on his bed right then and there.

At the sound of his growl, at the promise of his hands on my body, heat shot through me. My chest flushed.

Finally, I mustered the presence of mind to bend down, snatch the blanket off the floor, and hastily wrap it around myself. "Sorry," I mumbled.

Words seemed to have deserted him.

Distraction. Distraction. Let's pretend like nothing happened. I nodded at his chest wound, trying to think of something to say. "You know, it looks better already. The bleeding has stopped. Maybe it doesn't need the bandage."

After a moment, Adonis broke his silence. He crossed his arms with a wicked smile. "Never apologize for appearing naked before me. And certainly don't wear that blanket on my account. I prefer you without it."

Heat prickled over me, and I pulled my blanket tighter. "Can you ask your ill-tempered demon friend for those clothes now?"

"I'll send Drakon for her."

I shivered. "I don't suppose you have a shower in here, while I'm waiting. My room had a bathroom but no shower."

"Bath is in there." He pointed to an arched doorway, and I nodded, scurrying away from him with the blanket clutched tightly around me.

As I crossed into his bathroom, Adonis purred instructions to Drakon in an ancient language. Phoenician? Sumerian? I had no idea, but the angel probably knew more languages than I could count.

In his bathroom—a round, domed space—candles burned in iron sconces. A circular stone bathtub stood by one of the walls. Next to it, dry towels lay folded in a stony alcove, along with a few bars of soap.

I turned on the tap, and warm water rushed from the faucet, steam rising into the air. When I dropped the blanket once again, the castle's drafty air whispered over me. I stepped into the hot bathwater, watching it redden my legs, and slipped down into its welcoming embrace.

I rubbed the anemone-scented soap over my skin, cleaning my neck, my chest. I couldn't quite get Adonis's carnal expression out of my mind, or the promise of what might have happened if I hadn't pulled that blanket around me again.

He was Adonis—a creature known for his beauty. Of course I reacted that way to him.

Before the Great Nightmare had begun, Marcus and I had the perfect relationship. There were no questions, no mysteries. When he was upset, he told me, and he told me why. I knew that blood-hunger made him cranky, that sometimes his own snoring woke him up, that—despite being a vampire—clowns terrified him.

Adonis was the opposite. All mystery. Granted, I'd been learning a little more about him—that he hurt himself to stop the curse from setting in, that he dreamt of a great rebellion against the angels who controlled him. But he kept most of his secrets buried deep. What was that strange necklace he wore around his neck? What were those intense flashes of pain I sometimes saw in his eyes? What was his whole history with the fae?

I couldn't deny the allure of the unknown. Maybe there was a strange sort of power in that mystery, of things unspoken and unnamed. But danger lay there too.

A clicking sound on the floor pulled me from my thoughts, and I turned to see Drakon prancing into the room, tail slicing through the air. He clutched a bundle of clothing in his teeth. He dropped it on the floor, then cocked his head to stare at me, tail thumping expectantly.

I glared at him. "Off you go, hellspawn." So I might smell a bit like reptilian spit, but at least I wouldn't have to walk around naked under a blanket.

I stepped out of the bathtub, water dripping down my body—keenly aware that Adonis's bathroom had no door, that he could pop his head in at any moment. Not that he'd see anything new at this point.

I grabbed one of the towels from the alcove and quickly dried myself off. Frowning, I eyed the clothing on the floor—an extremely short black dress, some thigh-high boots. Tanit, it appeared, had enjoyed the 1960s. Not exactly my style, but I wasn't afraid of a little dark glamor.

Surprisingly, the boots fit well enough, and the dress hugged my body.

I wasn't about to ask her for underwear. Maybe one of those magic books in the library could summon some into existence.

When I crossed out of the bathroom, I found Adonis waiting for me, leaning casually against the doorframe, hands in his pockets. A dark, fitted shirt now stretched across his broad chest. His bleeding must have stopped quickly, because his shirt looked completely dry.

A sensual smile. "You do look amazing, though I preferred the previous outfit. When you're ready, Drakon will show you to dinner. Kur is desperate to meet the Bringer of Light."

Drakon. My favorite little monster.

Without another word, Adonis slipped into the hallway. But my mind wasn't on this new person—my mind was on the memory of Adonis's face when his pale gaze had roamed over my naked body.

CHAPTER 15

Through Adonis's windows, silver moonlight washed over the horizon. Just as in my room, I had a view of the slate-gray ocean, and the waves breaking on the jagged cliffs below.

Like its owner, the entire castle was breathtakingly beautiful. But it wasn't the peaceful, gentle beauty of the forests. It had an edge of terror, of brutality. I didn't belong in a place like this. I belonged in a simple cottage in the woods—just Hazel and me, and whatever the Old Gods would provide for us.

My stomach rumbled as I crossed the room. When I opened the door, Drakon was waiting outside, his head cocked. His tail cut through the air. Then, he rose and rubbed against my legs, scales sliding along my boots. I shuddered, suppressing my bile.

Of course Adonis couldn't choose a cute little puppy as a pet. Or a kitten. No, he wanted a red-eyed hellbeast with scales.

"No need to get too friendly there, Drakon. Care to show me where the others are?"

BLACK OPS FAE

Drakon's claws clicked over the floor as he prowled along the balcony, until we arrived at the wide, curving stairwell that led to the lower level.

I followed him through a vaulted hallway. Windows on my left overlooked the dark, churning sea. To my right, arches opened into the wider marble hall. Stained-glass windows in the panes were decorated with pictures of red flowers, white butterflies, and upside-down torches.

Through the colored panes of glass, I had a view of the sea.

Apparently, Drakon was growing frustrated with my pace, because he began to weave in between my feet, nearly tripping me as I walked.

As I moved farther down the hall, the scent of garlic and roast meat curled into the air, and my mouth watered. If Hazel had known we were headed for more delicious food, maybe she would have come with me.

At last, the arched corridor opened into an enormous stone hall.

There, I found Adonis sitting at a long, oak table near two demons. Tanit stood in a dark alcove, sipping from a silver goblet. She wore a short red dress and shiny thigh-high boots.

At the table near Adonis sat a male demon—this one in a throne-like chair, his feet resting on the tabletop. The demon's long, black hair flowed over his broad shoulders, and a few delicate green scales lined the tawny skin of his cheekbones and the backs of his hands. His pure-black eyes locked on me.

Light burned from iron lanterns hung high above us, bathing the room in amber. Drakon scurried over to Adonis, crawling into his lap. The Dark Lord stroked his pet's black, scaly skin.

Here, in his own castle, Adonis seemed a little different—

no longer staging the situation to intimidate, no longer seating himself on a dais or in a spiky throne.

Adonis's gray eyes pierced me, and his wings draped over the sides of his chair. He lifted his chalice. "Ruby. You've joined us, fully clothed." He nodded at the male demon. "May I introduce you to Kur."

Kur nodded, his inky eyes on me. "You're the one who woke everyone up last night." His voice was gruff. "Lucky for you, Adonis informed us we're not to kill you. Apparently he likes the way you look, and something about saving the world."

"Sorry. I was just looking for a book," I muttered.

Tanit examined me through narrowed eyes. "This one is really supposed to defeat the Heavenly Host?"

Adonis nodded at an empty chair next to him, already pulled out. "Join us."

Servants had laid the table with food—a bowl of apples and herbs, roasted with leeks. Browned chicken legs, covered in a delicate sauce that smelled of garlic and lemon, bread with mint leaves and olives, and salads. It looked very different from the meat-heavy pies I'd had in Kratos's castle.

I plopped down in the chair, serving myself apples and chicken. "So you all know about this plan, I take it? I'm hoping you'll fill me in."

Kur knocked back a long swig from his cup, then wiped the back of his sleeve across his mouth. "Ruby. I assume Adonis has told you of his plans to rule the celestial realm. But what are you hoping to get out of all this? What do you want?"

"Right now, I want this chicken, and then to work my way through the rest of the food. Beyond that, I want things to go back to the way they were. At least, as much as they can. I just want a simple home with my sister, free from demons and angels and everything else that might try to kill us. I want my human friends to be safe." My gaze slid to Adonis as I cut into the chicken. "I want the horsemen and dragons to leave us alone so normal people can rebuild civilization from the rubble. That's about it."

"You want a normal life," Adonis said quietly.

I helped myself to a bit of wine. "Simple pleasures are the reason that life is worth living, aren't they? Sunlight, good food, good company. I don't need to rule the heavens."

Adonis traced his fingertips over his wineglass. "You sound like a human."

I shrugged. "Or like a fae. Pleasure is the purpose of our lives."

Adonis's eyes flashed. "You might find that a bit empty after a while," he said. "Or at least you would if you'd lived as long as I have."

Tanit slowly walked closer, swaying her hips, her dark eyes locked on me. "How much time have you spent among humans?"

I speared another apple in the bowl. "I have more in common with humans than I do with demons or angels. Or even the fae. I just want what we all want—happiness."

I caught a faint glimmer of a ruby-red drop on Tanit's lips. I was pretty sure she was drinking blood.

"Happiness," she hissed.

"Now, how exactly are we going to defeat this Heavenly Host I've heard so much about?" I asked.

Adonis leaned closer, his intense eyes piercing me to my marrow. "Here's the first thing you need to understand, Ruby. You're not ordinary. You never will be. You've spent your life pretending to be a human, hiding your true nature. If you want to defeat the Heavenly Host, you'll need to stop running from yourself. If you're divided from yourself, the power of the Old Gods could tear you apart."

"I don't even know what that means." A dark memory

flickered in the back of my mind—dragons, ripping Marcus to shreds in front of me. If I'd been a hero like I was supposed to be, why couldn't I have saved him? My stomach clenched, and I pushed the thoughts away, strangling the life out of them.

I shook my head. "Anyway, I've been harnessing their magic already."

Kur folded his hands behind his head. "Listen, Ruby. Adonis tells me that you're our only hope. I've never known him to be wrong. But if he is, and if you fail, every living creature on earth will probably end up dead, slaughtered by the Heavenly Host. They'll just kill everything and start again. Earth will become a bone garden. Your fault."

My mouth went dry. "You guys really suck at pep talks, you know that?"

CHAPTER 16

"Look," said Adonis. "Assuming you can handle the power, our task is simple. We need the Stones of Zohar."

I remembered what I'd seen in the book. "Blue gems by any chance? That form a shield?"

Kur had resorted to simply drinking straight out of a wine bottle, which right now didn't seem like the worst idea. "Exactly. Only a Bringer of Light can wield them. They'll help you channel the power of the Old Gods. Your kind are the ancient and powerful enemies of the Heavenly Host. As long as you're not...divided from yourself or whatever Adonis was talking about. He's got some abstract sayings."

I nodded. "Garden of paradise and that kind of thing." At last, they were filling me in. "I need some concrete specifics. What's the power like?"

"We don't have a ton of specifics," said Kur. "We know in the right hands, the stones can repel the Heavenly Host. They can create a shield of some kind. And you can use them to fight the other horsemen."

"Okay," I said. "And where do we get them?"

Tanit smirked. "You're not the only spy, darling. While you were running around in the woods outside Hotemet Castle, I was discovering the location of the Stones of Zohar."

"She has yet to tell me," said Adonis with a hint of irritation.

Frankly, I was surprised Adonis didn't just threaten to vaporize her or something.

Tanit smiled. "Sadeckrav Castle. Aereus has been securely protecting them, just in case any errant Bringers of Light surfaced to find them."

I raised my eyebrows. "The horseman of war, right?"

"Yes," said Tanit. "He's wildly paranoid. He won't admit that he has them, and no one knows where he's keeping them. But my sources tell me he plundered them centuries ago, and he's always kept them close by. They terrify him."

Adonis tapped the edge of his glass. "He's unhinged. But I think speaking to him is on our agenda anyway."

"Why?" asked Kur. "He's a lunatic."

Adonis leaned forward. "True. But he's a lunatic we'll need on our side. If Johnny remembers what Ruby did to him, he and Kratos will be coming for us. And they could turn the horseman of war against us. We need to get to him first, to convince him that Kratos and Johnny are at risk of rebelling against the Heavenly Host. A lunatic ally is better than no ally at all."

"Sounds promising," I said. "What can you tell me about him? What are his weaknesses?"

Tanit knocked back a sip of her "wine." "Weaknesses? Not sure that he has any."

"Everyone has a weakness," Adonis replied.

"What does he love?" I asked.

"Himself," said Adonis emphatically. "That's it."

I nodded. "So he has an ego problem. Even more than the rest of you angels?"

Adonis glared at me. "Yes."

"Where is this castle?" I asked.

"France." Kur was frowning at Adonis's injured wing. "I'm not sure our angel of death will make it there just yet."

"It's nearly healed," Adonis growled.

I practically drained my wine. "So let me get this straight. We need to get some gemstones from the horseman of war, whose only weakness is his ego. And I need to use them to destroy the other horsemen, as well as the immortal, incorporeal celestial archangels known as the Heavenly Host. If I don't, every living being on earth will die, and it will be my fault."

"That about sums it up," said Tanit. "The dirty fae catches on quickly."

Adonis twirled his wineglass. "I wouldn't put it quite that way..."

I took a deep breath. "I don't want to come off like I have trust issues, but how do I know any of this is true? I'm supposed to put my faith in the word of one horseman and two shadow demons I've only just met. One of whom burned my underwear."

Kur nearly spit out his wine. "She did what?"

Tanit's forehead crinkled. "What's the purpose of underwear, anyway? I've never understood that."

Adonis let out a long sigh. "Since you're so interested in reading material, Ruby, perhaps a reference book would help. I take it you were looking for one last night."

"I guess it would be better than nothing."

Adonis stared at Tanit, who grimaced. "I'll get the books."

I speared a bit of chicken on my fork. "Tell me more about the Heavenly Host."

"Pricks," growled Kur. "Bodiless, ancient pricks. They're still angry that Azazeyl gave their precious Angelic language to humans a hundred thousand years ago. And for some reason, Adonis wants to be their god."

Adonis folded his hands behind his head. "A hundred thousand years of torment hasn't been enough for them. Not great at moving on, the Heavenly Host. They need someone new to lead them."

"How many of them are there?"

Kur finally pulled his feet off the table. "A hundred million angels."

My fists tightened. "A hundred what now?"

Adonis leaned closer. "Relax. We don't need to kill all of them. We just need to weaken the ten archangels, and repel them from the earth. The Stones of Zohar can help us do that. Without the archangels leading them, the rest of the angels will be trapped in the celestial realm."

I narrowed my eyes. "And then you just swoop in and take control up there. There are ten archangels and one of you. Do you really fancy your chances?"

"Against ten weakened, sickly archangels? I don't have any doubt." Adonis lifted his wineglass. "Leave this festering hole to the demons, the fae, and the humans, and I'll rule the hordes in the heavens."

"Festering hole. Cheers, mate. That's my home you're talking about." Kur snatched another bottle of wine off the table and uncorked it with his teeth. He spat the cork onto the floor. "You did promise us you'd come back regularly, or I'd never agree to help you in the first place."

I raised my eyebrows. "So you two are close, then? I hadn't expected…" I wriggled uncomfortably in my chair. "Well, I never expected Adonis to have any friends, to be honest."

A warm smile from Adonis. "I fell in with some shadow demons a few thousand years ago. Ancient protectors of the succubi."

Kur's eyes had taken on a slightly glazed look. "If Adonis hadn't already told me you were a fake, you might have had the rare pleasure of watching me drop to my knees when you walked in the room."

I looked down at my arms, half surprised to find I was still wearing the succubus glamour. "Oh, right. I can take this off now, I suppose."

Kur shook his head. "Best not to. Adonis hates the fae. I hate humans. Succubi are about the only thing we can agree on."

At the mention of Adonis's fae-hatred, my stomach flipped. Did he hate me, under all his flirtatiousness? It didn't seem that way.

Tanit broke the awkward silence by gliding back into the room, clutching two books to her chest. She moved with a disturbingly fluid motion, as though she were hovering just slightly off the floor. "One in cuneiform, and one in English so the young fae can read it."

She dropped them on the table next to my plate with a loud thud. "There. Your literary proof."

I stroked my fingertips over the black, leather-bound book on top, its surface etched in silver lettering: *The Bringer of Light*.

"This is the one I saw in your room."

Kur rolled his eyes. "Of course you were in his bedroom."

"It wasn't like that," I said sharply, cracking open the book. "I was dressed as a puritan witch judge."

I turned the book's yellowed pages, taking care not to rip them. The book was written in English, but it seemed to be Middle English. Still, as I scanned the text, I could figure out its meaning. The first section gave an account of everything I already knew—Azazeyl's fall from heaven, his soul fracturing into seven pieces that became the seven earthly gods.

Nyxobas, god of night. Emerazel, god of fire, and so on. Each god tormented by their punishment.

I turned the page, my pulse racing at an illustration of Azazeyl falling from the skies. Pain creased his beautiful features, and the wind appeared to tear at his wings.

When I turned the page again, I found an image of Nyxobas, god of night. His cowl cloaked his features. The artist had painted a midnight sky with silver stars around him. Just a picture of him was enough to fill me with a sense of dread—as if a void were beginning to eat at me from the inside out.

Shuddering, I turned the pages until I got to a chapter about the Heavenly Host. Just as Kur had said, the text mentioned a hundred million angels, organized into cohorts and legions. An archangel commanded each legion.

Okay. Demons and angels, we'd covered that part. Where did I come in?

I continued leafing through, landing on a page where the text was adorned with images of leaves, beside a picture of a tree whose gnarls seemed to form a sort of face. Silver light glowed around the tree—and a single, silver branch gleamed in the candlelight.

Of course. This represented the Old Gods. A quick scan of the text confirmed everything Yasmin had told me—the Old Gods had grown with life on earth, and were native to this world. They sought to free us from the scourge of the earthly gods, from the angels and demons who tried to control us. In times of crisis, they gave us what we needed through the earth itself.

A loud, exaggerated yawn from across the table interrupted my thoughts momentarily, and I looked up to find Tanit staring at me. "Is this really how long it takes a fae to read?"

Sighing, I returned to the text. And that brought me to

the final section—the one about the Bringer of Light. Here, the artist had painted an image of a silver-haired creature, her body incandescent. Blue gems gleamed from her forehead like rays of light.

My pulse began to race. I was supposed to be one of these godlike creatures? I was good with harvesting herbs and moss from the ground, but this seemed a bit much. I sucked in a sharp breath, focusing intently on the text.

Here, I found an account of the Stones of Zohar—gemstones mined from a watery grotto.

According to the book, Bringers of Light were born every few hundred years, and they served the Old Gods. A Bringer of Light, united with the gems, would have the power to fight angels, to reclaim the earth for the Old Gods.

Of course, it didn't give any details beyond that.

As I closed the book, a cloud of dust rose in the air. "Okay, I guess the story checks out in the old book. When do we leave?"

"As soon as my wing heals," said Adonis. "We just need to hope for two things. One, that Johnny fails to recover his memory anytime soon."

"And the other?" I prompted.

Adonis's eyes flashed with a pale light. "Well, let's just hope that none of the celestial angels manage to figure out who you are before we get to Sadeckrav Castle."

Tanit smiled. "We wouldn't want your pretty fae face splattered all over the earth."

CHAPTER 17

Adonis's powerful, dark wings practically trailed against the ground as he walked by my side over the rocky outcrop that overlooked the ocean. I pulled my coat tight around myself, tasting salt on my lips.

"So glad we managed to convince you," said Adonis. "I'd hate for the fate of the world to sink into an abyss just because of your trust issues."

"Yes, I'm on board."

The scent of brine floated on the wind, and along with it, Adonis's deliciously exotic scent slipped around my skin.

"You're going to be undercover again," he said. "But you're used to that."

"What's my role?"

"We had to go with something realistic. Kur sent word to Aereus, explaining that I've tamed a succubus concubine for my pleasure," he purred. "Obviously, it was the most logical thing to do."

I glared at him. "*Tamed?*"

"Taming a succubus is a common angelic fantasy. It's how you were able to beguile Kratos so easily."

"Right. That was the only option, I'm sure. Are you going to tell me why you're so desperate to go to the celestial realms? You've never lived there before. Why so eager to divest yourself of a human body?"

When he met my gaze, I found something unexpected there—just the faintest hint of vulnerability in his gray eyes. "I've been here long enough. I've done all I can on earth."

"I suppose it wouldn't be super awesome to have to stab yourself in the heart all the time."

"You're certainly catching on."

The marine winds toyed with my crimson hair. "It seems like you spent your time among shadow demons over the centuries. When did you join up with the other horsemen?"

"We didn't find each other until just before the Great Nightmare began. I've spent most of the centuries hiding my wings, disguising myself as a demon. I fought alongside Tanit and Kur in more wars than I can count."

Below us, the waves crashed hard against the rocky shore, and mist dampened my skin. "So you spent centuries pretending to be someone you're not."

"Something you're familiar with, isn't it?" His voice twined softly around me.

"I guess. You're not complaining about my disguise, are you? You hate the fae."

He studied me carefully. "Not all of them."

I walked by his side, our footsteps crunching over the gravel path. The path wound sinuously around the cliff's edge, wrapping around the ancient, gothic castle itself.

I folded my arms. "And what makes us worse than demons?"

"Demons lose control because they can't help it. The fae worship chaos, seek it out. I spent too much time among them."

"Why?"

"Let's just say my particular skill set appealed to them—death and pleasure." A haunted edge tinged his voice, and I knew he was only giving me part of the story—a sanitized version.

"Your kind are fascinating, I'll admit," he continued in his deep, alluring timbre. "The fae are as beautiful as you are brutal."

His description startled me. In fact, it was exactly how I'd describe him. "Beautiful?"

A slow, heartbreaking smile. "Yes." He paused, running a fingertip over my cherry-red hair. "Where's the real Ruby under all this?"

Warmth spread between my ribs. "I'm not sure you want to see the real Ruby. It's not just glamour that hides me. Glamour is an illusion—the hair color, the eye color, the ears. But you know the fae also shift. That's an actual, physical change. My canines grow, and my muscles become stronger, swifter. Some older fae stay in that state all the time. But a young fae like me—we don't keep control so well."

"Show me." A seductive plea and a command. "I want to see you under there."

A dark heat thrummed through my blood. I never shifted completely, not unless I went feral, and yet here, in the forlorn salty air, I found myself wanting to do as he said. "Like I said. It's not easy to control."

Amusement curled his beautiful lips. "I think I'll be able to handle it."

Why was it so hard to say no to him? Maybe because he'd spent thousands of years honing the skill of getting what he wanted. He used his voice, his beauty as a weapon.

I closed my eyes, letting the glamour fade with a sharp tingling over my skin. The sea air wrapped around me.

I opened my eyes, knowing that Adonis would be staring into pools of silver. Pale-gold hair whipped in front of my

BLACK OPS FAE

face. Still, I wasn't shifting. Who knew what would happen if I went feral with Adonis again?

Adonis reached out to brush my hair from my face, and the feather-light touch of his fingertips stroked against my skin, ice-cold and fire-hot at the same time. "But that's still not the real you, is it?"

"Just because I have a feral side doesn't mean it's the real me. Maybe this is the real me. Or my human glamour. Maybe it's Angela Death, the succubus, dressed in sequins on a stage. Maybe my disguises are the real me."

Without my glamour, I felt completely exposed before him, like I'd walked into his room naked, submitting myself to his judgment. I closed my eyes again, summoning my human glamour, hiding my ears, my inhuman hair, as the magic whispered over my skin.

I opened my eyes again, catching a flicker of disappointment in his gaze. I cocked my hip. "That's enough of that. I'm not a performing monkey. And anyway, I'm not as convinced as you are that you'd be able to handle me when I'm feral."

He peered down at me with a wicked smile. "Oh, but I would love to try." With his hands in his pockets, he moved deeper into the garden, and I followed. "Do you like it here?"

It honestly surprised me that he cared what I thought, like he was looking for my approval. "I do. It's a little bleak, admittedly." I gestured at the dark, craggy shoreline below us. "How long have you lived here? It's elegant, but it's…unforgiving."

"Nearly a thousand years, I suppose. But it has its own strange beauty." His eyes drank me in, the corner of his perfect mouth quirked in a smile. "Like the fae. Do you want to see?"

"How could I resist that description?"

The path twisted around the castle's walls, and thorny

shrubs crawled over the path around us. A vast canopy of stars spread out above us.

Adonis met my gaze. "Kur was wrong. You don't need to disguise your fae side around me."

He led me toward a crumbling stone wall.

"I lived among humans for my whole life. It's just an old habit, I suppose. I've always glamoured myself."

He pushed open an old, creaking gate. In the darkness, the silver seemed to burn brightly in his eyes. "But there's more to it than that, isn't there?"

"I'm not sure what you mean." As we moved through the gateway, I cast my gaze over an enormous, untamed garden, the plants and flowers silvered in the moonlight.

A jagged tree grew in the center of the garden. A stream ran past it, burbling out of the ground. It had carved a sinuous path through the plants. On the far edge of the walled garden, the stream poured under a low archway, cascading off the cliff's edge to the rocks below.

Myrrh trees grew by the riverbanks. Blood-red flowers dappled the grasses—poppies maybe—growing among blue and white anemones. The air smelled of wild thyme and marjoram.

One of the ancient walls had partially eroded, giving way to a view of the ocean. Moonlight glinted off the water.

My breath caught in my throat. "This is your private garden? It's beautiful."

"This is where I spent many of my days when I wasn't off getting tangled up in shadow demon wars. Reading. Writing. Drinking with Tanit and Kur, hosting visitors from the shadow realms."

Tall wildflowers brushed against my fingertips, featherlight. "Why would you fight with shadow demons? You're not one of them. Why would you be loyal to Nyxobas?"

"The god of night?" He snorted. "I have no loyalty to him."

I nodded slowly, my gaze trailing over the perfect planes of his face. "So what were you fighting for, then?"

"For my friends. They saved me when I escaped the fae realm. And I saved them, whenever I could." Adonis's exotic scent mingled with the heady perfume of the wildflowers.

"Let me see if I understand this correctly. You have close friends who you love, who you've been with for thousands of years. You have this gorgeous garden, where you read books, drink with your friends. I'm going to wager you've seduced a few beautiful women in your time. I know it must suck—like, seriously suck—to have to stab yourself in the heart. But isn't there another way? Do you really want to give all this up to float around in heaven?"

"The thing is, Ruby, angels were never meant to walk the earth."

I'd said the same thing many times over the past year and a half, but I still felt the impulse to argue with him.

He froze abruptly, staring up at the sky, and an icy chill rippled over my skin as the temperature seemed to freeze around me.

"Speaking of angels going where they don't belong..." Ice chilled his voice. "You need to get inside."

CHAPTER 18

*A*donis's voice had changed, became commanding. No longer was it the sexual purr of a lover, but the voice of a general.

I narrowed my eyes at the sky, but I could see nothing among the stars. "Can you at least tell me what's happening?"

"It seems some of the angels have found us. Not the archangels, but still a nuisance. Hide in my room. There's a secret passage behind the garden tapestry."

My heart began to hammer. "Are you going to fight a whole horde of angels?"

"Oh, you don't need to worry about me. Go."

I hurried back to the castle door, my fingertips brushing over the holster at my thigh. I still had the knife, though I wasn't sure how much good it would do me in a fight against a legion of angels. How many angels were we talking here, exactly?

I sprinted through an open archway to the courtyard. Distantly, the sound of trumpets pierced the air, and the noise rumbled through my gut.

I raced up the stairs to Adonis's room and flung open the

door. I scanned the room, searching among the old, faded hangings for one that looked like a garden. The tapestry of blood-red flowers hung just across from his bed.

First, I rushed over to the window. I peered through the glass, catching sight of a small horde of angels racing toward the earth, bodies glowing with golden light. If I narrowed my eyes, I could make out the swords glinting in their hands.

My mouth went dry. Were all these angels really after me? Being a spy was one thing, but I didn't have much supernatural war experience.

Adrenaline burned through my veins. I hurried over to the tapestry, then pulled it aside. Just as Adonis had said, a door stood inset in the wall. I pushed it open into a dark, narrow passageway. For just a moment, I froze, my heart thumping hard.

Complete darkness in here.

Which was worse? An angelic horde hell bent on my death, or a dark hallway? Clearly, the hallway was the better option.

With my heart slamming against my ribs, I began to run. I had no idea where I was going, just that it was away from the angel horde.

Dread coiled around my heart. If these angels knew I was here, did that mean it was all over? Did they all know? I couldn't hide from them forever.

I raced through the bowels of the castle, my fingers tracing the damp walls as a guide. At last, the passageway gave way to a wider hall, and the sound of screeching echoed off a high ceiling. I still couldn't see anything, and my blood began to roar in my ears. It sounded like I'd run into hell itself—and for all I knew, I had.

Air whooshed over my head as something swooped lower. A leathery wing brushed against my forehead. No—not leathery—scaly.

My heart threatened to gallop out of my chest, and the darkness felt as if it were closing in around me. The otherworldly shrieks echoed in my own skull. I pulled the knife from its holster. I'd never wished more for a flashlight, a match, anything.

In the darkness, images began to ignite in my mind—the dragons diving for us on the day the world had ended, their screams rending the air. Hazel, clutched tightly in a demonic talon.

And the one image I couldn't face—the one I'd been hiding from. Marcus, trying to save us, climbing onto the dragon's back. I knew what was coming next.

I crouched on the ground, clamping my hands over my ears. "No!" I whispered.

Another scaly wing brushed against me, a scrape of talons against my shoulders. Dragons were going to rip me to shreds, just like they'd done to Marcus.

A sharp, painful certainty coiled through my chest. Adonis had sent me right into my own personal hell, and I couldn't even see the way out.

I fell deeper, lost in the hell of my own memory. If I let the iron door break open on my memories, they'd consume me. Or else, the dragons would.

A flicker—just a flicker of the blood that had stained the pavement, and I felt as if my mind would rip apart.

I couldn't save him. I didn't save him.

When I opened my eyes, my breathing started to slow again. Strangely, light was blooming around me, radiating from my own body over the cave. Apparently, some of the Old Gods' power had stuck with me since I'd plunged that knife into the silver branch. My terror must have sparked it.

I swallowed hard, staring at the domed, stony cave. It wasn't some kind of hellish dungeon. It seemed to be a rookery for dragoniles, and they swooped in wide arcs below the ceiling. My breath caught at the beauty of them—stunning shades of violet, gold, and blue, their scales faintly iridescent.

I looked down at my own body, beaming with radiant light, then I gaped at the illuminated ceiling, the dragoniles. They seemed to delight in my light, unleashing cheerful squawks.

"A Bringer of Light." A deep voice echoed off the ceiling, slicing through the reptilian squawks.

Slowly, I turned around, my pulse racing.

There in the entryway stood an angel, dressed for battle. His sword hung strapped behind his back, and his golden wings spread out behind him. Long, blond hair hung over his powerful shoulders, and a smug smile twisted his lips. "I smelled your magic when you unleashed your light. I smelled the magic of the Old Gods. Animals, the lot of you. I raced here at the speed of the wind so that I might have the honor of putting you to death."

I tightened my grip on the knife, ancient battle fury pulsing through my blood. I'd have to kill this one before he called the others. "A celestial angel. I've heard about your kind. Is it true that if you're not an archangel, you're mortal on earth?"

For just a moment, his smile faltered. "Now why would the horseman of death be hiding one of your kind?" He rushed for me, fast as lightning. Just as I began to lift my knife, he pressed his sword against my throat. "Drop your knife. And tell me what you're doing with Adonis."

Stall, Ruby. Stall. I swallowed hard. "He's imprisoned me here. Something about not wanting me to mess up his apocalypse. I don't know what he's talking about."

He pressed the blade harder. "Drop your knife."

I let go, and it clanged to the floor. One way or another, I needed to get it back. Poison still laced its blade. He'd be dead in seconds. But given the way his sword was pressed against my neck, I'd need one *hell* of a distraction to get my hands on it again.

The dragoniles screeched above me, their wings beating the air.

The angel stared down at me, his eyes burning with a bright, heavenly fire. "You're telling me that Adonis is keeping you prisoner? Why wouldn't he simply kill you? You're a threat to the entire angelic race."

Think fast, Ruby.

"He thinks there are more of us." I needed to keep myself alive, through talking. "Adonis thinks I might know where these Bringers of Light are, just that the memories are buried deep in my subconscious or something. I have no idea what he's talking about, but he's definitely not on my side." I widened my eyes, letting my body tremble a bit. Truth be told—with an angel pressing a blade into your throat, it wasn't really that hard to fake fear. "He's awful to me. He keeps torturing me."

The angel's eyes flashed brighter, and one of his hands found its way to my waist. That last bit apparently fascinated him. "Torturing you? Tell me." His lips twitched.

Did I detect a hint of desire in his words, in his eyes? Fae were experts in pleasure, and I do believe I'd found this angel's weakness. Here on earth, angels were not only mortal, but vulnerable to primal desires—just like the beasts. And this one was a sadistic perv.

I thought I'd found my distraction. I let my lip tremble. "You want me to tell you how he hurt me?"

"Oh yes."

I swallowed hard. I didn't have any visible scars, so I'd have to get creative. "He locks me in here, knowing that I'm scared of the dark, that I'm scared of dragons." I widened my eyes, all innocence. "He uses his mind control on me and forces me to hold my head underwater until my lungs burn, or to contort my body in painful positions for hours. I've never felt so helpless. I've never felt such excruciating pain."

The angel licked his lips, his wings spreading out wider behind him. "What else does he make you do?"

"Sick, depraved things that I can't even speak about. And the pain. The *pain*. I can't bear it anymore. Can you get me out of here?"

The angel's fingers tightened on my waist. Oh, he liked that idea. Sicko. "Tell me more."

"He uses his angelic mind control powers to make me choke myself until my lungs burn."

"I want to watch you hurt yourself," he rasped.

I shot a quick glance at the knife on the floor. Pervy Angel still had a sword at my throat, and I wasn't able to reach for it. "I'm afraid he's broken me completely. But it's no use. I still can't remember anything about the Old Gods."

The angel's eyes burned with desire. He wanted what Adonis had. Right now, he'd give anything for that power of mind control.

He gripped the back of my neck, forcing his blade deeper into my skin. I winced at the sharp pain, and a trickle of blood ran down my throat. He kicked the knife away from me, and it spun across the floor with a scraping noise.

My blood roared in my ears. I wasn't getting to that damn knife this way.

Still, maybe there was another way out of this.

Angels could fall. All I needed was for him to give in completely to earthly desires, to lust and the thrill of power.

Lucky for me, this creep had telegraphed his weakness.

CHAPTER 19

"Please," I whimpered. "I'll do anything you want."

If a horseman fell, it would summon all the archangels from heaven. I could only hope that the fall of a regular, mortal angel like this perv would go fairly unnoticed.

He snarled. "I want you to hurt yourself."

Honestly. Couldn't he have had a nicer desire? Maybe massages with oil, long walks on the beach? Of course it had to be something like forcing women to hurt themselves to exert complete sadistic domination.

Demons got a bad rap. I was increasingly certain angels were worse.

"Hurt myself how?" I asked.

"You can start by falling to your knees."

Ugh. Males. Always the same.

I widened my eyes, trying to look shocked as I dropped to my knees. The cold stone bit into my skin.

A smile split his features, and something new appeared in his eyes—his golden irises darkened to black.

"Yes," he growled. "Good. Now pull off your dress."

Oh, you've got to be kidding me. Could I take out his knees and rush for the knife on the ground? Not likely. He looked incredibly powerful.

I pulled down just the top of my gown, giving him a view of my shoulders. Given that I'd still never gotten any underthings, that was as far as the dress was going. In any case, I didn't think nudity was the important part. It was terror and humiliation that excited him.

"I'd never shown another man my shoulders until Adonis kidnapped me," I pleaded.

A rumbling noise rose from his chest.

I let the fear shine in my eyes. "But I'll do anything to save my life."

His features were changing, teeth sharpening. Ash began to rain from the ceiling, coating our bodies, the floor.

The dragoniles circled above, their wings whipping at the air. Reptilian screeches echoed off the walls. They could sense a change falling over the room.

"Touch my sword," he said, a quaver in his ragged voice. "Run your fingertips along the blade until they bleed. Hurt yourself, succubus."

Bile rose in my throat, pure disgust. Ash began to coat me, falling on my dress, my bare shoulders. And the cold floor chilled my knees.

He was changing, though, horns growing from his forehead.

I reached up for the sword, running my fingertips over the blade. The steel sliced into my skin, drawing blood that ran down my palms, my wrists.

"Yes!" The angel roared, his wings spreading out behind him. His feathers were beginning to darken, the pale gold now tinged with the faintest charcoal gray. "How does it feel?"

"Painful," I whimpered. *Like your transformation is about to be.*

Above, the dragoniles swarmed faster. The light created by my body began to dim, but the dragoniles punctuated the darkening air with hot blasts of fire from their jaws.

So *this* was what it was like to watch an angel fall.

The angel gazed down at me. "You're mine," he growled. His body had begun shaking, convulsing.

Slowly, I rose, and he lowered his sword, his expression completely rapt. I suppressed the bile rising in my throat, my complete and utter disgust, and stared in mock horror at the blood on my hands. It wasn't a deep cut, but I played it up.

He moaned, and I fought down more nausea. I glanced at him, smiling darkly as I watched the transformation at work.

Now I had him exactly where I wanted him.

Blood-red streaks speared the black of his pupils, and claws sprouted from his hands. Two gleaming, ivory horns emerged from his head, and his wings began to shrink, the feathers shifting and smoothing into sleek leather.

As they did, pain began to contort his features. An agonized groan rose from his throat, and he fell to his knees. He clawed at his shoulders where his wings were changing shape, becoming more pointed and angular. His back arched, and his mouth opened. Golden light poured from his open jaw, racing for the ceiling, and his body twitched and jerked like a dying man on the gallows.

I couldn't say I felt sorry for him.

I ran for the knife, snatching it off the stony ground. Overhead, the dragoniles flew more frantically, swooping lower over the transforming angel, over me. I crossed the floor, and brought the knife down hard into his back.

The demon's body jerked one last time, then fell still, slumping on the ground. The bursting flames of the dragoniles cast blasts of warm light over the growing pool of blood. I pulled my knife from his back, catching my breath.

Too bad my victory was short-lived. A golden light brightened the air behind me, and I whipped around. There in the doorway to the dragoniles' rookery stood four angels, their wrathful eyes locked on me.

At the front of the group stood an angel with silvery-white hair, his wings the color of pearls. "We felt your power, Bringer of Light. And here we find you. Covered in blood, gleaming like a beacon." His deep voice echoed off the ceiling, and he pointed to the fallen angel on the stone floor. "You lured him to his doom."

I gripped my knife. How could I take out four angels with one knife?

"Didn't take much," I said. "He was awfully eager to fall."

Pearly Angel drew his sword. He stalked toward me, his footsteps echoing off the walls and ceiling through the cacophony of dragonile squawks.

My palms sweated over the knife's hilt, and I clutched it tighter. If only I had control over this light, I'd be in a much safer position right now. To be honest, the Old Gods were screwing me over a bit by giving me uncontrollable powers. Right now, this magical light only served to paint a glowing target on me. A giant neon arrow to enemy number one of the angelic horde.

I summoned a glamour to cover myself, but this time a sharp sting pierced my skin. *What the hell?* Maybe fae magic and Old Gods' magic didn't mix so well.

"Light?" I asked, playing dumb. "I don't know what you're talking about." Not a brilliant strategy. Just the best one I had right now.

Pearly shook his head, and firelight glinted over his sword as he prowled closer. "Little Light Bringer. You can't hide it from us now. We feel it. We've seen it."

Another angel, one with curly ginger hair, stalked closer, by Pearly's side. "Imagine this, Afriel. We come here to check on Death, who hasn't been slaughtering like he should. And instead we find something much more interesting."

Afriel cocked his head, gripping his sword in both hands. "His seal should have broken once the terror began. Does this creature have anything to do with that?"

Ginger's eyes blazed with cold light. "Don't move too quickly, Afriel. She might have honed her powers."

Fear shone in Afriel's features. "We need to kill her now, before she brings us all down." He stepped over the demon's body. "Look what she did to Xapham, the filthy little minx."

"So you didn't come for me, then?" I asked.

This was the first good news I'd had this evening. If by some miracle I made it out of here, none of the other celestial angels knew about me.

It was just the whole "getting out of here" part that I couldn't quite work out yet. I could throw my knife and take out one of the angels immediately. But then I'd be all out of knives.

I'd have to lure them closer until they were in range. It was my only hope.

The dragoniles swooped over my head, squawking wildly. Their fiery breath singed the air, burning strands of my hair. The situation seemed increasingly disastrous, like I might not have a way out of it alive…

As the specter of death crept over me, a cold, primal rage began to roil within me. My hunter's instincts took over.

I can hear your mortal hearts beating, angels. I want to pierce them.

Oh shit oh shit oh shit. Feral Ruby was about to come out, and if she did, I'd lose control completely. Feral Ruby didn't necessarily make the best decisions.

Afriel raised his sword. "You are quite the serendipitous discovery."

My glamour began to fade.

Then, as fury erupted in my blood, I began to shift, my ears changing shape, canines lengthening. Ancient power burned through my body, ready to explode.

"Come on, then," I snarled. A wild energy ripped through me. My pale hair whipped around my face as my body glowed brighter.

Afriel rushed for me, probably expecting me to run from him. But the hunter's instinct raged strong in me, and I surprised him by rushing for him, too, until I was pressed up close to his body. The sound of his heart seemed to echo in my own blood.

This close, he couldn't strike me with his sword.

Go in for the kill. Instinct propelled my knife into his chest, finding its mark between two of his ribs. I thrust the blade up higher—right into his heart. He dropped his sword, and with a lightning-fast reflex, I snatched it from the stony ground.

Pure, primal instinct overtook my body until I felt at one with the stones beneath me. *I am blood, moss, bones, and earth, a creature of the damp caves. I am the feet pounding the leaves as you run from me. I am the rhythmic terror of your blood roaring in your ears.*

My heartbeat slammed against my ribs like a war drum as I gripped the sword in my hands. From the corner of my eye, I glimpsed movement, another sword, metal. A threat.

Thrust. Kill. Draw blood.

Move away from the threat. I dodged back, eyes landing on the ginger one—the pulsing vein in his neck. Life—so much life pulsing in that body. I licked my canines.

Time to end it.

I needed to sink my teeth into those hot veins. To hear him scream.

I snarled, no longer able to remember how to speak. I'd make my message clear enough.

I rushed at the speed of storm wind toward my prey. Primal fear glinted in his eyes, and my sword found its mark in his chest. My lips curled with a dark smile at the feel of shattering bone, the tearing of veins.

Blood soaked my sword, spraying over my body. *Glorious. I am home.*

CHAPTER 20

Above me, the dragoniles pierced the air with their strange, primordial song, and it called to me, stirring my blood. Why had I hated the dragoniles so much? We were alike, these creatures and me. The beating hearts of beasts, driven to break, to kill—to drink the blood of our enemies.

With the angel's sword in my hand, I moved across the blood on the floor like a dancer, whirling and ducking, fighting the next threat. When I pivoted again, I found the next angel coming for me, black hair streaming behind him. *Kill.*

My sword clashed with the angel's, sparks lighting up the dark air. Another angel pressed in on me—and my twisted, bestial heart started to panic, a rabbit cornered by wolves.

From above, a black dragonile scorched the air with his fiery breath, singeing the angels.

Just enough to give me an advantage.

Smiling, I whirled my sword through the air, cutting into the angel's sword arm, thrilling at the destruction. How would he like the feel of mortality?

Blood-soaked soil, thunder rumbling over the horizon, lightning searing my blood.

I swung my sword again, hacking into his other arm, sword through bone, through flesh—

Fear flashed in his eyes, and he screamed, "Get away from me!" His terror sang through my blood like an aria.

Dimly, I wondered where the beautiful one was—the man with the blue-gray eyes and the broken wing. But he wasn't here.

I was here, and I wanted blood. I hacked through one of the angel's wings, creating a masterpiece of blood-stained feathers.

"Evil flee from me!" he shrieked.

At his words, an image—a distant memory seared in my mind like a brand: sharp, monstrous teeth, sinking into pale flesh, blood streaming onto the pavement.

I stumbled away from him as if I'd been burned. As I did, a blur of white moved for me—another threat. I gritted my teeth, swinging for him in a haze of steel and red. Our swords clashed, and his eyes blazed with silver light. He pressed in on me, his golden hair streaming behind him.

Kill. Prey.

He was the strongest among them, and my muscles burned, my sword faltering. My legs began to shake, blood pumping hard as his steel clashed against mine.

Kill.

A single thrust, and my stolen sword plunged into his heart. His pale eyes widened, a stream of blood dripping from his lips.

I pulled my sword from his body, and he slumped to the floor.

Light blazed from my chest, and the disturbing memory faded from my mind. Even with the din of the dragoniles howling around me, a sort of peace had overcome me.

Blood and gore glistened in the dim light of my body. The screams of the dragoniles hummed deliciously over my skin—wild beasts, the lot of us.

I'd left one alive, hadn't I? He'd escaped while I'd been fighting the last angel. An injured one had run from the rookery, his arms and shattered wing hanging off him. The hunter in me wanted to chase him down, to finish him off, but I'd probably lost my chance.

I glanced at the doorway—waiting for more angels to come through—*hoping* for more angels to arrive. I needed more to kill.

For just a moment I faltered, horrified at my own thoughts. Free from the risk of death, some of the feral rage began to slowly seep out of my body. It cast a silver glow around the dragoniles, one of them circling the air protectively above me. Drakon.

Footsteps pounded in the hallway outside the rookery, and I readied my sword, my eyes on the hallway.

Before anyone had a chance to arrive, a figure rushed into the room in a blaze of silver light. A silhouette of dark wings spread over the hall, and my feral bloodlust exploded once again.

Kill. Dominate. Devour. A bestial growl rose from my throat, mingling with the wild symphony of dragonile shrieks. My canines lengthened, and I rushed for the angel, sword ready to slash through flesh—

His hand shot out, grabbing my wrist.

My heart began to slow at the feel of soothing, myrrh scented magic.

In the silvered light glowing from my body, I looked up into a pair of stunning, gray eyes that faded to a midnight blue around the edges. I couldn't remember who he was, just that he was the most beautiful man I'd ever seen.

He squeezed my wrist harder, until I dropped the sword.

"Well, well, well," the angel purred. "*This* is interesting."

Feral Ruby still didn't quite have the power of speech, and another snarl escaped my throat, my lip curling.

He searched my face, like he was trying to interpret primitive scratches clawed into a tree. "Ruby." His voice wrapped around me like silk, and his grip softened on my wrist until it almost felt good. "Not your enemy."

Some of the battle fury raging through my nerves began to go quiet. The battle drum pounding in my ears began to still.

"Not an enemy," I repeated.

Footsteps echoed off the walls and ceiling, and I turned to see the two demons—the male and the female. Couldn't remember their names.

The male's mouth dropped open, and leathery wings spread out behind him. *"This* is the Bringer of Light?"

The female folded her arms, and her eyes blazed. "Is it just me, or is she covered in blood and ash, and surrounded by dead bodies?"

The large male nodded. "I'd honestly expected something a little more...civilized."

The demoness's hair writhed around her head, and she pointed at the fallen one. "Is that a dead demon?"

The beautiful angel searched my eyes, his expression probing. Gently, he ran a thumb over my wrist, and his soothing magic wrapped around me, pulling the fear, the violence from me.

Adonis. I breathed in his smell, and my gaze roamed over his broken wing, the place where I'd healed him.

"Are you in there, Ruby?" he asked softly. "Are you hurt?"

I nodded, finally remembering how to speak. "Yeah. It's me." My voice sounded too quiet, too tame for what had just happened. "I'm not hurt."

Slowly, the bloodlust drained from me completely, and Adonis released his grip on my wrist.

I looked down at my body, at the glowing silver light. It illuminated the stark spatters of blood all over my dress, although it was starting to dim.

Vaguely, I was aware of how I looked to Adonis, of the horror he must have felt at my appearance. Feral, bestial, covered in the blood of angels.

Why did I care what he thought, anyway?

I took a step away from him, surveying the damage, and swallowed hard. "So, you probably want me to explain this."

Tanit licked her fangs. "We slaughtered the angels outside. Or rather, Adonis did most of the work, while we watched on—"

"I killed plenty," Kur interjected.

"And then we heard the dragoniles calling us," added Adonis.

"How many angels were there?" I asked.

"Twenty," said Adonis. "It may take a while for the Heavenly Host to even notice that they've failed to return."

"The angels weren't coming here for me," I began. "They were here to check on you, Adonis. They want to know why your curse hasn't taken hold, even after the apocalypse has started."

Adonis stroked his fingertips across his chest. "Little messenger angels. Well, they're all dead now, so I don't imagine the message will get through."

Tanit nudged the dead demon with her foot. "Can we get back to what the fuck happened in here?"

I surveyed the carnage around me. "Oh. The bodies. Well, the fallen one over there was the first to arrive, and he said he could smell the magic of the light bringing." I looked down at the incandescent light that radiated from my body.

"It just sort of came out when I panicked. And I used his demonic transformation process to kill him."

Adonis's eyes flashed with a cold light. "How exactly did he come to fall?"

I curled my lip. "Weird torture fetish. I indulged it a bit until he lost control."

Adonis's eyes flashed with anger, and the air seemed to thin around us.

"Four other angels followed," I continued. "They could all smell my light magic. And then I went a bit feral, and slaughtered them in a brutal bloodbath. So that about sums it up."

Kur smiled at me, his dark eyes glinting. "Oh, I like her."

"You killed all of them?" asked Adonis.

I shook my head. "One of them got away, but I'm not sure he'll live. His arms and one of his wings were in tatters."

Dark magic whirled around Adonis. "Seems the magic of the Old Gods still fills your body. That's the good news. The bad news is that we now have another problem on our hands. We're racing against Johnny's recovery, and against discovery by the Heavenly Host."

I looked down at my body, at the silver light pooling from my skin.

Adonis nodded at the demon's body. "You've glossed over a thing or two. What do you mean, a torture fetish?"

Somehow, it felt undignified to go into it, but I supposed it was stupid to cling on to dignity when coated with a sticky mixture of blood and ash. "He wanted me to kneel on the ground, pull off the top of my dress, and cut myself on his sword. He really wasn't a very nice angel."

Adonis's gray eyes darkened, and his wings spread out behind him.

Kur scrubbed his hand over his mouth. "Oh, this will be interesting."

Violence glinted in Adonis's eyes. "He will suffer a painful death."

I blinked. "Pretty sure he's dead already."

"He isn't." Adonis's voice was pure ice. "I'd know."

Dark tendrils of his magic spread out around the room, and a claw-sharp filament of magic caressed my cheek.

As his power roiled around us, the demon on the floor began to twitch and moan. Slowly, he pushed himself up to his knees, his black eyes landing on me. He roared, the sound echoing off the hall. Just as he began to run for me, Adonis cut his wrist through the air. With that one sudden motion, he severed the demon's body in half at the waist.

The creature unleashed a half-strangled scream, refusing to die.

I closed my eyes, trying to block out the last of his shrieks as he bled out on the floor.

Glad I wasn't the only ruthless killer in here.

"Now he's dead," Adonis said quietly.

The stench of blood curled into my nose, sickly sweet. Dark, unwelcome memories prodded at the depths of my mind. An old memory—brutal, monstrous teeth sinking into a pale arm, blood staining the pavement—

My eyes snapped open again, and I took a deep, shaky breath. "Well. This night turned out well, didn't it?" I smeared some of the blood off my arms, watching as it dripped onto the floor.

The sound of the dragoniles screeching still echoed wildly around us.

"You may want to wash the blood off." Among the chaos of reptilian screams, Adonis's voice sounded oddly soothing.

"Brilliant idea." I was already heading for the door. "I need to get away from that horrific screaming."

Tanit's lips curled. "What's the matter, little flower? Can't handle a little blood?"

"Leave her alone, Tanit," said Adonis.

Kur waved at the carnage all over the floor. "Doesn't look like she's afraid of a bit of blood. We could have used her at the Battle of Plataea. She could have fended off half the Greeks where they'd trapped us."

Ignoring them, I crossed over the blood-slicked floor to the doorway, my entire body shaking. "Bath time for Ruby."

"Don't take too long," Kur cautioned. "We need to leave here as soon as we can in case that surviving angel manages to pass along a message."

Ten minutes ago, when I'd been feral, a strange sort of calm had quieted my mind. But now, dark memories roiled just below the surface, and a lick of dread danced up my spine.

The Heavenly Host might be coming for me. As archangels, they wouldn't be quite so easy to kill—at least, not without the Stones of Zohar.

I had no idea what might happen now, only that there was no going back.

CHAPTER 21

In Adonis's bathtub, I scrubbed a bar of soap over my skin. It smelled faintly of anemones, and formed a pink foam over my forearms. It felt good to clean the stench of death off myself.

We had two ticking time bombs on our hands now—Johnny, and the injured angel who could be limping his way back to the celestial realm.

In the bath, some of the battle fury began to seep out of my body, and the shaking in my legs went still. But when I closed my eyes, my mind flashed with images of the fight—the angelic sword slicing into flesh, through bones. When I'd fought the angels, I'd wanted more death, more blood. I'd wanted to hear the crush of bones under my sword's steel, to feel the hot rush of their blood in my mouth.

Adonis seemed strangely fascinated by the fae, but he also thought we were savage beasts, driven by the worst, basest impulses. That we worshipped a lack of control. After he'd seen me dripping with angelic blood and gore, I doubt his opinion had changed on that front.

Reddened suds dripped off my arm. Maybe the Old Gods

were sparking something in me—a complete rebellion at the presence of angels on earth. They didn't belong here—not the horsemen, nor the angels. The earth belonged to the gods of nature, not these nightmarish, heavenly creatures.

I rinsed off the pink, bloody foam in the bathwater. My jaw clenched as a dim memory flickered in my mind—sharp, bestial teeth ripping into flesh. As I ran the soap over my legs, my mind whirled with images of blood that turned to something darker—blood dripping down a pale arm, streaming over the pavement. Dragons, maybe. I was remembering a dragon attack.

No wonder Drakon unnerved me.

I clamped down hard on the unwelcome memory, gripping the soap so hard my fingernails dug into it.

This was no time to lose myself in haunting memories—I might have an angelic horde coming for me. I rose from the warm bathwater, letting the suds drip off my skin. As I unplugged the drain, goose bumps rose over my body.

The shock of the cold castle air pulled me from my dark thoughts, and I stepped from the bath. I grabbed a towel and dried myself off.

In the stone alcove, I had a fresh set of clothes laid out, courtesy of Tanit—a wool dress that looked like it would fall just below my ass, and wool stockings that would reach up to mid-thigh. And apart from the boots, that was it. I'd asked for something warm, and that was what she'd brought me. At least she'd found something made of thick material.

Freshly dried, and smelling of anemones, I pulled on the woolen stockings, the fabric rough against my bare skin. The dark dress hugged my body, sleeves reaching down to my wrists. I pulled on the thigh-high boots, then slipped my sheathed knife into one of them—the leather loops making a perfect holster. I'd reapplied the Devil's Bane poison to its blade.

My heels clacked over the floor as I crossed into Adonis's room.

Tanit and Kur sat on the edge of the bed.

Tanit leaned back. "Oh, the feral one is here. Ruby, did you manage to civilize yourself in there with a bit of soap?"

Adonis paced the stony floor. His sword—Ninkasi—hung over his back, ready for battle. His icy gaze met mine. "Tell us about the angel who got away. How bad were his injuries?"

I closed my eyes, shuddering as I remembered the flashes of savagery from our battle. "I think I cut into both of his arms, but I didn't take them off completely. I don't think he can use them. I sliced into one of his wings. He'd have a damn hard time flying, and if he were human, he'd bleed out. I'm not sure how mortal angels heal."

Adonis stroked his chin. "Drakon and I followed his trail of blood while you were bathing. It ends just at the edge of the cliff face. Either he plunged to his death in the ocean—or he managed to fly off to report what he saw."

Tanit's eyes burned into me. "He was half dead, his arms hanging off, wings severed, and you let him get away? Why?"

My jaw tightened. "It was four against one. And I started with a knife against their swords. I think I managed fairly well, to be honest."

Tanit rose from the bed, her predatory eyes locked on me. "I don't think the numbers were the problem, though, were they? Did you feel mercy for that angel fucker?" She laced the word *mercy* with disdain.

I shook my head. "No. Not mercy."

Adonis's midnight wings spread out wider as he assumed more command over the room. "This is hardly the time to nitpick a battle."

Tanit's dark eyes shone. "We're going all the way to France to search for the Stones of Zohar, just to hand them over to someone who can't handle the bloodshed."

Adonis raised his hand to silence her. "That's enough."

I sucked in a deep breath. "I can handle the bloodshed. I just go a little crazy when my fae side takes over, and it's hard to think clearly."

"I thoroughly approve of your crazy side," said Kur in his deep, rumbling voice.

Tanit wasn't letting this go. "It's not the craziness that I object to." She took another step closer. "With the Stones of Zohar, you'll be wielding an overwhelming power. You'll need to be able to control it, which means you can't be afraid of it. You can't be afraid of killing people."

"She'll be fine," said Adonis sharply. He handed me a leather bag, stuffed with Tanit's clothing. "Or at least, she's our best option."

"A ringing endorsement. Is someone going to tell me how we can get to this castle?"

"We'll be flying," said Tanit. "Only, you don't have wings like we all do, so Kur will have to carry you."

Adonis shot them an irritated glare. "I'll carry her."

"With that shattered wing of yours?" Tanit protested.

Adonis ran his fingertips over his feathers. "It's nearly healed."

"Don't worry," said Kur. "If he drops you, I'll do my best to catch you."

* * *

HIGH ABOVE THE ROCKY LANDSCAPE, Adonis pulled me in close. The February winds whipped over my skin, chilling me, and I nestled my head in closer to Adonis's warmth.

His heart pounded through his clothing, and his wings rhythmically beat the air. One of his arms was wrapped around my lower back, the other beneath my knees. His large hand curled around my thigh, practically encircling it. I clutched my little bag of clothes.

Something about his smell and the feel of his magic soothed my muscles, washing away all the violent images that had burned in my skull earlier.

A vault of stars arched over us, and my red hair whipped into my face. I brushed it out of my eyes. Stretching out far below us lay the vast, darkened wasteland of the post-apocalyptic UK. Every now and then, flashes of bonfires pierced the darkness, a few cities punctuated by flickering candles in windows. Those were probably the demon enclaves, since they now felt free to roam over the land unperturbed. Vampire cities, valkyrie havens, shifter dens…

I shot a nervous glance at Adonis's injured wing. "Do you really think it was a good idea to take me instead of Kur?"

Our gazes met. "Do you know that most women would give their right arm to fly with me?"

"Do you usually require that kind of a sacrifice?"

He ignored my comment.

A burst of flame punctuated the darkness, and my gaze flicked to Drakon. He soared above us, occasionally belching fire.

"Why *did* you want to take me instead of Kur? You've told me that you hate feral fae. And you've just seen a feral fae at her worst. Half naked, covered in blood and gore. Why insist on sticking close to me?"

"You don't seem like the other feral fae I've known. Violent, yes, but I can hardly object to that." His voice was smooth as a lover's caress. "Maybe I like it a little."

Was that a spark of warmth I felt in my chest? No—of course it wasn't. I didn't care what he thought.

"I wasn't raised among the fae. My parents taught me some of the old fae ways, but not the brutal parts, I guess." I tried to ignore the fact that the brutality just seemed to come naturally to me. "My mother taught me to carve weapons from trees, to live off what the forest provided us."

"What did they do?"

"They were spies among the Institute. Their work was dangerous, and my mother made sure I'd be able to look after Hazel if anything happened to them." That was my job, my destiny. "Except…"

"Except we came into your world, and the dragon-shifters, too."

"You know, none of the tree carving or berry picking came in very handy when faced with a hundred-foot-tall reptile." I didn't tell him how completely powerless I'd felt, but given the way he pulled me closer to his hard, masculine body, I thought he could sense it. "And I just want to get back to that old dream—the one about living in the forest off berries and venison. That probably sounds stupid to someone whose goal is to be worshipped by celestial angels."

"It doesn't sound stupid at all."

Drakon screeched at the night sky, and a chill rippled over my skin.

"I'm just glad I got my sister back." At the thought of Hazel, my mind wandered to Kratos. Sure—he was a monster. But monsters surrounded me at this point—and he was a monster who'd returned Hazel to me. Would the Stones of Zohar drive him from the earth? Maybe Adonis wanted to enslave him.

I knew angels didn't belong on earth—that they had to leave. And yet still, the question prodded at the back of my mind.

"What will happen to Kratos if the Stones of Zohar return him to the heavens?" I asked.

Adonis's body tensed, and he lowered his head so his breath warmed the side of my face. "Why are you worried about Kratos?"

"I just want to know what will happen to him. He found Hazel for me. I know he's a horseman, and he's at risk of falling, and he is forced to kill scores of people…but he did something kind for me. I owe him."

"Is that right?" Adonis's velvety voice had a hint of steel in it.

I frowned. "Yes. I mean, he searched for her, and he brought her to me, just because she was important to me. He even made me a dance studio."

He stared evenly at the night sky in front of us, his enormous wings rhythmically beating the air. "I see."

"Is there something you're not telling me?" My teeth chattered.

Instead of answering my question, he pulled me in closer to his chest. "You're freezing, aren't you? I can feel your body shivering." The sensuous tone of his voice slipped around me like silk.

One of his hands curled around my leg—the gap between my dress and my stockings. Slowly, the tip of his forefinger began a lazy stroke up my inner thigh. At his touch, a liquid heat slowly unfurled in my body, pooling around my belly, my ribs.

He kept his glacial eyes on the night air ahead of us, as if he were only half aware of what he was doing. I, on the other hand, was completely aware of every minute shift of his fingers, and my world narrowed to his light touch.

A slow, lazy stroke up and down my bare inner thigh, eliciting an ache in my belly. Another slow, gentle stroke. Sparks ignited up my spine, and my back began to arch. His plan to warm me up was working, and my body heated with every gentle stroke.

I pulled myself in closer to him, my breasts pressing against him, and he met my gaze. Once more, that carnal look burned in his eyes, and his fingers moved higher up my bare thigh.

I hated myself for it, but I desperately wanted to know what it felt like to kiss him. *Stay in control, Ruby.* He was born to kill and seduce.

If this went any further, at some point he'd realize that I wasn't wearing any underwear. And yet—who was I to stop him?

My breath came faster in my throat.

"You interest me, fae." Then, an unexpected question. "Why a succubus? You hide yourself as a human to blend into their world, but of all the demons, you chose succubus to mask yourself."

Again, that fingertip moved lazily along my skin, his eyes fixed straight ahead as if he was completely unaware of it. Did he realize that with every slow caress, a dark heat arced through my blood? I let my gaze trail over his full mouth, trying to remember how words worked.

At last, I cleared my throat. "Fae males like to dominate the females. To some degree, the same is true for angels, demons, humans... It's kind of a male thing."

Amusement glinted in his eyes. "Is that right?"

"There was one exception. Succubi ruled over men long ago. Shadow demons, human males—they all used to worship the demonesses of the night."

"Mmmm." His deep purr licked up my nape. "You envision yourself dominating men. I must admit. The image has a certain appeal."

"I mean, I don't dwell on it." Could he hear how fast my heart was beating right now?

The tip of his forefinger continued to trace lazy, exquisite strokes on my thigh, and warmth pooled in my core. I wanted to feel his lips against mine, his tongue licking my body.

"Do you feel warmer now, Ruby?" The way my name sounded on his tongue—instead of *succubus* or *fae*—sent a throbbing ache through my belly.

I liked being up here with him, feeling his arms around me.

I swallowed hard. "Yes. Warmer," I managed.

He lowered his face to mine. "This is why I didn't want Kur to take you." His voice was a purr against my neck, a dangerous invitation.

I had to stop myself from kissing his neck. What would he do if I pressed my lips against his throat, against that pulsing vein in his neck? I tried to imagine how hard it would be to wrap my legs around him from this angle.

It was a strange sort of torture, flying with him hundreds of feet in the air, desperate now to feel my body pressed against his masculine form. My gaze dipped to his sensuous mouth—the subtle curl of his full lips.

Another slow, lazy swoop up my inner thigh, and I let out a low moan. His body called to me, an inexorable magnetic pull. Tightening my arms around him, I moved my lips closer to his neck, an ache throbbing between my legs. His hand slid higher still. A cold rush of air—

Then, I slammed down the iron door on my desire. "Stop with the hands," I said.

I wasn't on this mission to enjoy myself, and definitely not to enjoy the pleasures of a dark angel of seduction.

My body went rigid, and I tugged down my dress. "I mean, I'm warm enough now, thanks."

A low, nearly imperceptible growl in protest. Maybe he tried to hide it, but Adonis had his own conflicts—his perfect masculine beauty masking a primal side.

The combination was disturbingly tempting.

CHAPTER 22

As we soared over the English Channel, icy wind bit into my skin. Adonis was no longer using his seduction power to warm me, and I was starting to regret it deeply. Particularly when a light, freezing rain began to fall, drenching my clothes.

Drakon circled around us, igniting the dark air with his fiery breath.

"I told you about myself," I said. "Now you tell me about yourself, then. You're Death, supposedly. You can kill with a flick of your wrist, and you have. But you have a problem with the savagery of the fae."

"Some creatures deserve violent deaths. Others don't. The fae don't discriminate in their ecstatic states."

"Ah. So you've got a moral code."

"Morality," he said. "Shockingly, it's quite important to angels. Sacrificing the few to save the many, brutally punishing those who deserve it. And do you know what? The second bit is my favorite part."

"Of course it is." I shivered. "I'd hate to be the recipient of one of your morally righteous punishments."

"I don't see that happening."

"Any idea how far we have to go?" I asked.

"Another hour, maybe."

I glanced down over the dark, churning sea, and it sparkled faintly in the moonlight. If Adonis decided to drop me for any reason, I'd freeze to death quickly. Maybe I should minimize the "Are we there yet?" questions.

"Close your eyes," he said quietly. "I'll wake you when we're over Paris."

I'd never sleep here, hundreds of feet in the air. Freezing, and with wildly sexual thoughts blazing in my mind.

Still, as I leaned against his powerful chest, the rhythmic beating of his heart lulled me into relaxation, and his soothing magic whispered over me. Slowly, sleep began to claim my mind, and I dreamt of a river carving through a wild garden dappled with red flowers.

* * *

A GENTLE NUDGING on my side woke me again, and my breath caught in my throat as I stared down at Paris. Or at least, what was left of Paris.

The Eiffel Tower still stood sharply in the dark landscape, silvered in the light of night.

While I'd been sleeping, rain had soaked my body, and I clamped down on my chattering teeth.

As we flew deeper into the city, warm lights burned in the ruins of Paris's buildings—rookeries, just like the ones that had sheltered me in London. Around us, pale creatures flew through the air on gossamer wings. As one of them swooped close to us, I caught a glimpse of his face. His eyes were milky white, and curly gold hair spilled from his scalp. The creatures looked eerily like children, but with haunted expressions, mouths gaping slightly open.

"What are they?" I asked.

"Cherubs. They're Aereus's version of the sentinels. They watch everyone, report to him."

"So Aereus will know the moment we arrive."

"Oh, he'll definitely know."

Adonis's wings beat the air rhythmically, then flattened out as he began to take us lower. The night air kissed my damp skin.

At last, we got to the center of Paris, where a vast palace stretched out below us—an expanse of ornate honey-colored buildings, joined together in a rectangular shape. A ruined garden spread out before the palace—all dead plants and broken statues.

In the center of a sandstone courtyard between the palace buildings, light blazed from within an enormous, glass pyramid.

"The Louvre," I said. "We're going to the Louvre?"

"Aereus always admired it. And when he got the chance, he made it his own."

"How enterprising."

"I should warn you that Aereus has his own effect on people."

"I think I can guess. Johnny, angel of famine, makes people hungry, Kratos the Conqueror makes us want to submit. You make people..." I swallowed hard, wishing I hadn't begun that sentence. "Yearn for things." *Vague. Good.* "And the angel of war will probably bring out my violent side."

A wry smile. "Not that it appears to take much in your case." His breath was warm against my ear. "Do you remember the role you're supposed to play?"

"Submissive succubus lover, her wild side tamed by the sexual prowess of the great and mighty love god Adonis."

"You've actually elaborated a bit there, not that I object to the description. It sounds entirely realistic."

I didn't think he could see the roll of my eyes in the darkness. "Just one of these days I'd like a spy scenario where I get to be the all-powerful Empress, and a beautiful man has to cater to my every whim."

A wicked smile. "Depending on your whims, I'm sure we could arrange something."

At his words, that heat surged again in my blood.

We seemed to pick up speed as Adonis carried us lower toward the Louvre, and the wind rushed over us. We glided to a smooth landing in the courtyard beyond the pyramid, swooping down gently before a towering set of doors. Drakon screeched to a halt beside us.

A line of milky-eyed cherubs stood before the doors, their bodies glowing like starlight in the dark.

Adonis wrapped his arms around me, his wings surrounding me like a shield.

"Aereus is expecting us," Adonis said in his commanding voice.

"The Dark Lord," the cherubs spoke in unison. "Welcome to Sadeckrav Castle."

A gentle thudding behind us turned my head. Kur and Tanit landed, their leathery wings folding behind them.

Eyes wide and gleaming, the cherubs glided to the side, and the front doors creaked open with a groan into a vast hall with an arched ceiling. Marble columns and alcoves lined the walls.

I'd been to the Louvre before—long ago, on a trip with my parents. And I didn't remember it quite this way. Aereus had definitely made it his own.

Torches burned in brackets along the stone walls. Statues of a war god—Aereus, presumably—stood over a marble floor.

Without Adonis's arms around me, a chill had spread through my body, and my teeth chattered. My wet hair felt positively icy on the back of my neck.

From a shadowy hallway, five humans emerged, each with an iron collar around their neck, each dressed in a simple gray tunic.

I bit my lip. Considering they weren't chained to anything, the iron collar served no practical purpose. Maybe they were chained up when they slept, or maybe Aereus just wanted to give them a harsh reminder of their servitude.

Four cherubs glided around us, their wide eyes peering up at us. "Dark Lord," they said in unison. "We understand you have arrived to discuss important matters with our master. You must rest now. The human servants will take you and your lover to your room. Please, follow them."

Eerie little buggers.

The humans stared at Adonis, their eyes wide with terror. Two of them stepped forward—the two largest men, one bearded and over six feet tall, the other a younger man, his body lean. They trembled as they stared at Adonis.

Nervously, they beckoned us down another expansive hallway, lined with stately columns. The other humans beckoned Tanit and Kur in the opposite direction, splitting us up.

My high-heeled boots echoed off the stone walls as we walked, and I summoned more of the charcoal glamour of a succubus to waft off my body in tendrils. Drakon's claw-tipped feet clicked over the floor behind us.

The path that the cherubs took led us past long, winding marble halls, the walls festooned with paintings of deeply unnerving battle scenes. Swords cutting off heads, blood spattering battlefields—*Saturn Devouring His Son,* the god's eyes wide with insane bloodlust. I shivered, maybe from the icy rain, or maybe the decor.

At the end of a long hall, the cherubs paused at a door

that swung open, revealing a small room with a simple bed in the center of a stone floor. White sheets, a few pillows—literally no other furniture in the whole room apart from a clawfoot bathtub. The place didn't have windows, just a few iron sconces protruding from the sandstone walls.

After all that grandeur, I'd been expecting something more luxurious than this. Aereus, clearly, was trying to make a point.

Adonis turned to the cherubs, his eyes darkening, and the candles wavered in their sconces, nearly snuffing out.

"*This*," he hissed, "is the room Aereus wants me to stay in?"

The bearded man shrank away from Adonis. "He thought you might be comfortable here. With your friend."

An eerie, animal stillness had overtaken Adonis's body, only faint whispers of his magic moving in the air around him. Nothing, I was coming to realize, was more dangerous or terrifying than the quiet stillness of an angel.

CHAPTER 23

"Aereus has done this on purpose, to prove a point," said Adonis. His lip curled in a snarl, then with a lightning-fast movement, he had the bearded man pinned up against the wall.

Drakon spread his wings and hissed, a stream of fire pouring from his mouth in the direction of the humans.

Sweet earthly gods, all this over a room?

"Relax, Adonis," I snapped, before changing my tone to be sweetly seductive. "This will be perfect for us. No distractions, just a bed and a bath to keep us occupied."

Adonis didn't appear to be listening to me, his hands wrapped around his victim's collar. Instead, he leaned in closer to the man. "I want you to go back to Aereus and tell him that this is perfect for me, and that I love it." Despite the gentleness of his words, icy rage poisoned his tone.

He dropped the man in a heap on the floor. The other servant seemed to have slunk into the shadows, probably hoping Adonis would forget he existed.

Within a moment, both humans had scrambled off, their

BLACK OPS FAE

footsteps scuttling over the floor as they ran. Adonis slammed the door.

When he turned back to me, his expression was one of complete serenity, his body entirely at ease.

I cocked my hip, trying to calm the chattering of my teeth. The flight's rainstorm still chilled me to the bone. "Did you really just violently assault someone over the furniture?"

Surprise flickered in Adonis's eyes. "He's fine, isn't he? And I don't care about the furniture, but the other horsemen expect me to act in a certain way. I'm supposed to be the Lord of Death, and all that." His movements smooth and easy, he prowled closer to me. "Surely you understand playing a role, Ruby."

I nodded. "I get it." I sat on the edge of the bed, desperate to pull off my boots and crawl under the covers. "So who gets the bed?"

"Plenty of room for both of us."

I swallowed hard, then lowered my voice to a whisper. "We're not really lovers, Adonis. We're just going to play the part."

Behind him, his wings shimmered away—the first time in days I saw him without them.

He pulled off his shirt, giving me a view of his chiseled chest. The network of scars over his heart interrupted the sharp lines of his tattoos. Already, he was sliding between the bedsheets. He leaned back on his hands, eyeing me as I stood there hugging myself.

"Can you turn around?" I asked, shivering. "I want to change out of my ice-cold dress."

"I have seen you naked before. In fact, the image is seared deeply into my fondest memories."

"Close your eyes," I barked.

He did as he was told, and I pulled off my drenched dress, my skin frigid and puckered in the cold air. I rifled through the leather bag until I found one of Tanit's dry dresses, and I slipped it on over my naked body. Then, I snatched the sheathed knife from the bag.

I hugged myself, my teeth still chattering. "So where am I supposed to sleep, now?"

Adonis opened his eyes again, and his gaze roamed over me as if imagining what he'd missed. "If you don't want to sleep next to a godlike being, that's your choice. There's always the floor, or the bathtub."

I shivered, and the warmth of the bed called to me.

Adonis cocked his head. "But I can see that you're freezing. You'll need me to warm you."

I tightened my fingers into fists until the nails pierced my skin. "Fine. I hope you're okay with sleeping with the torches lit," I added. "Because I'm still not into the whole darkness thing." I shoved the knife under the pillow. "And if you do anything I don't want you to, I have a poison-tipped blade under my pillow."

"Of course," he purred. "I'll only do things you want me to."

Don't fall for his charms, Ruby. He was like this with all women, of course. Definitely the kind of guy you couldn't trust. The kind who kept secrets, who never told you what he really felt about you. The kind who'd leave the earth to rule the heavens at the first chance he got. Typical.

Still shivering, I crawled into bed next to him, trying not to look at his perfect body. I was painfully aware of the fact that I was still going commando. I'd have to make sure my dress didn't shift too much during the night.

In any case, I definitely wasn't going to dwell on his smooth, tan skin, his powerful arms, or that perfect mouth that could torture me with excruciating pleasure.

I cleared my throat. *Shut down those thoughts.* "Since we're here for a reason, and that reason is to spy on Aereus, maybe it's time we figure out a specific plan. What else do I need to know about him?"

"Aereus is competitive with me."

"Hence the room." I lay down stiffly, keeping my eyes trained on the ceiling. Every one of my muscles was tensed.

"He's furious that my curse hasn't set in, that I inspire more fear than he does. He will want to steal you from me like the spoils of war."

Adonis leaned on his elbow, looking over at me. I tried to ignore that his searing gaze was roaming over my shoulders. I pulled the sheet tighter around me, clutching hard to it.

"That explains how I can capture his interest. Maybe he'll want me alone." Already, the gears were turning in my mind, and I started to envision myself functioning as a honey trap. "Any clue at all where he might be keeping these Stones of Zohar?"

"No. As you've seen, the palace itself is enormous. But they're so powerful, so valuable to him, that I'd guess he keeps them close to him, locked up safely in his bedroom or his office of war."

I took a deep breath. "I can probably contrive to get into either of those."

A troubled expression crossed Adonis's beautiful features. "He's dangerous—not just for who he is, but for what he can inspire in you. He'll draw your violent thoughts from you like nectar from a flower. He can sense inner conflict—and he can exploit it. I want to keep a line of communication open with you if you're alone with him."

"How exactly?"

"If you allow it, I can link our minds, so I'll be able to hear your thoughts."

My jaw dropped. "You must be joking."

"You can control it to some degree, but I'll be able to hear if you're in danger."

"I'm guessing it's not reciprocal. You'd never agree to me hearing your thoughts."

"It doesn't need to be reciprocal. I don't need you to save me. In any case, it's only temporary."

"I haven't agreed to anything."

Adonis's dark eyebrows furrowed. He reached for me, tracing his fingertips over my collarbone. His touch left a trail of tingling heat. "Goose bumps. You're still freezing."

He ran his fingertips over my skin, and his magic began to whisper through my blood, warming me and soothing me at the same time. Even from that light touch, my back began to arch, my breath speeding up. I knew a flush had spread over my chest, giving away my real desires, even if I wanted to keep them hidden.

He leaned in close, his breath warming my neck. I felt as if my body were straining against the dress. I wanted him to touch and tease me with his fingertips, to let them roam over my thighs again. *I knew this was a bad idea.*

Slowly, his fingertips trailed over the neckline of my dress, gently tugging it down.

"I want to see all of you," he rasped, inching down my dress.

I arched my back, a silent invitation, and he tugged the fabric down to expose my breasts. The look on his face as he took me in was positively *starved,* like he'd emerged from a famine to find a succulent feast before him. He kissed my throat, his mouth searing, teasing me with a hint of teeth, and I felt my legs opening. I groaned.

I wanted him, *needed* him to touch me, so badly I was practically shaking. One of his hands moved up the inside of my thigh, and liquid heat pooled in my core, between my legs. Already, my hips were rocking, anticipating his touch moving higher…

From a corner of the room, Drakon let out a growl, and

my body jolted. I pulled away from Adonis, pulling my dress up again.

What was I doing? This was all wrong. He was a power-hungry, maniacal death angel. I slammed down the iron door on my desires, and elbowed him away from me.

"This isn't a good idea." Granted, my body was screaming at me in rebellion, but I wasn't going to let him lure me in.

Adonis rolled over, disappointment etched across his gorgeous features. "Is there a reason a pleasure-loving fae would deny herself what she wants?"

I pulled the sheets up around me, my body suddenly freezing at the loss of body heat. "How about the fact that you've straight up told me you're evil?"

Candlelight danced over his skin, and he closed his eyes, inhaling deeply. As he breathed in, he pulled the light from the room, dimming the torches to a low burn—just enough to keep me comfortable.

My body still buzzed with the excitement of his touch. *Forget about how good that felt. Think of something vile.* I pressed my fingernails into the back of my hand, summoning instead images of blood and violence, of Saturn ripping the head off his child. And when I slept, I dreamt of blood spreading through a field of white anemones, staining them red.

CHAPTER 24

"I may not be entirely objective, but I do feel the bath would be better with two people in it," said Adonis.

"Oh, really?" I splashed the soap off my skin.

Wingless, Adonis sat in a chair facing the other direction. Drakon had been banished to the hallway.

"There are delicate parts of your body I could attend to better than you can." The sensual promise in his voice made my pulse race. "You can trust me on this."

At his words, a flush spread through my body. "I can manage."

I tried not to imagine his hand sliding gently between my legs, exploring my body, and I fought the burning ache. I tried not to imagine the sweet release of giving in to him completely.

"Stop distracting me," I said. "I have to meet the horseman of war. Alone, of course."

Adonis snatched a silver flask off the bed and unscrewed it while keeping his eyes straight ahead. Despite trying to tempt me with his words, he was acting like a perfect gentleman. "He's trying to send me another message. He wants to show that he can take what's mine."

"What's *yours?*"

"As far as Aereus knows, you're my succubus—a demoness I've claimed as my own. We've come here, purporting to seek his help, and he'll want to use it as an opportunity to put me in my place. It enrages him that I remained un-cursed."

"When I'm finished with him, should I meet you back here?"

"If you learn anything—or even if you don't—go to Tanit's room and wait for me there."

Honestly, I didn't want to ever leave this bath—especially not to meet yet another possessive, domineering horseman. The warm water licked at my bare breasts, and I found myself staring at Adonis's powerful back, imagining running my fingertips over his chiseled shoulder blades.

I loosed a long sigh. Yep, I wanted to stay in here forever, thinking about how Adonis's fingers had felt on my body. Almost unconsciously, I began tracing the path his fingers had taken up my leg, staring at the back of his shoulders.

Adonis folded his arms behind his head. "I want to hear your thoughts when you're with him."

I froze. "Oh. That again?"

"If I leave my mark on you, it will allow me to hear your thoughts. Not every single thought—not all the filthy thoughts I'm sure you're having about me right now while you wash yourself and stare at my back."

I cleared my throat. "Don't be ridiculous. I'm not sure why everyone thinks Aereus is the one with the ego. Wasn't Adonis the legendary figure who got trapped mooning over his own image in a lake? Is that who you're named after? It's fitting."

"That was Narcissus," he said sharply. "Not even close."

"Anyway—you want to read my thoughts?"

"I can link us. You'll be able to feel me, a little. And I'll be able to hear if you're in trouble. You can scream for me in your mind."

"So…is this a permanent thing, or what?"

"Only if you want it to be. In any case, it's the only way you should go in there on your own. You don't know what he's capable of. He's quite fond of torture. Mental. Physical. All kinds."

I cringed. "Give me a minute to think about it. I'm not looking forward to meeting him, but going alone is probably for the best. All that I know about him is that his ego is his greatest weakness, and if I can flatter it, I might be able to get him to talk. If you're there, you'll suck up all the attention in the room like a black hole of narcissism and ruin it all."

I stepped out of the bath, and water dripped off my skin onto the stone floor. I grabbed the towel to dry myself off, and scrubbed at my hair.

On the bed, I'd laid out one of Tanit's outfits—a short, silver dress with long sleeves. And by the dress, my most important item: the poison-tipped knife.

Adonis sipped from his flask. "Can I turn around now?"

"Not yet. I'm completely wet and naked."

A bit cruel, maybe, but I enjoyed watching his entire body tense, fingers tightening around his flask.

I pulled the dress over my freshly cleaned body, completely bare under the luxurious fabric that fell midway down my thighs.

I pulled on the thigh-high boots, then slipped the sheathed knife down the side of one of them. "You can turn around now."

Adonis rose from his chair, and a deep curiosity burned in his pale eyes when he turned to me. He prowled closer. "Do you agree to what I asked?"

BLACK OPS FAE

I crossed my arms. I'd hardly make a very good spy if I let someone I didn't trust invade my thoughts. "The whole mind-intrusion thing. Not a fan. Couldn't I just wear a wire?"

He shrugged, a smooth gesture. "I'm not familiar with that technology. But I can tell you that you're about to meet with one of the most dangerous beings who has ever walked the earth, and it might be wise to have an even more lethal ally backing you up."

"Yeah. Not really into it. How about I just call for you?"

"His rooms are often sealed so screams can't escape." Adonis's eyes darkened. "I once watched him trap two human women in his torture room for hours. Just for his own amusement. When he emerged, not a single piece of them was recognizable. He radiated joy that day."

I swallowed hard.

I leaned against the wall, still trying to gauge how much I trusted this self-professed dangerous being. He'd held back from telling me the truth about things. He wanted an insane amount of power for himself.

But—I didn't get the sense that he'd lied to me. And more —he was asking permission, when he really didn't need to. We'd already established that he could control my mind if he wanted to, yet he never did it. "It's definitely temporary?"

Another step closer, and he was standing right next to me, so close now that his magic slipped over my skin, kissing my bare thighs.

"Just temporary," he confirmed.

I let out a long breath. In this world, maybe I had to pick and choose which monsters I wanted to trust. The lesser of two evils, as it were. "Fine. Do what you need to do. And if I find out it's not like you described, I'm carving the thing off."

Without another word, he slipped his fingers into the sleeve of my dress and gently pulled it off my shoulder.

Goose bumps rose over my skin, and I gasped at the feel of his fingertips on me.

"What are you doing?" I asked.

"I need to leave my mark on you, in a place where no one will see it. It won't hurt." His voice skimmed over my body, lighting me on fire. "Much."

I nodded mutely, the power of speech deserting me.

Adonis leaned down closer, and in the next moment, his mouth was on my shoulder, his kiss searing me. Involuntarily, my back arched into him, and liquid heat swooped through my core. Pure ecstasy lit up my body, until I was only dimly aware of my leg hooking around his to pull him closer, or of my fingers threading through his thick hair. His tongue flicked over my skin, then a hint of teeth. I moaned lightly.

Visions burned in my mind of Adonis pulling my dress all the way up, of his hands and tongue exploring my body. Wild heat arced through me.

Then, a sharp pain scalded my flesh below his mouth, snapping me out of my fantasies.

"Ow!" I clenched my fingers tight.

Slowly, Adonis pulled his face from my neck, his eyes burning with desire. It was at that point I realized that I hadn't threaded my fingers through his hair, but through his soft, midnight feathers, and I'd entirely wrapped my leg around his, sliding my foot higher until my dress rode up, practically to my hips.

"You're piercing my wings with your fingernails." Despite the complaint, an erotic tone suffused his voice. "Although I guess I kind of like it."

Reluctant as I was, I unwrapped my leg from Adonis and pulled my fingers from his wings. "Sorry."

When I looked down at the place where he'd marked me,

I found a small, black tattoo—a perfect circle with a sort of dash in the center.

"That's your mark?" I asked. "What is it?"

"Theta. The eight letter of the Greek alphabet."

"Okay, but…why?"

His arms loosened around me, but his eyes remained locked on the mark on my shoulder. "Thanatos. Death. It's what I am. It's who I am."

I pulled up the shoulder of my dress. "I like the name Adonis better."

A faint smile played over his lips. "So do I."

"And now you can hear my thoughts?"

"Unless you're capable of guarding them from me, I'll hear your thoughts. Particularly if you shout."

Oh sweet heavenly gods. Had he just heard…? "Were you privy to my thoughts just a moment ago?"

That slow, seductive smile. "I didn't need to hear your thoughts to know what you were thinking."

A thin sheen of sweat had risen over my body. "Right." I smoothed out my dress. "Let's just forget about that, okay? That was some sort of magic, obviously, when you left the mark."

Adonis just looked at me, that infuriating smile on his perfect lips.

"I have to go." I moved quickly for the door, trying to gather my thoughts. In the hall, cherubs glided over the marble floor, heads cocked, white eyes on me.

Focus, Ruby. Adonis's mouth on my neck had just ripped the world right out from under my feet, but I had another horseman to meet, and I needed to keep my wits about me if I was going to have any hope of manipulating him.

* * *

I STOOD BEFORE AEREUS, in a large hall with a dais that towered high above me. Golden wings swooped from his back over his throne, the feathers blending to a deep maroon at the tips. A crown of chestnut-gold hair shone from his head, lit up from behind by a stained-glass window. Sunlight streamed in from the windows, gleaming over his golden breastplate. The room smelled of roasting meat.

Aereus studied me intently, tapping the armrests contemplatively.

The longer he stared at me, the more my muscles tensed. In fact, as my gaze slid over the humans lining the side of the hall, I picked out a ruddy-faced man with dark eyes. Something about him sparked my rage, and for a single, dizzying instant, I envisioned myself ripping open his rib cage and pulling his still-beating heart from his chest...

Simmer down, Ruby. Already, Aereus's power was beginning to affect my mind—and the way he was watching me, I was pretty sure he was doing it on purpose, testing the results. Above him, the stained-glass window depicted another image of Saturn devouring his son. A god so ruthlessly driven by power that he was willing to consume his own living child to preserve his throne.

Seemed to be a favorite motif for Aereus.

I licked my lips, desperate to taste blood there.

"Tell me about why you've come." His commanding voice boomed over the hall.

Why was he asking me and not Adonis? Maybe he didn't trust Adonis. I could start planting the seeds of our plan now, anyway. "You know, the Dark Lord hasn't really discussed his plans with me, but it was something about Johnny and Kratos rebelling against the Heavenly Host. Johnny ripped Adonis's wing—I know that much. Oh! And something about Kratos starting to fall? Does that sound right?"

Aereus's primal snarl slid through my bones. "Fall? Kratos?"

I shrugged, feeling minuscule before him. "Adonis thought they were angry about their curses, that they might rebel against the archangels in heaven. Whatever you call them. And he thought they could be coming for you."

As soon as Johnny and Kratos descended from the skies above the Louvre, Aereus would know. And with any luck, he'd be on our side when we had to face them.

Blood-red veins glinted in Aereus's eyes. "Coming for me?"

Fury rippled off him, stirring my rage once more, until my mind swam with visions of teeth tearing at flesh.

This was a dangerous game for a feral fae. A succubus had more control than I did—pure seduction and elegance. A bit of soul-stealing through sex, but relatively blood-free. But a feral fae in the presence of the horseman of war? Not a great situation.

Aereus cocked his head, moving for the first time in minutes. "You look hungry, Succubus. Do any of the humans appeal to you?"

The feral snarl that escaped my throat echoed through the hall. "I feed from human males, and there are plenty in here. But none particularly strikes my fancy."

A faint accent tinged his words as he spoke. "I'd heard that Adonis had managed to tame a succubus, but I wasn't sure I believed it. I suppose some think Adonis is the most adept seducer in the world, but frankly, I find it hard to believe. Death surrounds him."

It was quickly becoming clear that despite his angelic demigod status, despite ruling over a medieval palace with chained humans at his beck and call, despite all of his powers—this man's ego was in need of some serious stroking.

All alike. You men are all alike.

Another white-hot burst of rage tore through me, and for just a moment I envisioned myself with immeasurable strength, ripping the arrogant angel from his throne, hurling him to the ground, and crushing my boot into his neck. My mouth watered.

Aereus begs for his life as I thrust a blade between his ribs...

"You look as though you've become lost in a fantasy." Aereus's voice boomed over the hall.

"It's hard not to fantasize in the presence of greatness." I shrugged, looking down at the marble floor—a succubus who could be overwhelmed by the right godlike presence. "I can feed from humans, but they don't excite me the way real power does." I lifted my eyes to his in an invitation.

A satisfied smile spread across Aereus's chiseled features. "So it's not Adonis who excites you in particular."

Slowly, I ran my fingertip over the front of my chest, tracing the curve of my breast. "It seems to me like your palace is bigger than his." While volcanic rage surged inside me, I schooled my features—coy, compliant on the outside. I needed him to bring me into his inner sanctum, to find out where he kept his most important objects.

I bit my lip, swaying my hips slightly from side to side. "Where do you rule from, Aereus? When you want to summon a war between the humans, when you want to drive them to destroy each other—do you make your decisions from here? From that throne?"

He shook his head, and a phantom wind skimmed over my skin, dry and hot as the desert air.

"Not from here, no."

Tuning in to my glamour, I focused on the tendrils of dark magic emanating from my body. I sent them spiraling through the air toward Aereus. "Can you show me your war room?"

He studied me for an uncomfortably long time before nodding curtly at a guard behind me.

When he rose from his throne, his body cast a long shadow over the floor.

Wordlessly, he descended from the dais. With each footstep, the floor trembled as if he were an actual giant. Just after he passed me, he cast an impatient look over his shoulder. "I'll take you to my war room. But first, a detour through my garden."

"A *garden?*" Given the whole *war god* thing, I'd been expecting something a little more brutal from him than gardening.

As if reading my thoughts, Aereus replied, "It's not as tame as it seems at first. In fact, it's how I control my servants."

My throat went dry. I really didn't want to be anywhere near this angel or his garden.

CHAPTER 25

I followed Aereus through a heavy door, and I squinted in the bright light outside. It took my eyes a few moments to adjust.

At first, the garden's wild beauty struck me. It wasn't the stark, elegant beauty of Adonis's garden, but a vibrant riot of color—roses in shades of violet and pumpkin, cherry-red, deep amber, mulberry, and indigo. I breathed in the heavy floral scent.

Sunlight gleamed off the golden sheen of Aereus's wings, sparking over the reddened tips of his feathers like fire. His brutal magic sizzled up my spine, bringing with it images of death—a bleak forest of soldiers impaled on spikes, their bodies casting long shadows over desert sands. The vision dissipated from my mind as quickly as it had arrived.

His footsteps crunched over a winding path, and he led me deeper into the garden. Patterns in the mosaic path stretched out far ahead of us—images of swords and crowns, Greek letters and wild animals.

I'd suggested I wanted to see his place of power. So why

had he taken me to a rose garden—and what did he mean that he used it to control his servants?

Only after a few minutes did I notice the dark gleam of barbed iron in the garden. I swallowed hard. Only one reason for barbed iron, as far as I knew.

In the depths of the garden, Aereus led me to a spiked, iron wheel, its surface stained rust-red. *Not rust.* My stomach dropped.

Aereus stood before it, a merciless smile on his face. "I was born in the Roman Empire. I once watched a man broken on the wheel. A vision I never forgot. The power a man can exert over another is thrilling."

The blood draining from my head almost left me dizzy. "You must have been a soldier."

"I helped to defeat Hannibal. I razed Carthage."

Desert air skimmed through my hair, and I twirled a lock of it around my fingertips. "I can only imagine how the armies of Carthage would have trembled before you." I blocked out the fury roiling in my chest. "And do you use this wheel for anything now?"

"It's how I keep my human servants in line. They don't wear chains, but they know not to rise up against me. They wouldn't dare. Sometimes, I kill their loved ones instead of them."

I plastered a serene smile onto my face. "How thrilling. You must be like a god to them."

His eyes flashed with a fiery light. "I am a god to them. I'm a god to your kind, too."

Bile rose in my throat. Never before had I felt it so strongly, the sense that these angels had to get away from us. I'd do anything to rip them from the surface of the earth.

As my thoughts raged, a silky-smooth presence caressed the depths of my mind. Was it Adonis?

I'm fine, I mentally telegraphed to him. *Just disturbed. Deeply fucking disturbed.*

As we walked the garden's winding path, we turned a corner, and my stomach dropped. Across from a row of wild roses, a line of guards stood. Their spears glinted in the sunlight. Instead of human forms, they had the bodies of enormous scorpions, with sharply pointed tails that curved over their heads. They stared at me through inky pools.

Masking my fear, I pointed to them. "What are they for?"

"Ah. They guard the poison garden. I grow a collection of dangerous plants here—extremely toxic. The guards simply ensure that no one dies accidentally."

"I see. How kind of you to look after your servants."

As if he gave a flying fuck. If I had to guess, Aereus couldn't stop the Old Gods from growing Devil's Bane in his garden. He didn't want any humans getting their hands on it, trying to destroy him. In fact, I could just about feel the warm glow of the Old Gods around me.

We moved farther along the path, and I ran my fingertips over the rose petals. The closer I looked, the more I found signs of death within this garden—iron devices with jagged rows of teeth jutting from the earth, designed to tear at flesh, to crush bodies. Among the flowers, bones—human, demon maybe—protruded from the soil.

Now, when I studied the mosaic on the ground, I realized the patterns were formed from teeth—human and animal, some painted black to create the designs.

I tried to choke down my disgust, but a wave of rage unfurled in me. I closed my eyes, pretending to breathe in the scent of his garden. Inwardly, I was envisioning myself strapping Aereus to the iron wheel and smashing his limbs with one of those spiked iron mallets. I'd crush *his* bones. I'd thrill at his screams. I'd rid the earth of this angelic scourge…

Easy, Ruby.

Once again, Adonis's presence stroked the depths of my mind like a lover's caress.

I'm fine, I screamed at him, unable to keep the wrath from my mental communications. *You angelic fuck.*

Taking a deep breath, I refocused on the garden around me. I was supposed to be charming the angel, not envisioning his gruesome demise.

I just…honestly had no idea how to relate to a two-thousand-year-old, omnipotent sadist.

"Those were the good days, weren't they?" I ventured. "The Roman Empire's glorious expanse over Europe, Asia, Africa…"

"My legions brought the Roman eagles over the farthest corners of the earth."

Aereus pivoted over the bony mosaic path, leading me farther into the garden, where someone had created sculptures from human bones, each one pierced with iron spikes. Roses climbed some of the sculptures. A strange, perverse sort of beauty in this garden of death.

Who had these bones belonged to? Servants who'd displeased Aereus? I could pull the knife from my boot now, ram it into his neck…

Charm him, Ruby.

What was it Adonis had said? His depressing angelic aphorism? Something about seeds…

I moved closer to Aereus, then flashed him my most charming smile. "This reminds me of a saying. The seeds of destruction grow within the gardens of paradise."

Aereus stopped walking, then turned to look at me. The wind toyed with his red cape, his hair. "So you know that expression? It's an angelic concept that I take very seriously." He gestured around him, pride beaming from his features. "That saying inspired all this. Glorious, isn't it?"

"It's good that you angels have come to earth to teach us.

When you're done purifying the earth, we can begin again, creating a true paradise from the glorious destruction you've wrought."

"I was born for this. Born for war. Born to rule as an archangel on earth, just as the Heavenly Host rule as archangels in the celestial realm."

At the mention of them, a shudder danced up my spine, and I glanced at the cloudless skies. Had that injured angel made it back to them, or had he bled out before he had the chance?

Would the terrifying archangels be coming for me soon?

Whatever the case, I didn't have much time to screw around admiring Aereus's plants. I *needed* those stones as soon as I could get my hands on them—even if I didn't quite know what they did, or how to use them, or any of those somewhat important details.

I plucked a red rose, then began pulling the petals off one by one, hoping to enchant him. "So this is your beautiful paradise. Will you show me from where else you rule your kingdom? The real destruction? I want to know where you keep your most powerful, dangerous treasures. I want to *touch* them."

CHAPTER 26

I followed after him, heels clacking on the marble floor. In the large hall, sunlight streamed through the windows onto walls painted the color of dried blood.

As we reached the imposing oak doors, they creaked open of their own accord. I walked behind Aereus in the hallway, and his essence crackled over my skin. A hot current of rage roiled under the surface of my mind. How could the humans let themselves cower in here as slaves? Why didn't they work together, rise up against their oppressors? If they worked together, they could find the Devil's Bane, poison him again and again.

They scurried and shuffled in the shadows, hoping to remain unnoticed. A woman, her filthy hair hanging in tangles over her shoulders, hurried past us, her eyes downcast. She carried a bundle of rags in a basket.

Simpletons. Every human we passed was potential prey. How easy it would be to sink my feral teeth into their necks. How easy to punch my fists through their chests, snapping their ribs, to rub their blood over my bare skin...

A gentle, soothing presence licked at the hollows of my mind—*Adonis?* Apparently he could feel my rage.

I mentally cursed myself. It had been Aereus's magic clouding my mind. I didn't hate these humans. I hated *him.* But the horseman of war provoked a will to dominate the weak.

The iron collars around their necks probably served to dampen some of their rage. But as humans, they wouldn't be as vulnerable to fury as a feral fae.

Aereus shot me a sharp look as we walked. "Ruby. Is that a violent side I can sense?"

Put on a good show, Ruby. Always put on a good show.

I flashed him a sweet smile. "I think your powerful presence might affect me a little."

He smirked. "Does the Dark Lord affect you?"

"Not the same way you do. You're a god of war, the beginning and the end. War has shaped all of history, hasn't it? The reason why angels fell to earth in the first place, the explanation for nearly every advancement in human history. War. Nothing is more powerful."

Aereus's approval was a low rumble that trembled through my gut. When he spoke again, his voice echoed off the high ceiling, off the marble columns surrounding us. "Tell me why you think Kratos might fall." In the bright light of the hall, blood-red streaks shone in Aereus's eyes. "He's lived for nine hundred years without falling. Why now?"

I shrugged. "I think he's developed a taste for succubi."

"I can understand his temptation. And Johnny—he really attacked the Dark Lord?"

"I saw it happen. He looked crazed, like he'd lost the ability to speak. He'd been on a drunken bender, maybe poisoned himself with something. Mud and grass covered his body. There was something distinctly wrong with him."

"It's good that you came here to tell me. Only I can help you."

Flatter his ego. "I don't think Adonis wanted to admit it, but he was worried he couldn't handle them on his own."

"Fool." Aereus snorted. "He'd never admit something like that."

At the end of a glass-ceilinged hall, Aereus led me to an iron door. I balked at the sight of it. Touching the iron would drain my energy completely.

Aereus stroked his enormous fingertips over the iron surface, and his body glowed with a golden light. He whispered in the Angelic language.

Angelic was the language of magic—passed down from one generation to the next. In fact, it was the ancient language of fae and demons alike. I'd studied it, like I was supposed to, but I wasn't fluent.

Adonis would be, though.

Mentally, I repeated each syllable as loudly as I could so Adonis would hear it.

When Aereus finished the spell, the iron door groaned open, revealing a dim, windowless room. Torches burned in some of the alcoves, and a long table stretched across the center of the stone floor. Weapons hung from brackets in the walls.

Across the table, stacks of papers lay scattered, and my gaze wandered over them. The writing looked like Angelic, which meant I had no idea what it said.

The moment I stepped inside, the door slid shut behind us, scraping over the floor. At this point, I was pretty relieved about the mark Adonis had left on my shoulder, because I'd never be able to get out of here on my own if I needed to. Even if I went feral and pulled the knife from under my dress, the iron door would stop me.

The single mercy of the closed iron door was that the

murderous rage clouding my mind seemed to have dissipated a little. Apparently, Aereus's magic mostly affected how I felt about weaker creatures, people I could dominate.

Aereus stood at the head of the table, staring at me. The torchlight wavered over his breastplate and his red-tipped wings.

I traced my fingertips over the wooden table in the center of the room. "This is thrilling."

Violent energy pulsed from his body, and he took a step closer to me, his armor gleaming in the warm light. "Your little succubus body reacts to me, doesn't it? You feel my power."

I feel like I want to tear your eyes out, if that's what you mean. "Yes, I can feel it."

"That's because you're at war within yourself."

He lumbered closer, then ran a meaty finger down the front of my chest. Inwardly, I shuddered, but I tried to hide my disgust.

"I sense your turmoil, Ruby. Deep in your chest."

I stared at him, trying to control my own aggression. What the fuck was he talking about?

Aereus closed his eyes, breathing in the air. Then, he gripped my shoulders. "You want something, but you deny yourself. Guilt eats at you, doesn't it? You left someone behind. What was his name?"

Stop intruding in my mind. I didn't want this monster talking about Marcus, or thinking about Marcus. He had no right to invade my memories.

He gripped my shoulders tighter. "You're scared of someone. Scared of a monster that you can't get rid of."

Now I had no idea what he was talking about, and I slipped away from his grasp. I schooled my features into a perfect mask of calm. "We're not here to talk about me," I said serenely. "I'm not interesting, Aereus. I want to know about *you.*"

That seemed to do the trick, and he arched a golden eyebrow at me. "Of course you do."

I sat coyly on the edge of the table. "What happens in here?"

"Since the Great Nightmare has begun, I've started wars on three continents. I've inspired bloodlust across the globe. I've recreated the conquests of Alexander the Great, riding into Persia and India. For the past year, I've planned my bloodshed from here."

He crossed to an alcove, where a chalice glowed with golden light, and he plucked it from its resting spot. "Do you know what this is?"

"Some sort of magical chalice?"

"Azazeyl, the fallen angel, drank from this the night before the angels expelled him from the heavens. The night before he fractured into seven gods. No angel was ever more powerful, more beautiful—no one ever more tormented." A dark satisfaction dripped off his words.

"Amazing," I breathed, eyes wide. "What other ancient treasures do you keep in this room?"

Aereus crossed to the wall of weapons, lovingly stroking a long spear. I tried not to think of the phallic implications as he caressed it.

"The sarisa belonging to Alexander the Great, the weapon of his Diadochi army. Conquest has imbued this weapon with power."

This was all fascinating, and at one point I'd have been thrilled to find myself standing before Alexander the Great's spear. Now, I could think about only one thing—how to rid the earth of the angelic scourge.

Ignoring the fury that surged in my blood, I sauntered

over to him. "Alexander the Great was amazing, I'm sure. But no one could rival an angel for skill in war."

His body glowed with fiery light, and I fought the urge to turn and run from him, or to grab Alexander's spear right off the wall and ram it through his body. "I was born to create war."

I cocked my head. Time to test his reaction. "And nothing can stop you, right? There's nothing on earth with the power to stop an angel from his quest."

He crossed to me, and a sharp pang of dread pierced my chest. I didn't want him too close to me. "Nothing," he repeated—but his tone lacked conviction.

For just a moment, his eyes flicked to a darkened corner of the war room. He was thinking about something there.

And that was exactly where I needed to look when I returned later.

Aereus moved closer, boxing me in where I sat on the table, and planted his hands on either side of my hips. "Tell me how war thrills you."

My gaze darted to the door. This would be a great time to get the hell out of here, if I didn't have a giant angelic asshole breathing down my neck.

Put on a good show, Ruby. "I can feel the power in this room, all around us. Once, I fed off the worship of humans, and I remember that feeling. It's coming back to me now."

His wrathful power intensified, choking me like a fist at my throat. Even though I'd never be able to take him in a fight, my mind began to burn with images of his bloody demise.

"In the old days," he began, "I took what I wanted. I'd have you bent over the table right now, that little dress up around your waist. I'd show you what you're missing with Adonis."

For just a moment, Aereus's eyes began to darken—the

first hint of a fall. Then, he gripped the oak table so hard it began to splinter.

Swiftly, I slipped off the table, ducking under his arm.

"From what I understand, you can't get too close to me, can you?" I said. "Or you'll be at risk, just like Kratos. And I know you have the power to resist that temptation." I began traipsing over to the corner of the room—the place where I'd seen him looking.

There, a wooden bookshelf stood, crammed with faded texts.

Books? I'd been hoping for a box of some kind—something that might contain stones.

"I can't get too close to you," he roared. "But Adonis can, can't he?"

I turned to face him, backing up against the wall.

This topic *clearly* pissed him off.

"Only temporarily," I said. "I'm sure his curse will torment him soon enough."

Aereus's lip curled. "I've been cursed for five centuries." Rage dripped from his voice. "What good is war without the spoils?"

It took me a moment to understand what he meant —*women* were "the spoils."

Once again, I had to bite down on a searing flash of rage that threatened to overtake me.

Okay. *How do I get out of this situation?*

I touched my chest, feigning horror. "Five centuries of abstaining! How terrible. No reason to sabotage your success now, though, is there? Perhaps you should get back to ruling your palace."

I started to make a move for the door, when Aereus lunged for me, pressing his hands to the wall on either side of my head. Veins bulged in his thickly corded arms.

"I want what Adonis has. I can't touch you. But I can see you. I want you to take off your dress."

I clenched my jaw. I could let my feral side come out, inflicting some serious damage with my poison-tipped knife. But that would disrupt the entire mission. I'd come here for the Stones of Zohar.

This seemed like a good time to use that mental link I had with Adonis.

"Adonis!" I screamed within my mind. *"This would be a good time to interrupt!"*

I needed to stall. I took a deep breath. "Oh my, your arms are very strong, aren't they?" The words tasted like poison on my tongue, because I could think of nothing but ramming my knife into his stupid, fat neck, right into his throbbing jugular.

"Yes," he growled. "Strong. Take off your dress. Let me see Adonis's prized possession."

Before I could get another word out, the sound of shearing metal pierced the air as the iron door twisted away from the frame.

I let out a slow, relieved breath as Adonis strode into the room, bathed in light, his midnight wings trailing behind him. As soon as he stepped inside the space, my muscles began to relax a little, and Aereus released me.

Adonis shoved his hands in his pockets, completely at ease, as if he'd just happened upon us at a picnic.

His eyes shone with amusement. "Ah. There you are. I thought I felt a current of primitive, mindless rage spilling through the door, and I knew it must be my old friend Aereus."

"He was just showing me his war room," I explained hastily, as if we'd been caught unawares. "It's all completely innocent."

Aereus's entire body had tensed, and he unleashed a wild roar that trembled through my bones. "You broke my door."

Adonis blinked. "That? It didn't seem to have a doorknob, so I found my own way in. I suppose it's not there to guard against other angels."

I'd mentally telegraphed the spell to Adonis, and I was sure he could have used it. But that would have given away our mental link.

"Now I'd like my succubus back." This time, Adonis injected venom into his voice.

I needed to satisfy Aereus's primitive ego to smooth things over.

"Did you know that Aereus has caused thousands of wars?" I cooed.

Adonis's eyes shone with icy rage, and shadows thickened around him. "Get back to our room, Ruby."

I smoothed out my dress, crossing over the floor as if I'd been chastened.

The moment I stepped into the hallway, the roars of wrathful angels rumbled over the hallway, and the walls shook with the sounds of divine bodies slamming against marble.

CHAPTER 27

I stood in Tanit's room, waiting for Adonis and his demon friends to arrive. The eerie cherubs had guided me here—just as Adonis had suggested—but I'd found it empty. I could only hope Aereus hadn't broken Adonis on one of his iron-spiked garden features.

From the expansive bedroom, I stared out over the Jardin des Tuileries, at the charred stumps of trees and the frozen earth. Aereus had put all his efforts into his death garden, completely neglecting the world outside the Louvre.

Outside, a group of cherubs drifted past the window, heads cocked. As I'd moved around the castle, I'd tried to study the cherubs' movements. Sometimes, they glided together in groups, speaking in unison. It was as if they shared some kind of mental connection. If I had to glamour myself as a cherub, I'd never be able to work as a synchronized drone among their numbers. They seemed to patrol the same paths within the Louvre, their movements predictable and unified, the product of a shared mind.

But occasionally, a taller cherub with silver-streaked hair would float by on her own. The taller ones seemed to move about more freely, taking on some sort of supervisory roles. I never heard them speak, but their pale eyes held a keen intelligence I didn't see in the smaller cherubs.

Behind me, the door creaked, and Adonis crossed into the room. Tanit and Kur followed close behind him.

At the sight of Adonis unharmed, my chest unclenched a little. "How exactly did that situation resolve?" I asked. "It sounded like you were both breaking the walls with each other's bodies. I'm surprised your wings are intact."

Adonis rubbed his chin, narrowing his eyes at me. "Of course my wings are intact. I can hold my own in a fight. One scuffle with Johnny and everyone's acting like I'm broken. I'm an immortal who's lived for—"

"For four thousand years, since the Amorite conquest of Ur," Tanit chimed in. "We know."

A few bruises marred Adonis's skin, but he seemed to be healing quickly. "As to how I resolved things with Aereus, after we battered each other senseless for a while, I simply told him that we needed his help to keep Kratos in check." Adonis leaned against the wall, folding his arms. "He seemed to like the idea of being needed. Pathetic, really."

His pale eyes stood out sharply in the room's dim light.

Tanit and Kur dropped into large armchairs on the other side of the room, their bodies illuminated with the twinkling light of a chandelier. Tanit had definitely landed herself a better room than ours.

"It's a good thing we're not being kicked out," Tanit said, eyeing me sharply. "So far, you've only found a bookshelf. Is that right?"

"An important bookshelf," I corrected. "Why keep a bookshelf in a war room? Aereus is obviously not a reader. He's more of a 'sticking sharp things in people' type than an intellectual."

Kur leaned back in his chair. "I see it didn't take you long to work out that Aereus is an idiot."

"I need to get back into the war room," I said. "When I asked if anything could stop him, his eyes definitely went to the bookshelf. He was thinking about it, and it made him nervous. Maybe there's something hidden within the books."

"Maybe," said Kur without much conviction.

"You're not going back in." Adonis's inky magic tinged the air around him. "I already regret leaving you alone with Aereus in that room. He's worse than Kratos. This time, I'll go on my own."

I crossed my arms. "And how will you get in there discreetly? You can't even glamour yourself."

Adonis tilted back his head. "I have other skills. Aereus has invited us to dinner tonight to discuss the fallen angel problem. I just need you all to keep him distracted, while I use shadows to cloak myself. As long as he's with you, I know that he won't be surprising me in his war room."

Kur threaded his fingers behind his head. "I could challenge him to a wrestling match. I've noticed he likes throwing men around."

"A wrestling match," I repeated. "At this dinner party."

Kur sneered. "Nothing can keep him occupied like a chance to prove his physical prowess."

"That's a start," I said. "And maybe Tanit can flirt with him. I already took one for the team earlier, and I'm not eager to revisit it."

Adonis smirked. "Let him think that you both belong to me, and that he has a glimmer of a chance of stealing you from me."

Tanit hissed, her eyes flashing with blue light. "I belong to no one."

"We all know that," Adonis soothed. "But you can play the part. Let Aereus think he's stealing something from me."

I paced the room, the cogs turning in my mind. "If we both moon over him and ask him about all his glorious war stories, we'll have his attention completely rapt." I met Adonis's gaze. "All you have to do is return with the stones, without anyone noticing."

* * *

WE SAT at a long banquet table laden with food, my stomach already full of shortcrust pie and fruit. Torches lined the stone walls, and below them, a row of human guards stood pressed against the walls, their faces gaunt and scared.

I cast a nervous glance at the ceiling.

You know how sometimes people use the "sword of Damocles" as a metaphor, a threat of an impending demise hanging right over your head?

Tonight, we had literal swords hanging over heads as we ate. On the high ceiling above us hung an assortment of weapons—battle-axes, broadswords, maces—all of them dangling from iron chains that I could only hope had been forged with care.

The dinner hadn't begun until ten p.m., which had given me plenty of time to search the entire palace from top to bottom, glamoured as a cherub. I'd found no stones, no references to stones—just a crapload of violent art festooning the walls. The hours glamoured as a cherub had cost me—sapping my energy with magical effort. Now, fatigue burned through my body.

So I sat at dinner, with my most charming smile on my face, trying to block out our utter failure so far.

A human female, her neck ringed with an iron collar, refilled my glass of wine.

Tanit sat on the other side of Adonis, candlelight gleaming in her dark eyes. "So glad Adonis took me with him on this trip." Her toneless inflection suggested otherwise. "You know, being the lover of the angel of death doesn't always come with many travel opportunities."

Aereus's lip curled as he gripped his copper chalice. His hand clenched, bending the metal in his fist. "Two lovers? You have two?"

Adonis flashed a satisfied smile. "Why not? Might as well enjoy myself until my seal is broken."

Okay. We didn't want to go too far down this path or we'd end up with shattered walls, broken angel bodies, and no allies.

I took a final bite of my pie. "I'm just so glad you're agreeing to help us. If the other horsemen come for us, I'm not sure what we would do. But with you two working together, you can simply unite against them, imprison them until they come to their senses."

Aereus leaned back in his chair, surveying us. "Then you should stay here. Sadeckrav Castle has superior magical fortifications to your humble pile of rocks, Adonis. We'll figure out a way to capture them, to weaken them with…" His gaze darted around the room, uneasy. He didn't want anyone to know about Devil's Bane. "We'll weaken them, until the mortification of their bodies reminds them of their mission here on earth."

"Good," said Adonis. "All your iron toys will come in handy."

Aereus smiled. "Yes. We will make them submit. No one must rebel against the mission of the horsemen. You and I both know that. The heavenly horde rule as archangels in the heavens, while we may rule as archangels on the earth."

Adonis lifted his glass. "As it was meant to be."

Tanit leaned in to Adonis, then stroked her hand up his thigh. "You two are both so *strong.*"

I narrowed my eyes. She didn't need to go *quite* that far

with her hands to prove that she was his lover—Aereus had already bought that story.

Not that I cared.

I glanced at Kur, giving him a quick nod. Time to get this show on the road, so Adonis could make his discreet exit.

CHAPTER 28

Kur spread out his arms, flexing his muscles within his leather clothing. "I've heard you're known for your wrestling ability, Aereus... Is it true?"

Adonis lifted his wineglass, staring at the wine as he sloshed it in the chalice. "You know, I do think Aereus may have spread those rumors himself."

Gods below. He just couldn't help himself, could he?

Aereus gripped the edge of the table, face reddening. "Just as you spread the rumors about your legendary seduction abilities?"

The easy smile never left Adonis's features. "Is that what you tell yourself?"

Aereus's snarl told me he didn't believe his own claims. His anger curled off him, rippling over my skin. Unconsciously, I'd started gripping my knife, ready to plunge it into something. No one else seemed quite as affected by Aereus's magic as I was. But then again, none of them were feral.

The horseman of war's face had become dead serious, flecks of red burning in his eyes.

Kur cleared his throat. "Wrestling. How about it?"

Aereus turned to him. "No one has ever beaten me in a wrestling match."

Kur cracked his knuckles. "Really? *No* one?"

"No one." Aereus's tone brooked no argument. "Do you doubt me?"

Kur leaned back in his chair. "It's just that I've never lost a wrestling match, either. And I've wrestled some of the high lords of the shadow kingdom."

Aereus's lip curled in a snarl. "But you've never wrestled the horseman of war, have you." His chair scraped across the floor as he rose, and he marched into the center of the hall. "It's not often that I have a formidable challenger, though a shadow demon could never win against an angel such as myself. These two shadow demonesses have probably never witnessed prowess such as mine. We'll wrestle now. Let's find out how long you can last."

Kur rose from his chair. "Do think now is the best time for this?"

"Right now." Aereus held out his arms to either side. "Servants!" he barked.

Instantly, two male servants hurried over to him, pulling off his brocade coat. The swiftness with which they executed this maneuver suggested that this was something Aereus did often.

Kur strode into the center of the floor and held out his own arms. Another set of servants pulled his coat from him. Then, the angel and the demon pulled off their shirts, tossing them on the ground.

Kur's body rippled with muscles, lines of green scales glinting in the torchlight. Still, Aereus had at least a foot on him. The horseman's skin was a deep gold, his muscles thick as oak trunks.

In unison, they paced to opposite ends of the hall, then pivoted to face each other.

Tension sparked in the air as they glared at each other, and Aereus's magic hummed across the room. The hot, arid feel of his magic sparked an ancient wrath that burned within my ribs, stoking embers of rage. I gripped the chair, restraining myself from running into the wrestling match to try my own mettle. They'd crush me—I knew that. But the stupid part of me wanted to fight.

In fact, I was beginning to think that angels' magic gave me a bit of a death wish.

"You know the rules, don't you, Kur?" asked the angel. "When I throw you to the ground, I will be declared the winner."

"Likewise." Kur's grin was cocky. "If I throw you to the ground, I win. I'm ready for it."

In the next moment, they ran for each other, feet pounding over the stone floor. They collapsed into each other with the force of hurricane winds, arms grasping for each other's shoulders.

As they began to grapple with each other, eyes blazing with aggressive intent, violent impulses gripped my body. Aereus's power was overwhelming me. My gaze darted to one of the human servants who stood pressed against the wall. My muscles tensed, thighs clenching, lip curling in a snarl. It would be so easy to break her neck...

Adonis brushed his fingertips over my knee, soothing some of the rage out of my system. I hadn't even noticed as he'd slipped next to me. He really *could* move discreetly within the shadows. In the depths of my mind, his silky presence brushed against my thoughts, and his magic swept over my body like a balm. My muscles began to relax, thighs unclenching.

I nodded at him, letting him know it was okay for him to go now while Aereus was completely distracted.

As I looked at him, he seemed to fade away before my

eyes, shadows cloaking him. I felt his presence move from me—disappear, really. Only someone who'd already been paying attention—like me—would notice the departure at all.

Kur slammed Aereus into a wall, and the entire building trembled. The horseman of war roared like an injured beast.

I tightened my fingers on the chair. *Please tell me Kur understands that he has to let the angel win this.*

They threw each other into the walls, cracking stone. Clanking metal filled the air. I glanced at the ceiling, where the weapons jostled violently in their chains, banging together.

I nudged Tanit, then pointed at the ceiling. "I think we need to move."

"Good point." She reacted swiftly, and in the next moment, she'd taken shelter in a doorframe.

In another second, I was by her side, crammed into the arched doorway.

The angel and the demon gripped each other's shoulders, grunting and straining, fingers digging into flesh. Groaning, Kur pulled Aereus's neck down into a headlock, trying to dominate him.

I leaned into Tanit, whispering, "Kur knows he needs to lose, right?"

Tanit cocked her head. "Demons can be irrational when it comes to domination."

"Wonderful," I muttered. Maybe a bit of a reminder was in order.

"Aereus seems to be winning!" I shouted, despite all evidence to the contrary. "How thrilling to see an angel dominate a demon!" I punctuated each word carefully.

The interjection actually seemed to work, because in the next moment, Kur released his grip around the angel's neck. Then, Aereus was able to grip the shadow demon by the shoulders.

With a wild roar, Aereus threw Kur onto the ground. The crack of demon bone against stone echoed through the hall.

Victorious, Aereus lifted his arms above his head, his muscled body glistening with sweat. "Victory is mine once again! The angel of war reigns supreme!"

I suppressed the urge to roll my eyes, instead forcing myself to clap. Honestly. I'd never expected ancient angels to act like such children.

Kur pushed himself off the ground with a groan. As I crossed back to the table, still clapping, Kur shot me a withering look that spoke of his resentment. Even if we'd all agreed to the plan ahead of time, it killed him inside to let Aereus win.

Without uttering a word, Kur collected his shirt and jacket from the human servants, sullenly dressing himself.

Still shirtless, Aereus dropped into his chair, breathing heavily. Sweat slid down his chest.

One of us would need to get up close to him, to block his line of vision. I gave Tanit a nudge.

I was pretty sure her groan was audible only to me as she rose from her chair. "In the shadow kingdom, the high lords never told us about the angels." She sat before him at the edge of the table, her dress riding up. Given what she'd said about underwear earlier, I was pretty sure Aereus's eyes wouldn't be leaving her body anytime soon.

She ran a fingertip over his bare chest. "I never knew you had inspired so many heroes in human history. Genghis Khan, Alexander the Great..."

"You see, my little shadow demonesses? Your males can't compete with me."

"Amazing," said Tanit, a little too deadpan. "Such power. Tell me about the wars you've fought."

Aereus stared up at her, transfixed, and began to launch into the tales of his historic exploits. With every word, a little more of that primal rage began to seethe in my blood. Now that Adonis had left the room, I had no one here to calm me. I gripped my wineglass tightly, taking out my anger on its stem, until a smooth presence kissed my skin once again.

It took me a moment to realize Adonis had already returned, shadows darkening the air around him. My clenched thighs and fingers began to relax once more. I met his gaze, and he shook his head—nearly imperceptibly. But it was enough to tell me that our plan hadn't worked.

My heart sank. Our death warrants may have been signed, and we were no closer to protecting ourselves from the archangel onslaught.

CHAPTER 29

Wordlessly, two cherubs led us back to our room, while I restrained myself from asking what, exactly, Adonis had seen in the war room.

At last, when we reached our room, I rushed inside and closed the door hard behind us.

I gripped Adonis's arm. "You gave me a head shake. What did the head shake mean? Please tell me there is a chance the head shake meant 'I found the stones and everything is fine.'"

"Unsurprisingly, the head shake meant 'no.' I did not find the stones. Just a book I already have, and Aereus's relics."

I wasn't letting this go. I'd been *certain* something lay hidden there. "What's in this book?"

His steely eyes betrayed nothing. "It's about the Bringer of Light. When you caught Aereus looking at the bookshelf, it's likely what he was thinking about was this text. But the book doesn't contain any information we don't already have."

I studied his chiseled features, so beautiful I could hardly think clearly around him. "I need specifics. What do we already know, exactly?"

"It's merely a description of the stones' origin."

"Please tell me you took it with you."

"I didn't need to take it. I have my own copy. I bring it with me wherever I go, searching for clues in its text."

I thrust out my hand. "Show me."

A dark power rippled off his body. He wasn't used to being ordered around. "You won't be able to read it, but if you must see it…"

He turned away and lifted up the mattress. He pulled out a thin, dark volume—one with no lettering on the front. "I don't think you'll discover anything I haven't already."

I took it from him and sat on the bed. The spine cracked as I opened it, and I began scanning the yellowed pages. I couldn't read the text, wasn't even entirely sure if it was Greek or Phoenician, but luckily for me, it came with pictures. Images of vines coiled around the edges of the pages, and artists had depicted page after page of flowering plants, each one labeled in that ancient language.

"What does it say?" I asked.

"It gives an account of the Old Gods, of the gifts they provide to combat the angels. The Devil's Bane that grows where archangels walk the earth, the sacred rowan tree that channels the power of the Old Gods. And the Stones of Zohar, mined from gleaming blue gemstones."

I turned another brittle page, uncovering an image of a grotto—one I was sure I'd seen before. A river carved through a rocky landscape, its banks dappled with blood-red anemones. I'd seen it in a dream, I thought, when I'd flown in Adonis's arms.

"This looks familiar."

"Does it?" Surprise tinged his voice.

"I've dreamt it." I studied the gentle curve of the river, the myrrh trees growing by its banks. "And it's not just that I dreamt it. The garden outside your castle is a version of this place. The red flowers, the river carving through the center."

"It's where I was born."

"Afeka. Right. Why is your birthplace in a book about the Stones of Zohar?"

Adonis leaned in to me, pointing to the cave. "Some say this cave is the entrance to the underworld, the realm of the Old Gods. I was born in their presence, surrounded by the stones that could kill me."

"Right…the seeds of destruction thing."

"This cave is where life mingles with death. It's where Aereus found the stones in the first place."

I traced my fingertips over the picture. "I didn't know the Old Gods had anything to do with an underworld."

Adonis's magic caressed my body. "That's the first thing you need to know about gods. All gods rule the realms of the dead. All gods demand sacrifices for their gifts. Even the Old Gods."

Frankly, that didn't sound ideal. I was about to reap a metric ton of power from the Old Gods. "A sacrifice. And what sacrifice will they demand from me for using their stones?"

He considered it, a concerned look in his eyes. "I honestly can't tell you that. I think they'll want you to change, to become something new. That's how the gods of nature work, isn't it? They sacrifice the old to make way for the new. Death gives rise to new life."

Among the plants by the mouth of the cave, the artist had painted a few shimmering blue stones.

I pointed at them. "This must be them. The Stones of Zohar."

"I remember them," he said quietly. "The color of the sky over Afeka."

I breathed in his exotic scent of myrrh. When an angel like him looks at a garden—he sees a place of death. No wonder Aereus's garden had unsettled me so much. From an ancient immortal's perspective, it was already dying.

My gaze trailed over Adonis's breathtaking, masculine features—then lower, over the pendant he wore at his throat. I touched it, gripping it gently between two fingers. He nearly flinched at my touch. Candlelight glinted off the amber.

"What is this?"

For just a moment, a sharp flash of pain lit his gray-blue eyes, then his gaze shuttered. An easy smile replaced the brief look of pain. "Just something I've kept with me a long time."

And there it was again. Adonis keeping secrets from me, even if he could hear some of my own thoughts.

CHAPTER 30

𝒞urled up in bed, I'd given in to sleep, to the bone-deep tiredness that gripped my body. In my dreams, I'd wandered through the grotto from the pictures in the book, surrounded by the sound of a rushing river echoing off stone walls.

A hand at my throat woke me, powerful arms pinning me to the bed—one encircling my neck, the other gripping my wrists.

My eyes snapped open with shock, and I looked up into Adonis's eyes—not icy blue, but the cold hardness of obsidian. His midnight wings spread out behind him, ready to fight, and his magic thrummed over my skin.

For a moment, fear gripped my heart. What the hell was he doing? Instead of his soothing presence whispering through my mind, I felt claws of rage, of panic.

"Adonis," I whispered.

His powerful body completely pinned me down, one of his legs pressed between mine. His hand enclosed my throat —but he wasn't pressing down. All I knew was that he had complete control here, and I had no idea what was going on.

I searched his eyes, expecting to find rage. Instead, I found only confusion. He hadn't fully woken yet, and his breath sounded ragged in his throat. He'd been dreaming of something terrible.

Within my mind, I called to him. *Adonis. Now would be a good time to help me.* With my hands pinned, I couldn't gently jostle him to wake him. Instead, I stroked one of my legs up the back of his. Slowly, I felt those claws of rage begin to recede, replaced by a soothing calm.

"Adonis," I whispered again.

He blinked, his muscles relaxing, and his eyes began to focus, returning to pale gray-blue. He pulled his hand from my throat, searching my neck. Gently his fingertips brushed over my skin. "Ruby?" he rasped. "Did I hurt you?"

"I'm fine," I said. "You were having a nightmare. I think."

Frowning, he glanced at my wrists before pulling his hand away from them. He rolled onto his side, propping up his head to peer down at me. "I was dreaming of the fae."

I swallowed hard. That made sense. He was in bed with a fae. "Not a good dream, I take it."

He shifted, sitting up in bed, his wings disappearing from view. Dim torchlight danced over the savage scars on his chest. He stared at the bed, looking lost in his thoughts. "More of a memory."

He'd shifted his body away from me, and the loss of the heat from his skin made me want to press up against him again. "Of what?"

His magic sliced the air around us in vicious swirls. "About when the fae king imprisoned me when I was young."

My throat tightened. "What happened?"

A deep, searing pain flashed in his eyes for a moment, before he masked it again. "After my parents died, the fae captured me. The king gave me as a gift to his consort. She used to say she wanted to surround herself with beautiful things." His voice had a sharp edge to it. "Most of the time, King Oberon kept me imprisoned within an oak grove. He used a certain magical enchantment to trap me there, and Devil's Bane to weaken me."

I tightened my hand on his, just a little. "Fae magic. Devil's Bane. Was that really enough to trap someone like you there? You're a god of death."

He searched my face, as if he might find the answer there. Then, his familiar charming smile curled his lips. "Maybe I wasn't always the powerful being you see before you today."

"What happened to you there?"

"At night, I slept outside on a bed of moss. When King Oberon brought humans to his realm, he'd command me to enchant the air, so the women were out of control with lust. They used me as an agent in their lurid rituals. They worship euphoria, ecstatic states. It doesn't sound so terrible, does it?"

Silver flecks, like starlight, shone in his gray-blue eyes. I almost thought I could get lost in those arctic depths. "Except there's a dark side to that ecstasy." His fingers flexed on the bedsheets. "The violent, primal side of ecstatic states. The fae euphoria."

Seemingly lost in his thoughts, he reached for me, brushing his fingertips over my hips, stroking up and down. "Sometimes, the fae turned on each other in their frenzy. But they mostly went after human females. They dragged women into their forested palace, seduced them in their frenzied states. Fae males like to dominate women."

"Yep. And that would be why my parents left the realm."

"Some fae feed from humans, just like vampires. Except instead of blood, they draw power from heightened human emotions. Ecstatic or devastated states. The humans' frenzy fed King Oberon's magical ability. The hunt filled him with power."

A cold shudder danced up my neck. "What do you mean 'the hunt'?"

He idly traced over my hip, lost in his own memories. "Another form of fae entertainment. They'd let human females loose in the forests, pretending to free them. The women would run, naked, thinking they'd been given a chance at freedom, thinking they could get home again. King Oberon drank in their terror. His body glowed with power. The fae males would work themselves up into an ecstatic, feral frenzy. Their eyes would gleam with silver, their canines would lengthen. Claws and horns would sprout from their bodies."

Shadows darkened his eyes, and his voice had taken on a haunted tone.

I swallowed hard. "And the women were the prey."

"Exactly. Their deaths were brutal, savage. The fae would tear them limb from limb. They'd feast on the women like beasts."

My stomach turned. "You obviously don't approve of the fae. You have your own moral code—punish the wicked and all that. So why stay with them? Why take part? You're a death god. You could have survived the Devil's Bane."

He didn't answer.

Compelled by a sharp need to touch him, I ran my fingers over the savage scars on his chest.

Ice glinted in his eyes. "I am the single most lethal creature to have ever walked the earth. I was never meant to be here. I can kill just by thinking, just by feeling. It's in my nature. It's what I am. When given the chance to slaughter the unworthy, I enjoy it. My captivity kept me from killing in greater numbers."

My fingers froze. "Do you actually kill people just for fun?"

"Not anymore. That was a long time ago." His features

softened as he looked at me. "I was like you, once. In love with beauty. Every now and then I remember that feeling. I get glimmers of it, and it makes me feel alive again."

"When?"

"When I look at the color of your skin, the flush on your cheeks, the heat in your eyes after I kissed you. The perfect, tempting shape of your body when you dropped your blanket in my room. The dirt smudged on your skin when you were a feral fae, caught up in passion."

At his words, my blood heated, and I pressed in closer to him, until my skin skimmed against his. Finally, I was getting some of the real Adonis, the truth behind his facade. I reached for his face, stroking it.

"Show me you—without the glamour," he rasped. "Show me all of you. When I kissed you on Eimmal...I haven't felt so alive in centuries."

"You hate the fae, but you're drawn to us."

He shook his head slowly. "I'm not drawn to the fae. Just to you."

I sucked in a deep breath, letting the glamour fade completely. My pale hair tumbled over my shoulders, and I took a deep breath, waiting to see his reaction. I felt completely exposed before him.

It was at that point I realized how close our bodies were —my dress riding up under the sheets, my bare thigh brushing against his leg. My pulse raced, heat flaming through my body. Adonis seemed to notice, too, because his breath grew heavier, eyes burning like starlight. He reached for the neckline of my dress, tracing his fingertips under the hem. At his touch, pleasure rippled over my skin.

My mind flashed with an image of Adonis pinning me down again—except this time, in my fevered mind, he was kissing me hard, my legs wrapped around his waist.

"Intense emotions still fascinate me." The unexpected

gentleness of his touch made me want to moan. Glacially slow, he began to tug down the neckline of my dress, studying the vivid flush on my chest.

I hooked my leg around his. I wanted to feel his hands gripping me, to feel his mouth pressed hard against mine. Instead, he was teasing me, silver glinting in his eyes.

I threaded my fingers into his dark hair.

With a slow, graceful gesture, he eased down the top of my dress to expose my shoulder, where his mark stood out starkly on my pale skin. He lowered his mouth to the mark, then ran his tongue over it, sparking a wave of wild heat arcing through my blood. Slowly, his mouth moved farther up my neck. Now, his fingers were gripping my hip possessively. Wild, liquid fire surged through my core, and I felt my back arching, my legs falling open.

Moving like honey over ice, he slid the collar of my dress down just a little farther, exposing only the tops of my breasts. My nipples hardened, my breasts swelling and straining against the fabric. I'd told myself I'd never let him seduce me, but right now, I didn't really care. I just wanted him to keep touching me.

His mouth moved lower, heating my skin, his tongue now swirling around my nipple. I wanted his mouth on mine.

"Adonis," I moaned.

He was drawing this out, stirring me to a peak of desire until I forgot how words worked.

Another slow tug at the top of my dress, this time a little more forceful as he kissed me deeply. He pulled down the front of my dress until my breasts slipped out. Adonis let out a low growl, his eyes raking over my body. He was still keeping a leash on himself, still restrained, and the kisses he brushed over my breasts were agonizingly light, even as his hands grew more possessive on my body.

I moaned, rubbing my hips into him. Of course Adonis

would turn pleasure into a strange sort of torture, until my mind and body screamed for him.

It was at this point I realized that his wings had appeared again behind him. I ran my fingertips over the feathers at the apex, and his muscles tightened. Now, he pulled down the front of my dress roughly, practically ripping it. A hint of teeth on my breasts, an exquisite torture. Another growl from deep within his throat.

I whispered his name.

He reached my mouth, pressing his lips against mine in a searing kiss. I moaned into his mouth, my tongue brushing his.

"Yes, Ruby?" His voice was a low, deep sigh.

I tried to find the words to tell him what I wanted, about the desperate ache that had spread through my body.

He reached down, his fingertips circling around to my inner thigh. As he traced upward, raw desire throbbed in my core. I stroked his wings again, and his body tensed against me, fingers gripping my thigh more possessively before releasing it again.

I couldn't take the teasing anymore—I wanted him to move faster. I pulled off my dress entirely, and the cool castle air kissed my skin. I wanted him to look at me—all of me—and I let my knee fall open in an invitation. For a moment, he leaned back, staring at me, torchlight dancing over the powerful planes of his torso. His potent magic licked at my body, caressing parts of me that burned to be touched.

Just as I was sure he was about to unleash the restraints he'd been keeping on himself, a sharp, piercing cry ripped through the air in the distance.

A reptilian cry.

The warlike scream of a full-sized dragon.

And all the heat warming my body chilled to ice.

CHAPTER 31

Within moments, alarms were sounding within the Louvre, and I had my dress back on. The voices of the cherubs penetrated the door, chanting in unison about a dragon.

Of all the things we'd anticipated—archangels from the Heavenly Host, the descent of the other horsemen—I hadn't expected dragons to attack.

Adonis was out of the bed in a flash, already pulling on his clothes. "I need to find out what's happening."

"I'm coming with you." My heart was still pounding hard now, but for a different reason.

Gods below. Talk about a bad moment to interrupt.

I grabbed my boots from the floor.

Maybe the interruption was for the best, anyway. Adonis wouldn't be on earth for much longer. What was the point in falling into his seductive trap now, when he had to go? I zipped up my boots, trying to think clearly. Adonis and I agreed firmly on one point—angels didn't belong here. Nothing could happen between us.

Adonis pulled open the door, his sword slung around his

back, and I hurried after him. Cherubs bustled through the hallway, and among their eerie whispers, I heard a few words repeated: *Dragon... Jardin des Tuileries... Succubus.*

I swallowed hard. Dragon. Succubus. *Hazel?*

Adonis strode quickly through the hall, and I hurried to keep up. When we reached the entrance, Aereus was standing in the center of an atrium, his wings and body glowing with golden light. Like Adonis, he'd dressed for battle.

"Any idea what's going on?" I asked.

Aereus's eyes burned with gold and red fire as he spoke to me. "Any idea why your sister has come to join us?

* * *

When the large, oak doors groaned open, I was greeted by a sight I didn't think I'd ever forget—my younger sister, mounted on a golden-scaled dragon whose wings shimmered in the silver light of the moon.

Hazel gripped the dragon's neck, her dark hair tumbling over her shoulders. A flush brightened her cheeks, and her eyes sparkled.

I stared at the dragon, my mind swarming with unwelcome memories. A dragon—clamping Marcus in its jaws, its teeth piercing his flesh, ripping him to shreds. Blood streamed over the pavement... My chest clenched, until I took a slow, steady breath.

Hazel flicked her hair over her shoulder. "Adonis. Ruby. I hope you don't mind the interruption."

Aereus stepped forward, his body towering over me. "No one told me you were coming."

Emitting a deep rumble, the golden dragon lowered his head, and Hazel slid off.

My heart thudded hard. Please tell me she had some kind

of plan here, that she hadn't just shown up on a dragon for the hell of it.

As soon as she slipped off the dragon's neck, the beast began to shift, with a snapping of bones and sinews that pierced the night air, until a man stood before us, his large body covered in gold armor. I shuddered, still repulsed by dragon shifters.

"Hazel," said Adonis. "You've come as a messenger, haven't you? To give us news about Johnny and Kratos."

Hazel crossed to us, her gaze on Aereus, features totally placid. "Exactly. I remained in Hotemet Castle, and Adonis told me I was supposed to let him know if Johnny or Kratos seemed as if they were going to fall." The night air whipped at her dark hair. "They've started to change, I think."

"Change *how*?" Aereus demanded.

She blinked at him, her features serene, and I knew she was about to enchant him. "They look different, like when you're staring at the water's warm surface on a hot summer day, and the lake looks black as iron, and the steam wafts off it, and you think you can see your past in it, you think you can see your mom's face, right? And you remember how sometimes she made you so mad but you couldn't do anything about it, and the steam curls around you. All those times you wanted things but you couldn't have them. And that's how you know the angels are going to fall, that their heavy, leaden wings are pulling them to the earth. That's why you need me here, Aereus. To fix things."

Aereus stared at her, his fiery eyes glazed over. "I see. Yes..." He blinked. "I can see why you'd think they were falling. I'm glad you've come to warn us."

She looked back at the starry sky. "You might want to set up some of your creepy cherubs to watch the clouds in case they show up anytime soon."

Aereus nodded dumbly.

Apparently, this little teenage fae was capable of manipulating one of the most lethal creatures to ever walk the earth's surface, and it didn't even seem to take much effort on her part.

"It flickers in and out," she added with a slight shrug. "Sometimes they get control of themselves. I just thought you should know."

Aereus beckoned her closer to him. "Another succubus. No wonder Kratos has been unable to control himself."

Mentally, a war raged in my mind. *She's sixteen, you creep. Back the fuck off.* But we were supposed to be ancient.

Adonis shot me a pointed look—no doubt he could feel my roiling anger. "Thank you for letting us know, Hazel. Now, you must be tired after your journey. You can sleep in our room."

Aereus's lip curled. "Oh, that's how it is, is it? One succubus isn't enough for you?"

Adonis's icy gaze slid to the horseman of war, but he said nothing.

Gross. Still, I could see why Adonis had made the suggestion. Hazel had obviously come here for a reason, and we needed to know what it was. We needed to speak with her alone. Now.

Aereus glared at Adonis, his magic tingeing the air around him with gold. "Sleep for a few hours. But in the morning, we must make a move against the other horsemen. We'll drag their imperiled souls here and pierce their bodies until they see the truth again. Until they once more understand that we must give up the temptations of the flesh in order to rule as gods on earth."

Adonis's eyes sparked with a cold light, shadows shifting and darkening around him. "Horsemen were born to make sacrifices." A hint of regret suffused his words, and I knew that he believed it, even if the rest of this was a sham.

Aereus's lip curled. "Kratos will feel his sacrifices in his flesh."

I swallowed hard, thinking of Kratos. Our ruse would never get that far, so I shouldn't be worrying about it. But the idea of this maniacal horseman of war torturing Kratos with his iron instruments made me feel sick.

Adonis nodded. "In the morning, then," he said quietly. He strode back into the palace, his night-dark magic trailing behind him. He moved swiftly, with the gait of a soldier, his footfalls clacking over the floor.

On the walk back to our room, the cherubs eyed Hazel, whispering among themselves. I bit down hard on the impulse to turn to Hazel, to demand to know what the hell was going on right now. At last, we reached our door, and I shoved it open.

Hazel plopped herself down on the bed, surveying the rumpled sheets. "You both sleep in this? Cozy."

I opened my mouth and closed it again. "Hazel. What are you doing here? You just… You summoned a dragon?"

She flicked her hair behind her shoulders. "Uthyr? I was one of his favorites. Like I said. I charmed them." She lifted the pendant from her neck—a dragon's tooth. "Remember? Uthyr gave me this to summon him if I ever really needed him."

Adonis leaned against a wall, his arms folded. "What's been happening at Hotemet Castle?"

Hazel sucked in a deep breath, and my stomach clenched. She hadn't come with good news.

"Johnny has slowly recovered his memories," she said. "He knows Ruby tried to kill him. He knows that she's not really a succubus, which means he knows I'm not really a succubus. Hence, I had to get the fuck out of there. What else? Oh yeah. He's on his way here to kill you."

My jaw dropped. "And what about Kratos?"

She screwed her mouth to one side, eyes narrowing as she thought about it for a moment. "I'm not entirely sure what his plan is, but he was angry enough to go on a bit of a rampage. He started breaking things and lighting things on fire. I befuddled them just long enough so that I could get out of there, but it wasn't a *great* situation, per se."

Shimmering, midnight magic burst from Adonis's body, and his wings emerged behind him, spreading out. "Did they follow you, Hazel?"

She shook her head. "I don't think so. If they'd been anywhere nearby, Uthyr would have smelled them."

Adonis snatched his sword, Ninkasi, from beside the bed.

"What are you doing?" I asked.

The air around us hummed with his magic, making my pulse race. "I'm going to search for them, and I'll stop them if they're on their way. I need to find out if they're coming for you. While I'm gone, find Tanit and Kur. Tell them what's going on. Tell them I'll be back as soon as I know anything."

I didn't want him to leave, for some reason, but I just said, "Come back to us soon."

He was out the door without another word.

CHAPTER 32

When he left, Hazel dropped down on our bed, exhausted.

I started to pace the stone floor. "Did you hear anything about their plans?"

She shook her head. "Something about archangels. Heavenly something."

A chill rippled through my blood. "The Heavenly Host?"

She pointed at me. "That's it. Johnny wanted to speak to them. To tell them Adonis was rebelling."

Even if that injured angel hadn't made it back to the Heavenly Host, Johnny could drag them here at any moment to destroy me.

I clenched my fists. "Did Kratos try to stop him?"

"Why do you think Kratos would want to stop Johnny? I think they're on the same side."

My chest tightened. "I don't know. He's a psychopath, yes. He left me stranded there after dragons ripped Marcus to shreds." The memory pierced my chest. "But then he did a kind thing for us. He brought you back to me."

She scrunched up her features. "Huh? Kratos?"

"Yes, Kratos. I told him I was looking for my sister, and he sent out a search party for a succubus in the dragon lairs. He didn't stop until he found you."

Her brow furrowed. "No, that's not what happened. First of all, do you know how much effort it takes an archangel like them to find anyone they want?"

I crossed my arms, wearing the floor thin with my pacing. "Not really, no."

"It took Adonis a few hours to find me. He's the one who turned up in the dragon's lair. When he did, he sent word to Hotemet Castle to say I was coming. Apparently Kratos took credit for it."

Surprise knocked the wind out of me. "Adonis reunited us?" I shook my head. "He never told me. Kratos didn't specifically tell me that he'd found you, but he certainly implied it."

"Oh. I thought you knew."

When I cast my mind back to Hotemet Castle, I remembered telling Adonis about Hazel, that I wanted her back. Adonis had said Kratos would never find her for me—that he'd want to keep me dependent on him. The next morning, my sister had been found. And it had been Adonis's doing.

For most of the time I'd known him, I'd been positive Adonis only ever acted for self-interested reasons. He'd done nothing to convince me otherwise, never mentioned that he'd been the one to find Hazel. Clearly, I wasn't the only one playing a part, pretending to be someone I wasn't.

My heart thudded hard, and I tried to focus on the problem at hand. Now, we had two potential problems headed our way: two horsemen, and the Heavenly Host. Still no gleaming blue gemstones.

I crossed to the bed and slid my hand under my pillow, snatching my knife and the holster. I slipped the sheathed knife into my boot. "Okay. First things first. I need to find Tanit and Kur and tell them what's going on."

"And what is going on? What's our plan? Run? Hide?"

I swallowed hard. "I don't know. Maybe I can speak to Aereus again. Find out what he knows."

"We have a dragon. I can take you anywhere you want. We could leave now, let the archangels sort all this out between them, and we charm whoever wins."

I scowled at her. "I'm not leaving without Adonis. And anyway. It's like you said. An archangel can find us if they want to."

* * *

With my arms folded, I continued my pacing in Tanit's room while the two demons stared at me.

Tanit's dark hair snaked around her head. "So the Heavenly Host know that you're the Bringer of Light, but they don't necessarily know that Adonis is working with you. He could be oblivious, for all they know."

"I think so."

Tanit cocked her head at Kur. "We could simply hand the fae over, if we must. We could say that we found her out, and Adonis had no idea, and the archangels can do with her what they like."

I paused, glaring at her. "I'm right here, you know. I can hear you."

She looked between Kur and me, reading our expressions. "What? I'm not saying it's a good idea. I'm just saying it's an option. We should consider all options. That's what brainstorming is, right?"

Kur shot her a sharp look. "Let's not sacrifice the little fae just yet. I have a feeling Adonis may not be thrilled about that particular option."

I bit my lip, desperation building in my system. "I'm going to talk to Aereus again. I'm going to see if I can get him to drop any kind of information about the stones, whatever it takes." A quiet panic had begun to race through my veins. I'd torture the bastard on his own instruments if I had to. "At least give me a few more hours before you throw me to the wolves."

"Be careful!" Kur called out as I yanked open the door.

I walked through the stone halls, closing my eyes and trying to tune in to the Old Gods around me. As a Bringer of Light, would I be able to sense the stones? I ran my fingertips over the stone walls, inhaling deeply. A faint smell of roses tinged the air, the bloom of Devil's Bane... Was that them?

I followed the lure of roses until the smell of roasting meat began to overpower me, and a primal violence churned in my gut. That meant only one thing. Aereus.

When I opened my eyes again, I found him towering over me, his eyes blazing with flames. His fire-tipped wings spread out behind him.

"Ruby," he growled. "A little black crow just delivered the most interesting message to me." He grabbed me by the ribs, lifting me from the ground, and his fingers tightened over my bones. "He tells me you're the Bringer of Light. Tell me. Does Adonis know?"

Sweet earthly gods, Hazel needed to get out of here. Fast.

Hot rage—Aereus's magic—sparked through my nerves. I wanted his revolting hands off of me. For just a moment, I envisioned my thumbs plunging into his eye sockets, blinding him.

"No. Adonis doesn't know," I managed to say evenly.

With a roar, he yanked me from the wall, then threw me through an open doorway. I landed hard on the stone floor, and pain shot through my bones.

From my prone position on the floor, I flicked my tongue

over my lengthening canines, blood roaring in my ears. I couldn't let my feral instincts take over completely or I'd never find out what I needed to know.

The sound of a slamming door echoed off the walls.

Aereus stood above me, staring down, and his immense body blazed with fiery light. "No one will hear you scream in here. Your friends won't be able to find you."

It was just as Adonis had said. Aereus liked to isolate his victims.

I began pushing myself up on my elbows. We were in a stark room—one with stone walls and iron chains and brackets inset into the walls. Sharp, iron instruments lay in the corner on the floor, tipped with old blood. Fear pounded into me like a fist when I looked behind me—a wooden table stood in the center of the room. Torture tools jutted from its surface, and crimson stained the wood.

My heart slammed against my ribs. If any one of those iron instruments pierced my flesh, there'd be no way out of here. The iron would work its way into my blood like a poison.

Before I could reach for the knife in my boot, Aereus lifted me by the neck. He slammed me into the wall, holding me aloft so my legs kicked futilely at him.

"I knew there was something inside you," he said. "A woman at war with herself. A woman fighting not to remember the truth, what she really is."

He closed his eyes, a deep growl rumbling from his throat.

Pain shot through my neck, and my lungs burned. Violent impulses gripped my mind, and in its dark recesses, blood ran down a pale arm, pooling on the pavement.

I kicked him hard in the crotch, but it didn't seem to faze him. My throat, my lungs were on fire.

I closed my eyes, screaming through the mental link to

Adonis. *Adonis. Now. I need you here now.* How far was he? Could he get here before Aereus tore me to pieces?

Aereus pulled down the shoulder of my dress, exposing Adonis's mark. He snarled hungrily at the sight of exposed flesh, pressing his enormous body into me. "So Adonis protects you, does he? Does he know what you really are? Does he know what you could do, my little poison flower? You could destroy us all."

Aereus pulled me away from the wall for just a moment before slamming the back of my head into the stone. Pain splintered my skull, and the urge to go feral nearly overpowered me.

One of Aereus's meaty hands was on my waist, moving up toward my breasts, and I choked down bile.

"Why isn't he coming for you now?" he hissed. "Adonis. Why isn't he here, when I'm taking what's his? He should be pulling me off of you."

He squeezed one of my breasts. Fury exploded in my mind. I kicked at Aereus, my glamour fading fast. He was choking me again, squeezing the life out of me. Mentally, I screamed for Adonis.

Aereus's fingers dug into my flesh, his eyes darkening. "If Adonis isn't coming for you now, then it means he's nowhere near us, is he? And you're at war with yourself still." Aereus pressed in closer, his magic overwhelming me. "A woman who thinks she enjoys pleasure, but she denies herself what she truly wants. A woman who won't let herself give in, won't let herself remember all the things she's done."

Adonis's image ignited in my mind, the memory of his fingers on my skin. Would my last thoughts be of the angel of death?

CHAPTER 33

Losing air. Can't breathe.

"What scares you the most, Bringer of Light, is that something terrible will happen to your sister. That you'll be all alone in the world, trapped at the edge of the dark, dark void. And there, you have to face the real monster, don't you? There, you'd have to face yourself."

I kicked him hard in the groin again, and he dropped me for a moment.

I sucked in a sharp, rough breath. "Don't you dare touch my sister."

A powerful backhanded smack cracked my skull, and I fell to the floor, my head throbbing.

"I'll tell you what's going to happen, Ruby." His voice was low, controlled. He pressed his boot into my neck, cutting off my air again. At least my hands were free now.

I reached for my boot, inching my leg up, closer to my hand. Aereus wasn't paying attention to my hands, focused instead on my reddening face.

"I'm going to kill you in the most painful way possible," he growled. "I'm going to delight in the sound of your screams as I break you on my iron wheel. I will revel in the beauty of your blood feeding my roses. Before you die, I want you to know that when I kill Hazel, I'll take even longer to rip her body apart."

Teeth in flesh, breaking bones. I'm not Ruby anymore. I'm your worst nightmare. I ripped the knife from my boot, then drew it across the back of his ankle. Just enough—just enough to weaken him, not enough to knock him out.

His eyes widened at the feel of Devil's Bane entering his blood. Then, he stumbled away from me, eyes bulging. Frantic, I gasped for air, my breath ragged in my throat from my position on the floor.

"Poison!" he roared. His boot slammed into my ribs, and I felt the crack of bone.

Maybe I hadn't given him quite enough poison. Slowly, I pushed myself up onto my elbows again, gripping the knife. Aereus stumbled toward me, stepping on my wrist.

I screamed with pain, dropping the knife. I rolled away from him, agony splintering my ribs where he'd kicked me.

Get up, Ruby. I forced myself to my knees, then rose, my eyes locked on the horseman of war.

He'd snatched an iron tool off the table—a sharp, clawlike thing. I couldn't let it anywhere near me. He looked a little unsteady on his feet, but he wasn't going down yet.

"You're not going to touch my sister," I hissed as a volcanic fury erupted in my mind.

Kill. Rip out his throat. Bathe in his blood.

My canines pricked at my tongue, and I darted across the room for my knife. Without realizing what I was doing, I found myself lifting the blade to my lips. I licked Aereus's blood off the knife. Devil's Bane didn't hurt the fae.

Ambrosia, rich and sweet as honey. I wanted more.

My gut tightened. *Stay in control. Get from him the information that you need.*

My prey staggered back, the iron tool gripped in his hands as the poison slowly took effect.

"I will make you submit." He lunged for me, and I sidestepped.

A vicious smile curled my lips as I started to feel in control. I lunged for him, fast as the wind through the trees, and nicked his skin again, then leapt away from him.

He grunted, fear glinting in his eyes, and he clutched his arm where I'd cut him. "How did you learn about Devil's Bane?" A thin line of spit trickled from his mouth, and he dropped the iron tool.

Earthy fog began to cloud my mind, and I tried to think clearly. I needed something from this beast… I needed…

Roaring, he flicked his wrist. A wave of hot, arid magic slammed me into the wall.

The blow sent a shock of adrenaline snapping through my nerve endings, and a bubble of clarity illuminated my mind for a moment. I threw my knife, and it landed in his shoulder. He howled.

This horseman could withstand a lot more Devil's Bane than the skinny one. I rushed for him, snatching my knife from his shoulder again.

Think, Ruby. Don't let the beast take over completely.

I scrambled to remember how words worked. "Tell me," I rasped. Something other than blood that I needed from him. "Tell me."

He staggered back, his features slackened. "Of course someone who looks like you would conceal a festering monster inside. The seeds of destruction grow in the gardens of paradise, do they not?"

"Garden!" I shouted, though I wasn't sure why. The

rational part of my mind was fighting for control. I bit down hard on the powerful urge to hurl my knife into his heart and just end it all.

He kept stumbling away—running from me, and my hunter's instincts were kicking in. *Kill the prey.*

I prowled after him, my sights locked on his slumping shoulders, his weakening body.

My prey grabbed another tool from the table—a sharp iron knife. The fucker wasn't giving up easily.

Mustering all the restraint I could, I grabbed a blade from the table, wincing at the feel of iron burning my skin.

"Garden." The word tumbled out of my mouth again. With lethal precision, I hurled the iron spike at my prey. It pierced his wrist, and he dropped his weapon.

I slammed my boot into his chest—hard—and he grunted. He'd tried to break me, hadn't he?

Fury erupted in my blood, and I kicked him harder this time—right in the ribs. He flew into the wall—not far from the chains.

Rip him to pieces. Drink his blood.

In the next second, I had my knife pressed against this throat. My lips curled back from my teeth. I needed to use words, couldn't remember them. I snarled.

"Knife," I managed to grunt. "Poison. More."

Good. Threat conveyed.

That damned peaty haze clouded my mind, the scent of dirt and moss. What was it I needed here? What did I need except this creature's blood and pain, and the glorious fresh meat filling my mouth, and the feel of fingers clawing into the dirt? What did I need apart from the beautiful, dark-winged man with the pale eyes?

Yes…him… I needed him to tear my clothes off and run his tongue over my body, needed him to grab me hard by the hips and fill me... Needed my fingers in the dirt, hands and knees on the ground before him.

I clenched my jaw tight. I couldn't think straight through the haze in my mind.

My prey rallied, punching me hard in the cheek, and I groaned, nearly dropping my knife.

A wild snarl tore from my throat. I gripped my knife tighter, swinging wildly to nick him again. I pierced his skin through his clothes, right below his elbow. He bellowed like an injured animal. And with that, my knife was at his throat once more, pressing harder this time.

Capture your prey. Then toy with it.

Without entirely realizing what I was doing, I found myself chaining the creature's arms to the walls with one hand. I kept the poisoned blade pressed against his throat, while my other hand snapped the cuffs around him.

He hissed at me, more bestial than angelic. In my feral state, I delighted in the fear in his eyes—this powerful man at my mercy. Fear rippled off him, so intense I could practically smell it. Fear was something even Feral Ruby understood.

No wonder he kept such fierce control over everyone. No wonder he tortured them, kept them terrified. They scared the shit out of him.

He was screaming at me, but I tuned out his cries, stepping back to look at my conquest.

That thing I needed from him... That thing that wasn't blood.

I closed my eyes, trying to clear the haze, but his words were drowning out my own thoughts.

"You don't know where the stones are, Ruby," he roared. "And without them, you can't kill me. I don't know where Adonis is. But I do know who is flying fast for my castle. The Heavenly Host."

I stared at the trickle of blood oozing from the nick in his throat, trying to make meaning out of his words.

"Flying fast," I repeated.

A sharp, panicked laugh escaped his throat. He rasped, the poison seeping deeper into his bloodstream. "You're not really there, are you, Ruby? Does Adonis know he's been fucking an animal?" He sniffed the air. "Can't say I wouldn't mind trying it myself, in your case, though I'd hate myself after."

I clamped my eyes shut, trying to gain control. The pig was right about one thing—I wasn't myself right now. I needed the roaring of my primal side to go quiet.

"Garden," I snarled, still unsure why I was saying the word. There was something I wanted to get at—an important idea of some kind.

Another little bubble of clarity began to penetrate the peaty haze in my skull.

I surveyed my victim. Feral Ruby had done well. If I hadn't poisoned the fucker, he'd be able to break right out of those iron chains. But the Devil's Bane had weakened him severely, and he was barely hanging on.

What had he said? I couldn't kill him without the stones.

Right. The stones. If the gods-damned Heavenly Host were actually on their way right now, I needed to find out where the stones were, and I needed to make the blue shield. Just like I'd seen in the pictures.

I stepped back from Aereus, marching over to the iron tools on the torture table. They would hiss and sting when I picked them up, but they wouldn't poison me unless I nicked my own skin. I walked down the line of torture instruments. Slowly, the power of speech began returning to my mind.

I stared at a two-pronged iron instrument. "Sharp," I said.

"What are you planning on doing?" Aereus bellowed. "The Heavenly Host are on their way. If you hurt me, your death will be agonizing. They'll keep you alive for centuries, torturing you until there's nothing left of your mind or soul." He was threatening me, but raw fear tinged his voice, and it warmed my heart.

A little more of the haze dissipated in my mind. "Which sharp thing?" I asked.

"You're not thinking clearly." His desperation reverberated around me.

"I want to hurt you."

"You can't hurt an archangel. It's against the rules of nature. We reign supreme over your kind. We are gods. You're a filthy beast who scrambles and fucks and feeds in the dirt."

I pulled the edge of my sleeve over my hand so I could pick up a three-pronged instrument, like a tiny devil's pitchfork. "This one."

Just enough haze in my mind right now that I could be brutal, but not so much that I'd forget what I was doing.

"What do you want?" he screamed.

I cocked my head. "No one can hear you in here. You told me that. No one will find you."

"Don't hurt me." He sagged in his iron chains. "What do you want from me?"

"Tell me where the stones are."

"You must be out of your fucking mind if you think I would tell you that."

I was looking into his eyes as I thrust the iron into his side, between his ribs. His scream rent the air. "I need to know. Now."

Aereus heaved a sob. "The seeds of destruction grow in the gardens of paradise. Heavenly Host, please come for me now, your humble servant. I need to rule as a god on earth!"

Garden.

That was why I'd been saying the word over and over.

Aereus, as he'd told me, took that aphorism very seriously. And I was his destruction, wasn't I? I'd lay his plans to waste.

He shook his head. "You can't use them. You'll destroy everything. You'll kill—"

I was out the door before he had the chance to finish his sentence.

CHAPTER 34

With the shield of glamour around me—a cherub's form—I prowled through the hall. I ignored the bruised, battered pain that throbbed along my ribs.

I'd disguised myself as one of the taller cherubs—the ones without predictable movements. With any luck, I could go where I wanted without rousing suspicion.

I moved swiftly through the hallway, heading for Aereus's garden. When I caught a glimpse of myself in a statue's armor, I shuddered at the sight of the milky eyes staring out from the face of a haunted child, silver streaks in my hair. The appearance of a gossamer white dress trailed behind me. A cold shiver rippled over my skin.

I moved on, gliding gracefully over the marble floor, past empty alcoves and into an arched hall. I wasn't sure what had once hung on these walls, but now they all featured war gods—Saturn, Mars, some of Zeus hurling lightning bolts from his fist.

My muscles began to ache as I moved, my ribs and neck bruised where Aereus had attacked me. This glamour, so different from my real appearance, drained my energy. My head swam.

When I turned the corner into the next hall, my throat tightened. A group of cherubs swarmed past a statue of Aereus atop his horse. Would they notice anything strange about me?

I kept my eyes straight ahead, the way I'd seen the taller cherubs behave.

The others passed me without comment.

At last, I found myself in the hall that led to the garden.

The idea of spending any more time in the torture garden filled me with dread, but I pushed through the door anyway. Cold air greeted my skin.

Outside, moonlight washed over the plants, the shards of bone. My footsteps crunched over the mosaic bones beneath my feet.

As I moved deeper into the vegetation, I tried to tune into the feel of the Old Gods. I closed my eyes, envisioning their blinding light—that pure warmth that had filled my body.

I slipped past the iron wheel, where Aereus delighted in torturing his victims.

With my eyes closed, I could feel the plants around me, and my fingertips skimmed over their leaves, thorns, petals, summoning that inner light I'd managed to capture once or twice before…

A dull, warm glow moved up my chest. The power of the Old Gods—still, it wasn't telling me where to find the stones.

A faint movement caught my eye—a bobbing tail—and my gaze flicked to the line of scorpion guards in one corner of the garden.

Bingo. Of course Aereus would guard the stones, and of course they'd be among the thorny, poisonous plants. I already knew he didn't give a flying fuck whether or not his servants poisoned themselves. He'd want to keep people from discovering the gems that could ruin his plans.

I moved closer to the scorpions, trying my best to go unnoticed—just a simple haunted-eyed cherub, out for my nightly patrol.

My gaze landed on the flowering, purple plants behind the guards. Devil's Bane—just as I'd thought.

I took another step closer, trying to peer through the thick, arachnid bodies of the scorpion guards at the plants behind them.

One of them grunted, moving forward. He gripped his spear and snarled. Still, I didn't think he saw me. Maybe he smelled me. After another moment, his body seemed to relax again.

My throat had gone dry. I *needed* to see what lay behind them without arousing suspicion, to find out if the stones were here.

I glided from the shadows—a cherub, nothing more. The scorpions didn't seem to notice me.

One more step closer, and—just soil. Disappointment coiled through me until—faintly—the soil began to shift, trembling. Light warmed my chest, and I stared as the unmistakable gleam of blue stones emerged from the soil, drawn by my presence. A wild euphoria bloomed in my chest. I ached to touch them, to harness their power. As soon as my eyes locked on them, I could feel them calling to me, demanding that I pluck them, that I feel their magic. They wanted something from me as much as I wanted something from them.

I could go feral at this moment and possibly slaughter the guards. But then—I'd never remember what I was doing here in the first place, and there'd be no point.

Adonis! I mentally screamed at him. *I found them. If you can hear me, I need your help.*

As I glided away from the scorpions, a pale, pearly light in the night sky pulled my attention. My heart slammed hard against my ribs. Focusing my keen fae vision, I made out the outline of powerful, feathery wings. I stared, my pulse racing, as ten gleaming archangels loomed brighter above us. And at their forefront, a scrawny, gray-winged angel. The horseman of famine.

My heart stopped.

The Heavenly Host were coming for me now—and Johnny was leading the charge.

Panic sank its talons into my heart, and I clamped my eyes shut. *Adonis!* I screamed through the mental link. *They're coming. The Heavenly Host are coming for us—now.*

Where the hell was he?

My gaze flicked back to the line of scorpion men. I didn't have any more time to waste. I had to kill them now, and I had to get my hands on the stones.

My hand twitched at my thigh, and I sank back into the shadows again to let my glamour fade.

I'd have to go just a little feral, and I'd have to catch the guards unaware.

Under the boughs of a sycamore, I let myself fade just a bit—a little of my primal side to give me extra strength.

My canines began to grow in my mouth, my body buzzing with wild energy. I breathed in the scent of Aereus's violent power all around me, and it electrified my wild fae body even more. *Keep a leash on it, Ruby. Stay in control.*

In the shadows, I yanked my knife from its holster, breathing fast. Scanning the guards, I made a quick calculation—kill the small one on the right, steal his sword, use it to slaughter the rest. Do it all as quickly as I could, without letting too much of the primal side take over.

A small swarm of cherubs moved along the mosaic path

toward me, their murmuring growing louder. They'd noticed something amiss here—that I wasn't one of them.

And they were about to notice something *very* amiss when I dropped my glamour. My gaze flicked to the skies.

It didn't matter. I had no more time to waste.

With a primal growl, I launched myself at the first of the scorpions. I lunged through the air, slashing my blade across his throat before he had a chance to react. Blood sprayed over me before my feet hit the ground. When I landed, I yanked the guard's sword off his fallen body.

Whirling, my blade crashed into the next guard's, the metal sparking in the shadows.

The scorpion roared, his tail pressing closer to me, and I lunged away from him.

Rip apart the enemy. Put him in the dirt.

As my sword clashed against his in a violent waltz, I wanted to taste his blood, to feel his veins and tendons ripping in my teeth. My sword arced through the air, an extension of my body, and the glory of battle fury trembled along my bones. I was made for this.

I drove my blade into his neck, then drew it out to kill again.

Dimly, I was dimly aware of another presence nearby—one forged of night and ancient power. One that I needed like plants needed water.

I couldn't remember his name—the beautiful one with the wings. For just a moment, my gaze flicked to him and I watched as he sliced his fingertips through the air in a brutal gesture.

The three remaining scorpions split down the middle, their severed bodies slumping to the dark earth.

I snarled. They'd been *mine*.

I moved toward the angel—the arrogance of him—didn't belong on earth—an abomination. His icy, alluring eyes designed to seduce, to confuse... Growling, I gripped my sword, ready to swing it into this abomination.

But he was speaking to me—pulling me out of my feral rage.

"Ruby," he said, his voice calming as a blanket of night.

A calm, soothing magic washed over me, relaxing the tension in my muscles. I lowered my sword. Slowly, my canines began to recede, and my gaze flicked to the sky again.

The Heavenly Host were pressing down on us, bodies blazing with light. "They're here." My voice trembled.

"Get the stones," Adonis said gravely. "This is our last chance."

Right. I rushed over the bodies of the scorpion guards, snatching the blue gemstones. Dirt covered their glittering surfaces from their burial underground. They *wanted* me to have them, to possess them. But what, exactly, was I supposed to do with them?

The sound of a door creaking open pulled my attention away. I had only a moment to register Aereus's presence before a brutal force knocked me into the air—a magic that burned my skin and smelled of arid desert winds. My body slammed down hard on the bony path, and I dropped the plant from my hands.

"Why have you killed my guards?" Aereus roared. "I told you the Heavenly Host would arrive!"

Another horseman—Adonis couldn't kill him. He could only try to slow him down—although given how he'd withstood the poison, that wouldn't be an easy task.

Adonis had drawn his sword, ready to fight Aereus.

The pale light burned brighter above us, washing over my skin—so pure and perfect I didn't want to fight them. No, I wanted to bathe in their glory….

The sound of steel against steel pulled my attention back

to the earth, my gaze landing on the two horsemen battling each other. Adonis's dark magic whirled around his body.

"You're after the Stones of Zohar," Aereus seethed, his sword cutting sharp arcs through the air. "I buried them deeply, but they rose in the presence of a Light Bringer. Why would you bring her here? You know what she can do to us."

Adonis grunted, meeting Aereus's blows.

I scrambled over the path, searching for the fallen plant, its leaves encrusted with gemstones.

"You know what they'll do to us!" Aereus bellowed.

There—among the bloodied soil—a glimmer of blue, the azure of the skies above Afeka. I reached for it, when another blast of hot, arid magic slammed into me with the force of a train.

My body shattered against a stone wall, ribs cracking. Pain splintered my entire body, and I groaned.

Adonis's roar sent a lick of fear racing up my neck. He viciously swung his sword through the air. He pressed in on Aereus with an increased ferocity—looking more feral than angelic.

The agony of my broken bones clouded my mind. I was on my knees, fingers on the mosaic path of teeth, blood streaming from my mouth. I rasped for breath, pain ravaging my body.

Gritting my teeth, crawling over the bony path, my mind so gripped by agony that my thoughts were no longer making sense... I could only stare at the teeth beneath my fingers, and wonder who they'd come from, if they'd died in this garden. Would I join them?

I shuffled along the ground, now only dimly aware of the angels moving closer.

If I died here, what sort of a disturbing design would they form with my teeth?

Blood dripped from my mouth onto the path. Adonis's

magic rippled over me, soothing the pain just a little. *I have to get to the stones.*

I glanced up to see him carving his sword through one of Aereus's red-tipped wings, and the howl Aereus unleashed pierced me to the bone.

Another inch forward over the teeth, crawling toward the glittering blue gems, and pain ripped through my chest, my legs.

Tentatively, I looked up to the skies, at the gleaming angelic horde, now only a hundred feet in the air, and my heart skipped a beat.

They're almost upon us.

I pulled myself a little farther along the path, still staring at the sky—staring, in fact, as a golden dragon soared through the air just below the angelic horde. I blinked at the sight of a female form riding on top of the dragon's neck, her black hair trailing behind her in the night sky.

Hazel?

Uthyr carved a sharp arc below the angels, then arched his back to breathe a hot stream of fire at the oncoming horde.

Idiot—what was she doing? They'd *kill* her. She was buying me time, and I couldn't waste it.

I grabbed the stones, and my body surged with warmth and light. My forehead tingled, and I fought the bizarre urge to press the stones against it.

I felt powerful arms around me—Adonis's arms cradling me, his magic soothing my body. Already, he was healing my bones with his power, numbing the pain. I inhaled deeply, able to breathe a little easier now. Adonis closed his fist around mine, enclosing the stones.

"Now," he whispered. "Use their power now."

I clutched them tightly, closing my eyes. I wasn't sure what I was supposed to do with them—but considering I couldn't move my body, I didn't have many options right now anyway.

They tingled in my fist, then a cold, soothing magic whispered over my skin. Light seemed to ignite me from the inside, blazing through my blood, ancient and pure. The power of the Old Gods flowed through me, my back arching with the intensity. The stones wanted something from me, as if they had their own consciousness.

Their desire whispered through my blood. They wanted me to protect the earth—then to return them home.

Pure strength infused my bones and muscles, and my eyes snapped open. I looked up into Adonis's eyes, and the voice of the Old Gods whispered to me.

He doesn't belong here. They don't belong here. Rid the earth of their presence, and bring the stones home.

Another part of me rebelled at the thought, wanted him here, but the gleaming light burned out those protests.

Still cradling me, Adonis pushed my hair out of my eyes. "Now," he whispered. "They're here. You can't stop—no matter what happens."

At his words, a spark of dread flickered through me. He knew something that he wasn't telling me.

"If what happens?" I asked firmly.

His eyes flashed. "*Now.*"

My gaze flicked to the skies, where the eleven archangels raced for us—for this garden.

Power snaked and rippled along my spine, and I flung out my arms. Light beamed from my ribs, burning with a white-hot intensity.

The angels froze in midair, and a dome of blue light arced over the earth. I closed my eyes, my skull whirling with images of caves and rivers, of oaks overgrown with ivy, sunlight burning through the leaves.

The power snapped and buzzed through my lungs, and

lower, through my belly. I gave in to it. Among the blazing sunlight, something darker lurked in the power of the Old Gods, too. The wolf taking down the stag, the plants growing from corpse-enriched soil.

My body a vessel for their power. And the stones were calling to me, too, urging me on. The Old Gods wanted them back, needed them returned to their original home.

It was always meant to be this way.

My body trembled, stones gripped tightly in my fist, until I felt as if my ribs might explode with a pure, wild ecstasy.

A crash pulled me from my reverie.

When I opened my eyes again, I stared up at the sky, my breath clouding around my head in the chilly air.

Beyond the dome of blue light, a horde of angels raced away from the earth. Fleeing—from my power. The glow around them seemed to weaken. Clouds began to roll along the horizon. But where was Johnny? He wasn't among them. Almost as if he'd just fallen from the sky.

It took me a moment to realize that I'd ended up hovering in midair, that my feet hung a meter above the ground.

When I looked down, my heart leapt into my throat.

Adonis lay on the path, his body completely still.

I dropped the stones, falling back to earth. The power of the gems had completely healed my body, but it seemed to have the opposite effect on Adonis.

Fat drops of icy rain began falling from the sky, chilling my skin.

I pressed my hand over his chest, feeling for a heartbeat. For a moment, I felt nothing. Then—a faint pulse, just below his scars.

His pale eyes opened, and I slid my arm under his neck, cradling his head. "Adonis?"

The rain picked up, hammering us harder now.

Adonis met my gaze, his eyes flaming with intensity for

just a moment. "You made me want to stay here longer. I need to know the real Ruby. But angels don't belong on earth."

My throat had gone dry, heart slamming hard. This didn't feel right. "What's happening? Are you going to be okay?"

He shook his head, almost imperceptibly, and his eyes began to close. Even close to death, he looked perfect—a god of beauty.

"The stones will carry me to the underworld." He spoke in a whisper. "It's where the horsemen belong. But I want to see you…" His words died out on his tongue.

He'd known.

All this time, he'd known what the stones would do to him—and he'd wanted me to use them anyway.

Sacrifice the few to save the many.

Sadness and a rising panic washed over me.

I'd freed the earth from the scourge of the horsemen, but when I looked at Adonis, grief pressed down on me all the same, suffocating me like heavy dirt. I pressed my hand over his heart again, desperate to feel a beat pulsing beneath my palm.

This time, I felt only the stillness of a grave.

CHAPTER 35

I tried to calm my panicked thoughts, to think of a solution.

My hand shook on Adonis's still chest, and I scanned the garden. Aereus lay on the mosaic path—not far from me. His torn wing had stopped pumping blood, and his heart no longer beat.

Dread slammed into my chest like a fist. I'd just killed them all. I'd killed the horsemen, and as insane as it was—I wanted to take it back. At least for this one.

I'd been so focused on Adonis, I hadn't even noticed that Hazel had landed nearby until I began frantically searching the garden, desperate for some answers. Desperate for a way to undo this.

Hazel's dragon had flattened half the garden, crushing trees beneath it. Rain battered Hazel as she slid off the creature.

Bursts of white streamed from the castle windows, racing for the sky, and it took me a moment to realize the cherubs were fleeing, soaring for the heavens in a mass exodus. The burst of power from the Old Gods had sent them racing away from us.

I pulled Adonis's body in close, embracing his head and his chest as though I could revive him with my body heat. A wave of sorrow washed over me.

This wasn't how it was supposed to end.

"What happened?" Hazel shouted.

I held him close to my heart. "I don't know! I used the stones." I heaved a sob. "They made a shield, just like they were supposed to. They wanted something from me. To be returned home, I think. The Heavenly Host took off, just like they were supposed to." Sorrow slammed into me. "But it killed the horsemen."

Hazel stared down at Adonis, her brow furrowed. "I think you're right."

His body felt cold as ice in my arms.

The shock was a fist in my throat. "I didn't know this would happen."

Deep in my chest, I felt something breaking, and I leaned over Adonis's body, grasping for the stones again, my hand shaking. He looked still and perfect as a god carved of marble.

Maybe I could fix this; maybe the Old Gods would revive him. The Old Gods provided, right?

I gripped the stones tightly in my hands, holding them over his chest—his scarred heart where he'd stabbed himself again and again, stopping his own seal from breaking. It was only now that I was beginning to understand the fuller picture of him, a man who viewed his role as one of sacrifice.

As I held the Stones of Zohar, light flowed through me—a dazzling summer light that tinged the air with honey. I put my hand on Adonis's chest, trying to channel the light into him, to stream it right into his heart…

A thin ray of blue light flowed into his ribs, and for just a moment, his back arched. But all I could feel through the stone's magic was a deep yearning to return home. The light dulled again, and Adonis's body went still.

Above me, the sound of rhythmic wings beat the air. Tanit and Kur were diving for the earth, rain hammering their bodies.

"What the hell happened?" Tanit shrieked.

Grief wrapped around me. The stones hadn't revived him—Adonis's body lay still in my lap, and my mind raced. He'd known, hadn't he? This had been his plan all along. He'd been talking about a sacrifice—all gods demand sacrifices. Maybe a part of him had wanted out of this endless cycle of euphoria and pain. Reliving the same self-inflicted wounds over and over.

Kur kneeled next to me, placing his hand over Adonis's heart. Inky magic coiled from his body, winding around Adonis.

I tuned out the driving rain and the wind, tuned out Tanit's frantic screaming and the painful thoughts hammering at the back of my skull.

I gripped the stones in my hands, closing my eyes. Their power ignited my blood with the pure, buttery light of spring rays filtering through oak leaves, illuminating dust motes in the air with their brilliance. I held Adonis's head, trying to channel that power into him.

I had to look up at the sky—couldn't bring myself to look at the ground. Teeth ripping apart an arm, a woman screaming. Whose teeth were they? I couldn't look at the blood staining the pavement...

The light called to me, the piercing light from above.

"Ruby!" Tanit screamed, ripping me from the vision. Her face wore a haunted, ravaged expression, rain pouring down her features in rivulets. "It's no use. That's not doing anything. He didn't tell us this would happen, but obviously this was his plan. This was his sacrifice. The Great Nightmare is over, and Adonis thought he had to go with it."

"I know. He said he was going to the underworld or something…" I mumbled. I clutched tighter to the stones. *No.* This wasn't how it was supposed to end. The good guys were supposed to win in the end, not die in the soil of a torture garden.

My mind whirled, searching for answers. I tuned out Hazel, tuned out Tanit's crying. I did my best to tune out Kur's rampage, vaguely aware that he'd moved away from us, that he was ripping things from the ground—the iron, the spikes, glass breaking, tearing through the garden like a furious god.

I stared down at Adonis, tracing my fingers over his chest again. A faint spark of hope lit in my mind. This death wasn't the result of dragons or fire. Adonis's death came from magic. And magic could always be undone, right?

If this was supposed to be a gift from the Old Gods, it was a gift I wanted to return.

I wanted to know *exactly* what Adonis had known. I wanted to know everything about the Stones of Zohar and the Bringer of Light.

I wiped the back of my hand across my face to clear away the rain and tears.

Nearby, Kur was ripping human bones from the garden.

"Kur!" I shouted. "I need your help!"

"With what?" he snarled, flashing a hint of sharp teeth.

"Can you read Phoenician?"

Stark pain shone from his dark eyes. "What the fuck does that have to do with anything?"

"I need you to help me learn everything that Adonis knew about the Bringer of Light. About the Old Gods," I shouted. "This isn't where his story ends. I'm sure of it."

CHAPTER 36

I slammed through the door into the bedroom where we'd been staying. Behind me, Kur carried Adonis's body into the room. Hazel sauntered in behind the two demons. At our arrival, Drakon yelped, fluttering his wings frantically.

My heart thundered against my ribs as I scrambled to find the book—tucked under the mattress, just where Adonis had left it. I pulled it out, and Kur laid Adonis's body on the bed. Panicking, Drakon crawled over to his master, curling up on his body, wings fluttering.

Kur sat down on the edge of the bed, ignoring the chaos behind him. I handed the book to him, and he began paging through it, muttering to himself in an ancient language. "And Adonis read this?"

"He's had it with him this whole time. He said he had it memorized. It's the same one that Kratos keeps in his war room. He only told me part of it—he left out the bit about how the stones would kill the horsemen. He said he wanted to rule the celestial realm. Same thing he told you." I shivered, my teeth chattering. I'd wanted to rid the earth of archangels, but this didn't feel like a victory.

Kur gripped the book hard. "This book explains that the Bringer of Light can harness the magic of the Old Gods to repel archangels from the earth. And her magic will kill all the living horsemen of the apocalypse."

Cold dread slid through my bones. Adonis had wanted me to act as his executioner. All along I'd thought he could lure me to my death through seduction, but I had it wrong. He'd been drawn to me precisely because he knew I could kill him.

Tanit tugged at her hair. "Of course he didn't tell us this. We would have stopped him."

There was a lot he hadn't told them. He hadn't mentioned how he kept the seal from opening. I'd been so sure that Adonis was only looking out for himself, that I'd failed to see the truth—Adonis had found a way to keep himself from slaughtering, to beat his curse.

There was still so much he hadn't told me, too.

"His story isn't finished," I said again, more forcefully. Adrenaline and wild desperation surged. "I'm sure of it."

Hazel leaned against the wall, her arms folded. "I told you we should have left things as they were."

Fury bloomed in my chest. "Shut up, Hazel. I'm trying to think." As it was, I could hardly hear my own thoughts over Tanit's sobbing.

"What did he mean his soul was going to the underworld? Is it…is it the one he told me about? Where he was born?"

Kur nodded slowly. "The Old Gods have claimed the souls of the horsemen. This book is written by one of their followers, lauding the defeat of the horsemen. Praising the work of the *Bringer of Light*." Contempt dripped from his words. "As you might imagine, there are no instructions on how to fix it."

I closed my eyes, wracking my brain for everything I'd learned about the Old Gods. The poisonous herbs that grew where horsemen tread, the power I'd felt surging through the silver bough, so raw and overwhelming it had almost driven me insane. The Stones of Zohar, mined from the grotto where Adonis had been born. The entrance to the underworld...

"Afeka," I whispered. "The stones want to be returned to Afeka."

Kur looked up from the book. "What?"

I stared at him. "His soul is in the underworld, where the stones come from, right? And I could feel the stones' desire to return there. They want to go back to Afeka." As soon as I said the word, the stones pulsed in my hand, as if affirming what I was saying. "Any idea where it is, exactly?"

"Lebenon," said Kur.

I nodded. "The Old Gods reside there. Maybe I can make a trade."

Hazel's expression was bleak. "Didn't Adonis warn you that every god wants a sacrifice? I don't think they're into making trades."

I glanced at Adonis, at his pendant that stood out like blood droplets against his tan skin. "The Old Gods want their magic rocks back. I can feel it, even now. Maybe they'll give us just one soul in return."

Hazel's expression was dark. "Or maybe they'll just kill you and take the stones."

Tanit pointed at Adonis, tears streaking her cheeks. "You need to fix this." Her voice was low, cold. "He thinks it was his job to sacrifice himself. It's why he stayed with the feral fae so long."

"I don't understand."

Fury seemed to ripple off Kur's powerful body. "Only the fae could keep his powers in check. Before he could control them himself, his emotions could spread waves of death around him—plagues, earthquakes, a frost on the crops. Just by feeling intensely—by growing angry or loving another person—death rippled off of him. Only the fae knew how to contain it, with their close connection to the Old Gods."

I felt the bone-deep chill of his words. He'd never wanted to kill, but death simply coiled out of him uncontrolled. I could hardly imagine the guilt, the stark isolation that must have plagued him all those years.

"Over time," Kur continued, "Adonis learned to control it better. He grew into his powers, the way a fae learns to control her hunger. He wanted to keep the world from his destruction." Sharp whorls of magic spilled from Kur's golden body. "Same reason he carved himself up every time the seal started to break open."

"You knew about that?" I asked.

"Of course I knew. I've known for centuries. Adonis always thought he needed to suffer in silence."

I wrung my hands. "He and Kratos both said the same thing. Sacrifice the few to save the many. That was their angelic sense of morality." I choked back the tears that threatened to rush out. I had to keep my thoughts clear. "I guess the horsemen were the sacrifices here. But I'm not going to let it end this way."

Kur met my gaze, his eyes suddenly piercing, body tense. "Do everything you can to fix this. Do you understand, *Bringer of Light?*"

I met his gaze evenly. "I understand. I am the Bringer of Light. And I'm giving back the gift the gods have granted me."

* * *

In Aereus's garden of death, I stared up at Uthyr's cold, reptilian eyes. His dragon form made my entire body tense. For just a moment, my mind flashed with the image of the dragon attack, the sharp teeth piercing bone, flames searing flesh. This thing was a ruthless monster.

I swallowed hard. At least, I thought he was a ruthless monster. Maybe I wasn't always the best at figuring out who the monsters were.

I closed my eyes, mastering my fears. Dragon or not, I had to get to Afeka.

With a noise in his throat like a deep rattle, Uthyr lowered his chin to the muddy earth. I looped my leg over the dragon's scaly neck, half terrified by the power in this creature's muscled back. Then I slid over his body until I found a spot on his spine where I could get a good grip on his scales.

Hazel climbed on in front of me, looking at ease on her perch. The creature's blood pumped below me, his muscles twitching.

What I hadn't expected was for Kur to climb on behind me, sliding over the dragon's hide like it was second nature to him. And given Kur's scales, maybe it was.

I turned to look at him. "You're coming?"

"I'm going to make sure you two fae don't fuck this up. Besides. It's a long way back to Afeka, and you'll both freeze to death without me. Probably fall asleep and slide off the damn dragon."

"Thanks for your vote of confidence."

My stomach lurched as Uthyr lifted off, his powerful wings thumping in the air to keep us a few feet above ground.

From the garden, Tanit lifted Adonis's body, like a supplicant offering up a sacrifice. Uthyr grabbed Adonis in his talons.

As we took flight into the stormy sky, I gripped hard to Uthyr's scales, using my thighs to hold tightly to the beast. The rain hammered against my skin, and Uthyr's wings stirred the air around us.

I tried to peer beyond Hazel, then beyond Uthyr's enormous haunches to catch a glimpse of Adonis, but it was no use from my vantage point.

Kur's powerful arms curved around me, keeping me in place. With the rain pounding in my face, I could hardly see where we were going, but the speed of flight thrilled me all the same.

I'd actually done what I'd first set out to do—I'd defeated the horsemen. I'd slain them all, driven the archangels from the earth. A shimmering, blue sphere still glimmered around the earth's surface, protecting us from the archangels' onslaught.

The Great Nightmare was over. Right?

It didn't feel like a victory. I couldn't let it end this way, not without trying to save Adonis, too. If his soul remained in the underworld of the Old Gods, I had to imagine he was trapped in some sort of hell.

The freezing rain made my teeth chatter. I slumped back into Kur, and he steadied me on the dragon's back.

"You two fae will get tired fast," he said. "We have a long way to go."

"Do you know where we're going?" I asked.

"Afeka is my home, too. It will take us almost a full day to get there."

Thank the gods Kur had come with us, because he wasn't wrong when he said we'd probably fall off this thing. If there was one lesson I'd learned from riding Nucklavee, it was that about three or four hours in, my thighs would be on fire.

Hazel's dark hair whipped into my face as we flew through the air.

"I don't suppose you have any of that magic that Adonis had? The kind that stops your muscles from hurting?"

"I have my own magic," said Kur. "I'm a demon of the night, and I'm going to put you to sleep."

I clutched tighter to Uthyr's scales. "Not sure that's a great idea, Kur. I'm kind of holding on for my life here."

"I'm not going to let you fall." As soon as the words were out of his mouth, a soothing, starlight-tinged calm swept over me, curling around my sister. Her slim body slumped into me, and Kur's muscled arms wrapped around me, holding me in place.

I sank deeply into a dreamless sleep.

* * *

I woke to the sun's rays warming my skin. When I opened my eyes, we were soaring over a rocky terrain, the land tinged with stunning shades of blue and green. A turquoise river carved through the land below. Despite everything that had happened, hope stirred within me.

"We're here," Kur said quietly.

I prodded Hazel in the ribs, and she jolted awake with a snort. "What?"

I leaned in closer. "Tell your dragon to bring us down. This is Afeka."

Hazel bent toward Uthyr's ear, whispering something to him. Uthyr's glimmering, membranous wings shot out, and he arced lower over the rushing river.

The wind whipped through my hair as Uthyr took us down to the river's bank. Around us, red anemones bloomed in tall grasses, and I breathed in the humid air of Adonis's birthplace. The dragon circled a few times above the grotto, where water rushed from a cave mouth over a rocky cliff face. It pooled below, a cerulean blue in the bright sun.

Uthyr swooped lower, aiming for a rocky cliffside above the river. Before he reached the ground, he hovered near the earth, his heavy wings pounding the air.

"What's he doing?" I asked.

"He's setting down Adonis," said Hazel.

At least he was being careful. A moment later, Uthyr gracefully landed on the path next to Adonis. Kur slid off the beast first, then helped us down. Fatigue ate at my muscles as I slipped off Uthyr's scales. If Kur's magic hadn't been here to soothe my body, I'd be lying on the ground right now, or possibly dead.

I crossed to Adonis, his body peaceful and perfect, his dark lashes stark against his golden skin. I crouched down, touching the smooth skin of his cheek.

"Do you know what you're doing here?" asked Hazel.

I shook my head. "No idea. I only know I'm taking these stones into the underworld, and I'm going to try to make a trade for Adonis's soul."

I rose, and the Stones of Zohar thrummed faintly through the leather satchel on my back, already urging me onward. I felt their power driving me, compelling me to move past the rows of myrrh trees. Here, everything smelled like Adonis.

Kur crouched down, lifting Adonis's body off the rocky earth. "We're both going to find him. I'm coming in there with you."

I squinted in the sunlight. "I'm not sure the Old Gods want demons in their realm."

"I'm coming," he said with growl.

A vernal breeze whispered over me as my footsteps crunched over the path. The grotto was the entrance to the underworld, but I felt life pulsing from it.

Kur trod behind me. As I walked along the cliff's edge, the turquoise water in the gorge below seemed to shift in color. I swallowed hard, watching it redden to the deep crimson of blood. A shiver rippled up my spine.

I wasn't entirely sure what that was about, but I wouldn't say the blood river seemed like a *good* omen.

As we walked on to the cave's mouth, distant cries skimmed past us—agonized cries. A woman weeping, a man's tormented screams.

Again—not a particularly welcoming omen in my book. I glanced at Kur, but he hadn't seemed to notice any of it.

At the cave's mouth, I paused, running my fingers over the arched, rocky wall by my side. I cast a nervous glance at the river of blood, dread pooling in my gut.

Awfully dark in there. So far, everything I'd seen of the Old Gods had been beautiful and full of life. The herbs growing in the forest, the gleaming silver bough, the scent of spring. Here, at the mouth of the underworld, I faced uncharted territory. Depths I really didn't want to plumb.

Pushing aside my fears, I reached into the leather satchel and pulled out the Stones of Zohar. I'd brought them back to their original home. My forehead tingled at the sight of them, and again I fought the overwhelming impulse to press them against my head.

They glowed in my hand, casting a dull blue light over the cave's interior.

Would the gods accept this as an exchange for Adonis's soul? I had no idea. Bartering with the gods for souls was, frankly, completely unfamiliar terrain.

I'd think of it as a sacrifice. That was what Adonis would say. All gods required sacrifices, and that was what I'd come to offer.

Distantly, those faint, agonized cries floated on the mountain wind. The cries didn't sound fully present, exactly. More like an echo, a memory of something from long ago.

My footsteps echoed off the cave walls. Fear began raking

its talons through my chest, raising the hair on the back of my neck.

Something from my past flashed in my mind— blood running down a pale arm, streaming onto the pavement. Teeth piercing the flesh... A woman screaming, a look of horror... Something I didn't want to think about.

Why did that memory keep haunting me? The dragon attack, maybe, of Marcus. No, it was something else, something with a woman. Whatever it was, the memory was a piercing staccato hammering at the inside of my skull, hot and crimson.

I slammed down the iron door. *Not now.*

As I moved deeper into the cave, Aereus's words began whispering around me. *There, you'd have to face the real monster.*

The light from the Stones of Zohar began to dim, now a faint glow. They cast a dull light over the glistening rocks around me, and icy water began running over my feet, growing higher and higher with every step. I tried not to think about the fact that it had looked bright red, or that I might be bathing in the blood of the undead. Where were the Old Gods in here? How far did I have to go?

I whirled around, alarmed to find that Kur was nowhere around me. My throat went dry.

"Kur?" My voice echoed off the stone walls. "Kur?" I called out more urgently.

No response.

Shadows smothered the stone's light completely. *Darkness. Darkness all around me.*

Icy fear raked its claws through my heart as slick, tight vines began snaking around my limbs, rooting me in place. Like a python, they climbed around me, threatening to suffocate me.

They dragged me under the water's surface.

CHAPTER 37

As the vines pulled me under, I managed to cling to the stones.

Holding my breath, I clutched them to my chest. My lungs burned. After a few moments, the waters receded again, the vines loosening on my limbs. I kicked until my head rose above the water, and I sucked in a ragged breath.

What the fuck is going on?

I scrambled for a foothold to stop the rushing river from carrying me with it, kicking and bucking until my tiptoes skimmed over the river bottom.

Stable ground. Thank the gods.

I gripped the stones tightly in my palm as the water rushed over my body. Music pulsed around me—a low, rumbling bass noise that trembled along my bones. Darkness closed in, and all I could see was the thick glistening of the rocks overhead.

Slowly the water receded, and the ground sloped upward. Another presence lurked in here, a female presence. The stones began to glow faintly again, casting a dim, blue light over a figure looming above me in a throne made of glinting rock.

A cloak of moss hung over her, and the scent of peaty soil curled off her. I couldn't quite see her, but for a moment, when the light of the stones flashed a little brighter, I had a sense of thin, wispy skin, like layered spiderwebs.

A voice echoed in my mind. *Bringer of Light.*

I cleared my throat. "I'm looking for Adonis."

Archangels should never roam the earth, the voice boomed.

I clutched the stones tightly to my chest.

A wispy huff of laughter. *Archangels should never walk the earth, Bringer of Light. His soul will remain here, with the other horsemen. See him if you must. You won't be leaving here, either. You're descended from the Old Gods, Ruby.*

Long ago, the Old Gods mated with the fae, creating a race of Light Bringers. You belong among us, now.

A wispy substance skimmed over my skin. "I'm part...Old God?"

The goddess pulled off her hood, and white light beamed through her translucent skin. From the shadows, more glowing beings emerged. Their naked bodies blazed with light, skin as thin as shed snakeskin.

You belong with us, Bringer of Light, my child. You may serve me here forever.

She reached for me, and I took a step back. *Oh, hell no.* Okay, so—*this* was the sacrifice. And it was one I wasn't willing to make.

The stones began to heat in my hands, held tight against my heart. Once again, I felt an overwhelming urge to press them against my forehead like a salve on a wound.

The goddess rose from her throne. Thin threads of silver hair curled over her shoulders, and her eyes shone like moonlight glinting off water. A cloak of moss draped over her shoulders, and a wreath of hawthorn encircled her head.

Her lips looked parched, skin dry and flaky despite the damp air.

Give the stones to me. Within my mind, her voice had a sharper edge. Desperate, almost. *I must drink from them.*

Was she out of her ancient, mossy mind? I wasn't giving over the stones just so she could trap me here.

I clutched them tighter to my chest, unwilling to part with them. At least, not until I regained some control over the situation. "Yeah, I'm not staying here with the army of the glowing, so we'll need a different plan. How about I give you these stones, and you give me Adonis's soul, and then I'll be on my way."

Rage blazed from the goddess's eyes, and she took another step closer. *I protected you. And now you want to bargain with me, for what's rightfully mine?*

When she stepped closer, I could see indentations in her skull—indentations that perfectly matched the size of the stones. She'd worn them once, a crown of sorts. These stones had once been a part of her, and they'd been stolen. Another step closer, her hands grasping for them—and my own skull ached to feel them pressed against it.

She heaved in a raspy breath. *I've been trapped here for a thousand years, unable to leave without my powers. Give them back to me.*

My utility to her was starting to become clear. She'd needed me to bring them to her. A messenger, working for her.

A lump rose in my throat, and I shook my head. I'd rid the earth of the horsemen. I'd protected it from archangels who wanted to slaughter us all. Was I about to undo that spell—just for one man? Adonis would never approve of it. A small sacrifice to save the larger numbers. But I needed a different kind of morality. I needed good to triumph over evil. I needed the heroes to live.

One last chance. "I want to leave here, and I want to take Adonis with me."

She snarled, long canines protruding. Claws emerged from the tips of her hands—long and curled, the color of aged tree bark.

The goddess was going a bit feral before me, and I took a step back from her in the icy water. My skull ached for the stones like a parched throat aches for water.

I could do it. I could use the stones' power for myself...

Snarling, the goddess lunged for me. I darted back, pressing the stones against my forehead, and my skin soaked them up.

My own voice echoed in my skull. *Gods don't run from themselves, Ruby.*

All at once, the rock around me seemed to fall away, and I was standing in the park in New York. Blood spattered the ground near my feet. I recognized this scene. This was the day the world ended, the day the Great Nightmare had begun.

I didn't want to look up. I knew what I'd see there—the dragon ripping Marcus to shreds. An unseen force gripped my chin, forcing me to lift my head.

Before me, a shadow loomed over Marcus, and the reptilian stench of ancient caves and rock dust pooled in the air. I whirled, just in time to see the dragon lunge.

I screamed a warning, but it was too late.

My world tilted as the dragon clamped Marcus in its jaws, teeth piercing his flesh. Blood streamed over the pavement, glistening in the afternoon light. My chest clenched with pure, raw panic.

Screaming, I leapt into the air, trying to get a grip on the dragon, but it was too tall for me, and my fingers slipped off its scales. *I can't protect him.* I slammed back down onto the ground, knocking the back of my head on the pavement.

With Marcus's body clamped in his jaws, the dragon shook his head back and forth, red streaming from his teeth.

Frantic, I hurled my knife at the dragon's eye. Somehow, I managed to hit it just at the edge of the iris, even as it flailed its head around.

I tried to slam the iron door down on the memory, tried to fight my way out of this hell, but there was no escape.

The dragon tossed Marcus into the air. Blood poured from his chest, his ribs. *It's too late.*

I screamed, not hearing my own voice.

I couldn't look down, couldn't stare at what the dragon was doing to Marcus. I had to bury those thoughts, lock them up in a mental coffin—but it wasn't working now. I had to see it, had to look at what had happened. The dragon had ripped through his ribs, his spine. His blood pooled over the pavement...

Until nothing was left of him but a pile of ash.

Ruby. Who do you believe the real monster is?

I started shaking my head, unwilling to make meaning from this. I heaved a sob. "I don't know what you mean."

The world around me fell away again. For just a moment, I glimpsed the dragons—a flash of blonde hair and flailing limbs. Teeth ripping at her flesh, her pale arms...

The image faded as soon as it had come, leaving me in the dark. I sucked in a sharp breath. Is that what I'd been imagining all this time? I hadn't been there when dragons had killed my parents—long before the Great Nightmare had begun. It wasn't a memory. And yet this image of blood on the pavement kept hammering at my skull, the piercing, red-hot staccato...

From the darkness, light bloomed around me. My mother towered over me. She was gripping my arm, trying to pull me into the house. She looked scared. *Why* was it so important to her that I stay inside?

Her blonde hair flowed over her shoulders, and I wanted to pull her outside. Spring blossomed in the air around us—the fae spring. February. Eimmal.

My canines lengthened, and a feral growl tore from my throat. *Hunt. Kill. Stop the heart.*

"Ruby!" my mom screamed, frantically tugging on my arm. "You need to get inside the house!"

Light shone brightly off the house's metal siding.

Her words began to blur into the red mist in my mind, lost in a haze of moss and peat, until I only knew that she was prey. My teeth sank into her arm, hot blood pulsing in my mouth, flesh tearing...

Blood streaming over the pavement.

It wasn't until strong arms pulled me off her that I saw what I'd done, that I heard my dad screaming my name. That I saw the horrified look in my parents' faces, as they realized what I was. *A monster.* They weren't as feral as I was.

The image faded, leaving me again in the dank cave. The stones had disappeared from my fingers, but their light seemed to pulse through my blood. A deep, throbbing rhythm thrummed around me.

Vines slithered from the ground, curling around my feet, my ankles—then penetrating my skin. Sharp pain splintered my body, shooting up my bones. My ribs, my skull fractured with the pain, and a flash of sunlight blinded me—burning away the image of blood staining the pavement. At last, the vines receded again, freeing my body. I gasped with relief.

Ancient, primal power surged in my veins. I opened my eyes again, and pale blue light blazed from within my skin. I wasn't alone anymore. Around me, shimmering forms moved—just wisps of scintillating outlines—shoulders and hair and fingers that glimmered like phosphorescence in the ocean.

The souls of the underworld—each with their own scent

I licked my canines, my hunter's instincts propelling me forward through the dank cave. I'd come here for Adonis, and I was going to find him. Already, the *theta* on my shoulder tingled, as if summoning me closer.

I broke into a sprint, running through the shallow waters as they rose around me. I followed the alluring scent of myrrh. Light blazed from the gleaming crown around my head.

Gods rule the realms of the dead.

In the far recesses of the cave, I found them—the four horsemen, lurking together—each one distinct by his smell, his aura. Four horsemen, their forms translucent. Adonis's blue eyes shone in the darkness. His eyes widened in surprise.

I homed in on Adonis, grabbing him by the hand, and pulled him closer to me—and his hand felt like pure warmth within mine. Light flowed from my body around his soul, wrapping us closer. "You're coming with me."

Those deep, blue eyes burned into me, shock written all over them.

Water rushed higher and higher around me, covering my body and surging over my skin. I lost my grip on Adonis, completely submerged in the icy waters--until at last, my head breached the surface. The water receded around me, and I pushed myself to my feet, frantically looking around for Adonis.

And there—at the cave's mouth—he stood with sunlight silhouetting his body. Alive again.

His back arched. Around his neck, snaked thorny vines—his seal, opening before my eyes.

Instinct kicked in, and I rushed for him and stroked the vines of magic with the tip of my finger, scraping it across the thorns. Blue light glowed from my fingertips. A sharp jolt of ecstasy surged into my body—life and death melding together.

The seal dissipated beneath my fingertips.

Adonis staggered back from me, his hand at his throat. A grimace contorted his features.

Then, he stared at me, his jaw open.

I touched my forehead, feeling the smooth stones that had become a part of my skin.

I cleared my throat. "I, um... I stole the goddess's magic rocks."

"You *stole* them." He blinked, as if awakening from a dream.

"I had to. It was the only way to get you back. Plus, she wanted me to stay here with a bunch of creepy Light Bringers to serve her or something."

He grabbed me by the hand. "I want to get you out of here."

I glanced behind me, relieved to see that no gods or Bringers of Light were following me.

"You've stolen the goddess's power," he said. "Now you have the power of a goddess. Do you understand that?"

Primal magic—the kind I had when feral—coursed through my veins. But I didn't feel feral anymore. I simply felt powerful.

"This magic feels native to me." River water rushed over my ankles. "I guess it is. The goddess said the Bringers of Light descended from the Old Gods."

Before we crossed out of the cave's mouth into the beaming sunlight, Adonis turned to me. Gently, he stroked the stones set into my forehead. "You found me in the underworld, and you pulled the curse off me. Why did you do it?"

I knew what he wanted. He was looking for some kind of well-reasoned, rational explanation about morality. Maybe some sort of plan. But I didn't have that, so I had to go with the truth.

"Because you're one of the good guys, and I didn't want you to die." I wrapped my arms around him, breathing in his smell. His heart pounded against my ear, full of life, and joy sparked in my chest. "You're not supposed to die yet."

His hand stroked up my back. "Ruby. You pulled out their souls with mine."

"Whose?"

"The four other horsemen. I felt their souls depart with me. The other horsemen aren't going to let this end here."

My body tensed. *Well, shit.* "I pulled your curse from you, didn't I? I'll free the other horsemen, too." My thoughts began to race. "And we'll just have to get them on our side. Five of us against ten celestial angels. They're not great odds, but...well, we've got a dragon." I could feel the words tumbling off my tongue, nearly nonsensical.

Adonis pulled away from me, his pale eyes beaming intensely in the dim light. "Our four deaths could have ended this all."

I shook my head. "I'm supposed to let you die to save the world. I know that. A few deaths to spare millions, or however many are left on this earth. But what if those aren't the only options? What if we change the rules?"

He stroked a fingertip down my cheek. "Do you know what happened when the last magical being tried changing the rules?" He leaned in, whispering into my ear. "He fell."

My stomach tightened. *Lucifer. Azazeyl.* It hadn't turned out well. In fact, it had led to millennia of death and destruction. "Admittedly, it's not the best precedent. But can we not dwell on the negative right now? I just hauled your ass out of eternal cave hell, and I have some brand new magical powers I need to try out."

When we stepped out of the cave into the beaming

sunlight, Adonis gaped at the river in front of us. Kur and Hazel were already rushing toward us, but Adonis seemed lost in his own world. He bent down and plucked a red flower from the ground, studying it, the expression on his face one of remorse.

The flower's crimson color perfectly matched the red pendant around his neck. *So that's what he'd been wearing...*

It was only then I realized Hazel was clutching my arm and screaming into my face.

"Ruby! What is going on with your head?" she shrieked.

"I stole the Stones of Zohar. They seem to have formed a crown on my head."

Her jaw dropped. "So what does it mean?"

I bit my lip. "I don't really know yet, Hazel." I stared at my hands, at the glowing light that tinged my fingertips. "I think we're going to find out."

CHAPTER 38

I lay back against the trunk of the myrrh tree in Adonis's garden, listening to the burbling of the spring. Sunlight washed over me, warming my skin.

A small, barren patch of earth stretched out from the tree to the stream, and I leaned over it, breathing in the scent of the rich soil. What could I do with this little patch of dirt?

I closed my eyes, summoning the warm power that pooled in my skull, then tingled down my spine. It settled between my ribs before streaming on through my arms, my fingertips... It smelled of moss, of damp leaves and wildflowers, and I felt as if I'd always had it within me.

When I opened my eyes again, light streamed from my fingertips over the damp earth. As I stared at the ground, tiny green shoots sprouted, curled like miniature ferns. I loosed a long breath, staring as they grew under the rays of blue light. As I gaped at them, the buds began to unfurl into crimson blossoms that trembled in the light.

When they'd opened fully, I let my light fade. I brushed my fingertips over the petals, smiling at what I'd created. I'd been toying with my powers for a few days, and this was the best result so far. Some kind of magical photosynthesis, I guessed. An antidote to the vast wastelands created by the Great Nightmare.

Gentle footfalls sounded behind me, and I turned to see Drakon padding over to me, his tail swishing behind him. When he reached me, he rubbed against my skin, his scales slick and slightly oily. I stroked his head. His eyes closed, and he nestled his head against me. Then, he crawled into my lap, crushing my legs with his weight, claws piercing my clothes.

"Ooof, Drakon."

He attempted to curl up in a ball on my lap, prodding at me with his claws. Apparently, Drakon hadn't figured out yet that there would be no way he'd fit on me, or that his scaly, clawed body on my lap felt extremely uncomfortable.

I nudged him off onto the grass, and he reluctantly prowled off me, then curled up into a ball by my side.

I smiled at him. Once, he'd disturbed me—a demonic reptilian beast from hell. Now, I was starting to like the guy. In fact—maybe I felt a strange kinship with him. We both had our bestial sides.

"My two favorite creatures." Adonis's smooth voice wrapped around me.

The sunlight washed over his deep, golden skin, and my eyes roamed over the finely cut clothes that hugged his masculine form.

Just the sight of him made my heart race. "Want to join us?"

"Sitting in the dirt?"

"It's more fun than you'd think."

A smile ghosted over his lips, and he sat by my side, his arm brushing mine as we looked out over the stream. "What have you been doing out here?"

I shrugged. "Nothing amazing. Just creating new life from my fingertips."

He cocked his head. "Testing your new goddess powers?"

"If a desperate need to garden arises, I'm your guy." I glanced at the sky, at the shimmering blue shield above us. "Any news on the other horsemen?"

Adonis squinted in the bright sunlight. "We've received a message from Kratos. He wants to come speak to us."

My shoulders tensed. "About what?"

"He wants to form an alliance. He wants his curse removed."

"What's going on with Johnny and Aereus?"

"Drakon located them. They're both in Sadeckrav Castle. If I had to guess, they're forming an alliance of their own, and they plan to kill us."

I swallowed hard. "They still want to rule the earth as gods."

"Can you imagine Aereus wanting anything else?"

"Conquest and Death against Famine and War. I like our odds."

The red pendant at his neck glinted in the sunlight, and I reached over to touch it. "This is one of the flowers from Afeka, isn't it?"

"Yes. It's nearly as old as I am."

"Why do you wear it?"

His expression darkened for just a moment, and he stared at the rushing water. Sparks of sunlight glinted off its surface. "I lived with my mother in Afeka when I was younger. She knew what I was—the horseman of death. But she thought she could keep me from my fate through love."

"She sounds like an amazing mom."

"She taught me to love living things. She taught me to identify plants, to grow flowers. She kept me away from humans, so I wouldn't hurt them. We lived in isolation—near humans, but never among them. Then the fae came for me.

They attacked everyone in the nearby city, burning, slaughtering until they got to us."

He met my gaze, and my chest tightened at the raw pain glinting in his eyes.

"I fought them off," he continued. "I killed most of them, trying to protect my mother. But they stabbed her in the side." His voice sounded hollow. "She might have lived. If a real healer had been looking after her, she *would* have lived. But I tried healing her myself. I thought I could do it."

I swallowed hard. "What happened?"

"Sometimes, if powerful emotions overcome me, I unleash death. I've changed, but...when I was young, I couldn't control it. I pressed her side, trying to staunch the bleeding. She was telling me to run, I think. Her blood covered my fingers, staining the flowers around her. She kept saying I should run, but—I was fifteen and she was the only person I knew." He didn't meet my gaze, just stared at the red flowers around us. "It was just us. She was the only person I knew. Where was I supposed to run to?"

A lump rose in my throat. "I can't imagine how scared you must have been."

"I was trying to help her. I was thinking about living on my own—just living forever in isolation. Then I felt the wave of darkness roll off me—that sweet release that soothed my nerves, like a blanket of night, like dreams sweeping over the horizon." His shoulders sagged, as if the weight of his unseen wings were dragging him to the earth. "I killed her. And everyone around us for miles. A vast landscape of death. That's what I was created to do."

I reached out, touching his arm. "It wasn't your fault."

"Her blood spilled over the white flowers, staining them red. They've been that color since then." He loosed a long, slow sigh. "I turned myself over to the fae who'd hunted me, the ones who served the Old Gods. I thought they could control me. Until one day, I realized I didn't need them anymore. I'd learned to control myself. You cannot imagine how much I enjoyed killing those fae, though…" He touched his necklace. "I've always kept this with me, one of the flowers stained red."

"It's a reminder of your mother, but—it seems like some sort of penance. Like you feel guilty."

"Of course I feel guilty. This is a reminder of why I needed to die. It's why I belong in the underworld. I am Death incarnate, and the archangels should have never put me here."

I slid my arm into the crook of his elbow. "But you are here, and I want you here. And you've changed. You've gained control over your power. We're not just one thing, Adonis. You're not just Death. Every one of us has many facets."

He turned his head toward mine, his face so close that his breath warmed my skin.

When I met his gaze, I felt a jolt of electricity rush through me. "I want you to teach me about all the plants your mom taught you. And we can grow them all."

"I can't think of anything I'd like to do more."

"What do you think will happen next?"

He plucked a red flower from the river bank and twirled it between his fingers. "We fight. And we rebuild."

* * *

We hope you enjoyed Black Ops Fae.

The final book in this series is Rogue Fae, which is in Amazon now.

Also, please check out our webpage for the full listing of books www.cncrawford.com

ACKNOWLEDGMENTS

Thank you to my amazing beta reader Michael, and to my editors, Robin and Lindsey.

Doc Wendigo, Shayne Rutherford, and Brian Jaramillo contributed their design expertise to our gorgeous ebook and paperback covers.

ABOUT THE AUTHOR

C.N. Crawford is sometimes one person, and sometimes two. We live in Vermont with our son. In this case, *A Spy Among the Fallen* series is written by Christine.

Christine grew up in New England and has a lifelong interest in local folklore—with a particular fondness for creepy old cemeteries. She is a psychologist who spent eight years in London obsessively learning about its history, and misses it every day.

ALSO BY C.N. CRAWFORD

A full listing of our books are found here:
http://www.cncrawford.com/books/